A LESSON IN MANNERS

Brice punched Henry, sending the young man onto his back.

"You shouldn't have done that." Cole's voice hushed the shrieking guests. He strode to stand over Henry and offered a hand up. "Is it a part of that badge to punch a kid?"

Henry refused Cole's and Ann's help and got to his knees on his own.

"You want part of this too, mister?" Brice muttered. "I don't want to shame you too in front of all these folks."

Cole stared at Brice. "You're a long way from there, friend."

Brice smirked. "I admire a man who has backbone." He twisted around slowly and spat out tobacco juice, then recoiled around a backhanded slap.

Cole caught the blow with his right hand, snapped Brice's arm rigid and wrenched it forward, locking the shoulder. He kicked Brice in the gut, exploding the wad of chaw out like a bullet. Brice dropped to one knee. Reaching his left hand to his right hip, Brice drew his pistol. Cole ripped the gun from Brice's grasp, kicked him to the ground and spun the revolver's aim back at its owner.

"Do you want part of this?" Cole growled.

Other *Leisure* books by Tim McGuire:
DANGER RIDGE

NOBILITY

TIM McGUIRE

LEISURE BOOKS 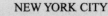 NEW YORK CITY

To My Family

Sons Cameron, Ryan, and daughter Erin:
This story's inspiration and my best accomplishment.

And to their mother, Joy, my wife:
*Lover, Partner, and Friend. You are the best
choice in my life.*

The most lasting gift given is knowledge.

A LEISURE BOOK®

June 1999

Published by

Dorchester Publishing Co., Inc.
276 Fifth Avenue
New York, NY 10001

ISBN 0-8439-4526-5

ACKNOWLEDGMENTS

A deep appreciation to the two people whose work I benefit from: my agent Cherry Weiner and editor Don D'Auria. Special thanks to the Pawnee Tribe of Oklahoma. To the Law Library of New Mexico, for answering my questions. My love to my mother, Jeanne; to my sisters Pat & Marilyn and brother Richard and all my family for listening to my ideas, and my friends at *Western Writers of America* who welcomed me into their realm. And to the *DFW Writers' Workshop,* with whose guidance and discipline this novel was born and raised.

The Appaloosa galloped. The rider clutched the mane, matching the pony's smooth stride. He blinked the desert's sand away to peer over his shoulder under the black hat's brim. Dust rising behind him signaled either a swirling devil or a pursuing posse. He lashed the reins on the animal's flanks for more speed.

Skill with a six-gun had saved him from ambushing bluecoats in Platte Falls, but two of them fell in the street. No matter his reasons, he had now drawn against his country. That fact had driven him out of Colorado for the sanctuary of Mexico.

Cactus thorns scratched his tanned-hide leggings as the horse darted through the valley. Pounding hooves echoed off canyon walls. The Appaloosa chased its faster shadow, huffing foam past the choking bit. Heat rising from the mesa distorted the cool water always just up ahead.

The border was a six-day ride, but it wouldn't be soon enough. The open made him an easy target for any army sharpshooter. A bullet could be waiting on him around the next bend.

He spurred his mount. Lather flew into the passing breeze.

His fate at the Little Big horn was the devil poking at his backside. That shroud hanging over his honor made him a wanted man. The truth of that day three years before was a story the army wouldn't hear.

Twenty more miles and he would be in the mountains. The shelter of the trees would allow him cherished rest he hadn't known in five days. More slaps of the leather might get him there by nightfall.

The animal charged over dusty streambeds toward a pile of ancient driftwood.

A lash would have the Appaloosa fly. He pinned his knees against the saddle. His fingers wrapped around the horn for the leap. Wind blew the sweat from his brow.

A clear horizon meant escape.

A hoof clipped the snare of twisted wood. The horse stumbled. The jolt tore him out of the crouch. The Appaloosa's head veered into the dust; only a death grip on the reins would save him from being trampled. Chin stubble stabbed his chest. The hat ripped away. His legs hurled into the sky. The sun bleached away his vision. Pain from behind brought darkness, then silence.

Chapter One

The sun's heat burning his eyelids told Clay Cole he was still alive. His throbbing head felt as if it were cracked open. Rolling onto his tingling right shoulder, he tried to get up, but the pain stinging his side robbed his strength. Slipping his left hand between his ribs and the dirt, he pushed his body off the ground and slid his knees under his weight. His expanding chest ached with every breath. There was no telling how hurt he was, but nothing felt broken.

An anguished neigh turned his head. The Appaloosa strained to rise. The shattered bone protruding from the leg prevented it or any further use of the animal.

He turned away, but his mind wouldn't ignore the sight. A long loud cry forced him to the task he had never planned but had to do. He stared in the dust at his fallen Peacemaker. He gripped the butt and flicked open the chamber gate. A live round was next into the barrel.

The Appaloosa's head arched over its side. Its bulbous eye watched him point the muzzle. He pulled back the hammer, but his better sense wouldn't release his thumb; the shot would be heard for miles. He holstered the gun, claimed a wobbling stance, and drew the Bowie knife from its belt sheath.

He limped around behind the horse; it would be easier for both of them if it didn't see him coming. More agonizing whinnies pierced the howling desert wind.

It was a fool's mind that had done this. Another result of his refusal to face up to his fate. One more reminder of what his life on the run had wasted. It had now cost him the best mount he had ever known.

Memories long since past filled his head. Renegade Sioux once caught him napping in the Black Hills. Luck kept his body clear from arrows in the dark, but a whistle brought the Appaloosa to him and he was gone like a shot. Their ponies couldn't keep up with the big horse's stride through the snow.

Then there was the time Old Jack Barton sent his gunnies after him. He was trapped between them and a horseshoe canyon in Utah. He had to turn and charge, firing over his horse's head, reins in his teeth, Winchester in one hand, the Colt in the other. The Appaloosa never flinched from all the lead flying. If it had reared and thrown him, he wouldn't be here this day.

There were many scrapes when that animal's faithful service had saved his skin.

Its low groan brought him out of the daydream. It rocked trying to regain its feet. The sight of that dangling leg touched fire to his insides. The only pity he could show would come from the mercy of the blade.

He had killed stock and game for food, and men in anger, and never thought twice. Although his heart slowed his feet, his mind knew killing was best done quickly.

He knelt next to the head, grabbed the bridle, and yanked up. He placed the knife at the throat. Second thoughts would only torment both of them.

Nobility

The sharp steel edge plunged deep. The Appaloosa struggled against his firm hold. Warm blood gushed against his hand as he turned his eyes to the sand. He inhaled the arid breeze as if gut punched, over and over, straining to keep breath in his lungs, tightening his grip on the bridle.

The pull from his grasp slowly ceased. A gurgling wheeze lasted only seconds. The weight of the head came to rest on his side.

His own stomach started to crawl up into his mouth, but a hard swallow and a deep breath kept him from losing what little moisture he had in him.

Despite the heat's sting on his skin, he couldn't bring himself to move. His shoulders drooped and his body sagged into the sand.

Horses are just property. The notion kept hammering into his head, but more times with the Appaloosa came to mind, and he reflected on what fate had changed.

He was a young man when he first saddled that Palousey pony. Folks took notice of it and him when he rode by, men with nods of admiration, and the women with discreet smiles. Even when he started running from the army, the Appaloosa served as a constant he could rely on being there, but he never thought about it at the time.

The years since had given him many scars, and at that moment he started to feel them all again.

All of this now served as a marker that the comfort of what he had known was slipping away. A piece of him died along with that horse.

He grunted the mucus from his throat, spat it out, and stood.

"Good-bye, Pepper."

Sweat seeping down his cheeks settled as dry grit on his chin. Only the Winchester and canteen filled his hands while he trudged through the loose sand.

He regretted leaving his saddle and gear strapped to the

horse, but he couldn't spare the energy to carry the weight. When he found another mount he could go back for them. He had covered the carcass as best he could with tumbleweeds, but he knew that wouldn't last long. Carrion was an easy meal in the desert.

Ahead lay mountains etched in outline through the purple haze. They crept up over the horizon with each step, the hollowness of the desert rang in his ears. A glance back showed the long wake of footsteps threaded between the cactus and brush.

Whoever was chasing him had given up the trail. Maybe there wasn't any posse. All he sensed were just the ghosts that would always be nipping at his heels.

He took the last swig of water from the canteen, gargled it in his throat, spat some in his hand to wipe his brow, and swallowed the rest. He licked his chapping lips. The heat quickly claimed the moisture and his throat was soon dry.

How long would he last? He couldn't rid his mind of the question. The army had taught him a man could last three days without water. He hoped they were right. The nearest town could be that far on foot.

He squinted his eyes tight, squeezing the biting salt clear of them. When he opened them, the sand reflected the blinding light. A quick step caught his balance. A deep breath reminded him of his injured ribs. The black hat trapped heat like a kettle, but he knew should he take it off; his brain would soon be stewed by the sun.

There was no shelter in sight. If he didn't find any during the day, he would have to battle the night's bitter cold in the open. He'd seen men catch the fever that way and be dead before daybreak. His mind hounded his unwilling legs to move on.

If only he were home in Kansas. His ma would take care of him. But the hacking cough of consumption had taken her almost eighteen years before. He'd never thought of her since his Union officer father had told him that to survive as a man, he would have to forget he had a mother. Four years later, he would see his father buried in Texas, felled by the last ball fired in the war.

His eyes sank to his own shadow on the sand. The demon's heat was playing tricks with his head.

In all the stink life had blown his way, he never had felt sorry for himself. All the days in the army and later on his own fighting with gun, knife, and fist had not made him shrink to crying, not even the lie about warning the Sioux at the Greasy Grass. That was all schooling a man had to have to live.

But he needed a bottle to help him bury the woman that wanted to be his wife and to drown the desire to hold his unborn child. Those were the cruel tests of manhood that he had passed.

It had brought him here. The canteen and rifle slipped from his hands. His ma's sweet smiling face appeared in his shadow. It was the same smile she always had when she talked about her boy. She was telling the story she loved to tell, about when she first held her only son. With her husband off at war in Mexico, she had only a Pawnee squaw midwife to assist in the birth during a cold autumn night.

When the squaw placed the child in his mother's arms, she uttered words in her native tongue: *"Ti Wahuks Te."* His ma asked what it meant, and the squaw told her that he had the eyes of a great one, "a bringer of life, a maker of miracles."

His ma asked for a word she could tell folks so they could understand. The squaw smiled and told her "Rainmaker."

A silhouette of a bird emerged from the shadow. His mother's smile was gone. A glance into the cloudless sky brought the first sight of death flying overhead. He felt one more kick from fate's boot.

"I leave you my damn horse and you come looking for me?" he yelled at the buzzard. He waited for the bird to circle, but it kept gliding farther away as it descended behind a small dune. The scavenger must have seen an easier meal, but a single bird seemed peculiar. The only reasons buzzards lighted on the ground were to pick bones, or . . .

He took a step, then another, then another, and soon he was at a sprint toward the rise in the sand. As he ran through the loose footing he struggled to keep his balance. If he fell, he was unsure if he would get up.

As he came over the dune, he sighted a long dry streambed and the black bird at the edge of a small pool of water. His legs buckled, but he kept them moving as he started down the side. When he stepped on solid ground he collapsed onto his knees in the water. The scavenger took wing into the sky.

He drank from his cupped hands, splashed his face over and over, but it didn't relieve the heat fast enough. He plunged his head under the surface of the water.

He was still alive. Another slip from death's grip. Although he would still have to find shelter and food, he didn't want to think of anything but the ecstasy of the water's caress on his scorched flesh. He wished he were a fish so he wouldn't have to leave the pool's cool embrace, but his lungs demanded air.

He lifted his head and took a breath, rolled his shoulders, and dropped into the water as if it were a bed. He sunk to the bottom, leaving only his head above the surface. As the sting began to leave his skin, his eyes focused on a mounted figure at the top of the dune.

His reflex to rise forced the rider to draw a gun from its holster and aim at Cole.

"You just hold it right there, mister, or I'll make that your grave," the rider yelled. He ambled the horse down the dune and dismounted at the water's edge. "You must have the mind of a jackass to be wandering around out here without a horse."

Cole silently agreed.

"That looks like a nice side arm you got there. I think I'll have it."

The muzzle trained at Cole's head made him comply. He

carefully lifted his Colt out of the water. The rider stretched out his hand, and Cole tossed the revolver. The rider caught it and began to admire the weapon. He turned the butt and saw the engraving.

"Army pistol. Are you a soldier or something?"

Cole shook his head

"My, this is a nice one. Good balance. Every man could use a gun like this one. Now stand up and let me get a good look at you."

Cole rose from the pool.

The rider chuckled. "You are a big fella. What's your name?"

"Cole."

"Mine's Billy Mansfield. Ever heard of me?"

Cole shook his head again. He felt that boot against his backside again. "No. But I'd guess that posse back there was chasing you."

"You're a smart fella, too. You know of the National Bank of Santa Fe?"

Cole shook his head again. "No, but you'll tell me about it."

"That's right. You're looking at the man that just robbed it. Got more than five thousand dollars."

"What about that posse?"

Mansfield grinned. "Those fools couldn't find their own shadows. I left them in those canyons some miles back. But you never know, they might double back this way. Some of them may have had a good look at me." Mansfield looked at his yellow shirt and brown pants, then at Cole. "They wouldn't be looking for a fella dressed in a green shirt such as that. Guess I'll have need for your clothes, too."

Cole thought about his Bowie knife. He had hit a man's chest before from a longer distance. His once-steady hand quivered from the strain of enduring the desert. His wet fingers might slip from the blade's handle. Mansfield couldn't miss at the short range.

17

Tim McGuire

Cole started unbuttoning his shirt. The rough cloth scratched his burnt skin as he pulled it from his shoulders. A wag of Mansfield's gun barrel signaled what was wanted next.

Cole slipped the end of his gun belt through the buckle and pulled open the hank knot that kept the holster tight to his leg. Once the belt was free, he flung it at Mansfield's feet. He unlaced the leggings and peeled them from his calves.

Few minutes had passed when they finished trading clothes. Cole stretched the yellow shirt across his chest to button it. His own dark-green shirt appeared too big on the slim outlaw.

Mansfield threw his tattered hat to the dust and crowned himself with Cole's black curled-brim hat. "A little big, but they'll do," Mansfield said as his grin turned to a sneer. "Now there's one more thing to do." He cocked the Colt's hammer.

"A shot out here will have that posse come running," said Cole as he stared at his own gun's barrel.

"And they'll find their bank robber. With their justice done, they won't bother worrying who done shot him." Mansfield aimed the Colt.

Despite the heat, Cole felt a chill. He saw Mansfield's trigger finger bend.

He dove but felt fire against his head, then the numbing clutch of the cold dark.

Chapter Two

Singing angels coaxed Cole toward a bright light. Rays flushed away the dark. The serenade echoed inside his mind, becoming a single voice as he approached the entrance. It was a child's voice. The call echoed over and over, providing a rhythm for the stroke of a blacksmith's hammer slamming against the anvil of his head. The face of a boy emerged from the blurred glow.

"Hey, mister. Are you alive? You all right?"

Cole's throbbing skull floated. He squinted in an attempt to relieve the assault of the blacksmith. He focused on the young boy. The events he last remembered circled in his brain. The Appaloosa, the knife, thirst, a buzzard leading him to drink from the shallow pool, the slim outlaw Mansfield holding his own forty-five Colt at an aim between his eyes and firing.

"Where is he?" Cole mumbled.

"Where's who?"

"Where's my gun?"

"Gee, I don't know, mister. Don't look like you got one."

Cole looked at the bleary face of the youngster, the eyes concentrating on his own face. "What are you looking at?"

The boy spoke in a wondrous voice. "That's the biggest shiner I've ever seen. And it's still growing."

The remark brought Cole's notice to his right eye's collapsing view, a hooded squint through the crack of darkness. The notice brought more torture from the blacksmith. He had to concentrate on something else.

"Who are you?" he barked.

"Noah."

Cole mashed his eyelids shut to be sure he was truly alive, then opened them to brown eyes peeking through long brown hair that appeared several months uncut. Suspenders held up dark trousers, black shoes were laced above the ankle, and a thin blue-striped shirt was buttoned all the way to the collar. Memories of being drenched in sweat because of a shirt such as that came flying back, along with those of unblemished peach fuzz framing wide-eyed amazement. It was like looking into a twenty-year-old mirror.

"Who?"

"Noah. Noah Hayes. Same name as the President, but Mama says he ain't no kin to us."

"Where did you come from?"

"I live here."

Cole quickly surveyed the surrounding desolation. "No games, boy. How did you get here?"

"Honest, mister. We got a farm just over that rise." Noah pointed to the dune Cole had come down for the water.

"How far?"

"I don't know. Not very far, I guess."

The throbbing turned to a sting. Cole pressed his hand to the pain, and a red-stained palm confirmed the wound. He dipped his head gently into the pond, but the now tepid water did little for the irritation.

"You suppose you could take me to your place to get

some fresh water, maybe a band of clean cloth for this?''

The boy's face lit up. "Sure. I can take you there."

Cole rose from the pond, eagerly helped by his new friend.

"My mama knows a lot about doctoring. She could fix your eye in no time at all. Once my leg was bleeding real bad, felt like it was cut off from falling out of the old oak back of the barn. My mama came quick and had the blood stopped before I could stop crying. It felt so much better, I didn't near mind when she cut down the branch that broke and whopped my britches with it for climbing up that tree.''

They both came over the dune. Cole used the boy's shoulder as a crutch while young arms wrapped half around his waist.

"Hey, mister. What's your name?"

"Co—. Clay."

"Well, it's nice to meet you, Mr. Clay."

"No, just Clay. You can call me that without the 'mister.' ''

"How come you were way out here?"

Cole steadied himself against the boy while he tried to recall. "I lost my horse."

"Is that how you got that shiner?"

Cole felt a threat to his pride as a horseman. "No. I got shot.''

"Wow, you got shot! Who shot you?"

"It weren't the cactus."

"Wow. Were you in a gunfight? Did you get shot by a gunfighter? A real, true, live gunfighter?''

"No.'' The irritation of his swollen head gave way to one coming into his ears. "It wasn't no gunfighter. It was some two-bit bank robber I let . . .'' His pride stopped the words, but he had to give a reason. ". . . I let get the jump on me.''

Green and amber growth blotched over the white sand. Relief seemed closer, but it still wasn't in sight. The few silent steps didn't last long.

"Well, why'd he shoot you? Are you a banker? I heard

21

Mama sometimes say some bankers deserve to get shot.''

"No, I ain't no banker." The question strained Cole's patience like a stretched rope. "The thief surprised me when I wasn't looking. He stole my clothes and my gun.''

"How did you get them clothes?''

"They're the thief's.''

"And he took your horse too, huh?''

The rope snapped. "My horse went lame,'' Cole shouted. "Are there any more things you need to know? If so, I ain't telling.''

"Sorry.''

The meek apology intensified the blacksmith's hammer, shaming Cole for raising his voice to the only person helping him now. "My fault, kid. My head hurts bad.''

"That's okay." The young enthusiasm returned. "It's not far now, the farm. Mama will fix you up in no time. Did I tell you how good a doctor she is? And after she gets your eye patched up, she can cook you supper. Yesterday we butchered a hog for Sunday supper. She cooked the liver, and we had 'falfa and beets. I don't like the beets much. But the rest of it was real good. She said she would stew the leavin's for tonight. There's not much better than my mama's hog stew.''

"I'll bet," Cole replied. "A hot meal would be worth a bag of gold dust right now.''

"Gold?''

Cole chuckled "Just talkin'." He looked down at his young friend. The delight in the boy's face eased the throb in his head. A remembrance of his own youth when he saw his pa riding in after weeks being gone. The wild stories his pa used to tell about Indians and outlaws were better than any gifts that were brought home. There was always something special about when a boy would talk to his pa. This sounded like one of those times Cole remembered, and that didn't seem right.

"Your ma and pa been farming here long?''

Nobility

The boy's face drifted away. "Yeah, but my pa, he's gone on a trip."

"Where did he go?" Somehow Cole knew the answer.

The boy took a deep breath. "He went west to replace the stock that got killed that winter. But that was a long time ago. My sister was still sucking at the tit then, and she's almost six now. Mama told just me that my pa might not be back. That I needed to learn on my own about being a man, because there were some things she couldn't tell me about." He looked up Cole. "It's hard not knowing some things."

Cole understood, but his tongue couldn't mold the words. A nod had to suffice.

Noah's face turned to the front. "We're almost there. Can you see it?"

Cole saw the apex of a barn come out of the dusty horizon.

"Maybe after supper you could stay over with us until you're all mended and feeling better. Mama could fix up a place in the barn. She's real strict about people staying in the house, but I know she'd let you stay in the barn with the stock."

Cole laughed inside. "That'd be right nice. Wouldn't be the first time I slept on straw. But I think you'd better ask your ma first."

"Oh, I know she'd let you stay. Mama always is telling me how being polite to others is what the Lord Jesus preached. And I know she wouldn't mind me offering."

Their approach brought them through a cornfield. Cracked ground showed the tops of the roots. The stalks had started to turn brown, and the silks protruding from the small husks appeared singed.

Beyond the cornfield was a weathered A-frame barn. A vacant three-rail corral squared out from the side. A pen with two hogs stretched out from the back. Next to it was a wagon resembling a buckboard, only this one seemed to have been altered for farm work with high side boards and a wider, longer bed. Yellow-leafed plants wilted over a small white fence between the barn and a brown-planked farmhouse. Smoke wisped from the chimney. In front of the house sat a welcome sight.

"You can wash at the pump," the boy offered as they both walked toward it.

A small girl in a brown dress came out from the house. She looked younger than the boy. She came upon both of them which such speed that the young host waved his hand as if he were defending Cole from harmful attack. She stopped suddenly, and her face cringed as she stared at Cole. "What happened to his head?"

"Go back to the house, Evie."

"Who is he? What's he doing here?"

"He isn't here to talk to no stupid girls," the boy disdainfully ordered. "Leave him alone."

"She ain't harmin' me none, boy," Cole murmured.

Noah shot a look of betrayal up at Cole, then snapped it quickly back at the girl. "I found him. Go away, Evie. He doesn't want to talk to you."

"I don't have to. Mama said this farm belongs to all of us, not just you."

Cole ignored the children's squabble and went to the pump. He grabbed the handle and rapidly stroked it.

The boy eagerly offered, "I can do that. Sometimes it takes a long—"

Water gushed out the spout.

"Wow," the two kids uttered in unison.

"Not even Mr. Taylor can get the water out that fast," Evie remarked.

Cole knelt under the flow. The near-frigid relief splashed on his head and ran down his neck and chest. He sucked in mouthfuls, washing down the dust. For the moment all the pain on his brow and his mind was flushed onto the parched dirt.

The last drip splattered on his forehead, and Cole wobbled as he rose, still dizzy from the wound.

The boy smiled. "I can't wait till you meet Mama."

"Noah Joseph!" came a shout from the house.

Cole turned to see a woman standing in the doorway pointing an old musket rifle at him.

"Move away," she said as she raised the weapon to her shoulder.

Cole's hand flinched to his side, but the familiar feel of leather and iron wasn't there.

"Mama, don't shoot him," Noah cried.

"You hush your mouth and get in this house. Evie, you too." A quick breeze flapping her blue skirt and the apron at her waist didn't distract her, and she maintained her aim at Cole. Her blond hair, combed in a bun, kept her eyes clear to aim the old musket. The thin arms coming out of the white blouse sleeves didn't seem strong enough to hold the rifle much longer.

If she fired, it was likely the shot would do her as much harm as Cole, but staring at a barrel trained at his head for the second time in a day kept him from taking the chance.

"But he's hurt bad, Mama."

"He'll be hurting a lot worse with a hole in him."

"You best do what your ma says, boy."

The girl scampered inside the house, but Noah slowly made his way to the porch, all the while looking at Cole.

"You get off my land and tell Owen MacGregor that I ain't leaving. I told him if he sent any more of you I'd shoot them on sight."

Cole raised his hands palms out. "I just came for the water. I mean no trouble."

"I've heard the lies before. If you're not with MacGregor's men, then you're another saddle bum looking for free food. I got none to spare so as to attract more like you. I saw you get the water, so start walking or I'll shoot you where you stand."

The boy looked at his mother. "Mama."

"I said hush, Noah."

Cole nodded. "I'll leave, but first I'd like to thank the boy for his kindness. I'm beholden to you, Noah. I owe you."

"Don't play tricks with his mind. Go on," the woman said without allowing the muzzle's line on him to wander.

Cole walked by the pump and headed past the house, not turning his back but with his hands still lifted. When he was out of sight of the porch he had a mind to go back and show his innocent intentions, but a mother protecting her young, no matter the animal, was unpredictable. A ball in the gut was a poor substitute for a meal. It would be best if he kept walking.

Chapter Three

Lucille Jean-Marie Fontenot peered at the two queens in front of her, then glimpsed her poker hand. Her concentration wandered from the cards, not because of the noise of the crowded tables but because of the dwindling twilight closing in outside O'Malley's Shipwreck Saloon.

"They'll be here soon," she lamented.

The queens peered toward the door.

Dueling Dottie cracked a grin. She was the usual choice of the spenders. Although born Margaret Barrows Caine, she preferred her professional name, bestowed on her by a drunken trail hand enamored with his view through her transparent chemise. The story most passed on was of the cowboy loudly proclaiming that his purchased companion for the night had a chest reminiscent of holstered dueling pistols with dots as big as silver dollars.

Bellowing Betsy had a less glamorous past. She, like Dueling Dottie, had been a veteran of many a cow drive passing by whatever town she was in. With those experiences came the marks of the trade of a lover for hire: two missing teeth, a slanted nose, and a slight limp when it got cold. Her years had taught her one sales tactic that proved productive: the more whiskey she could get her client to drink—along with one fraudulent hooting bellow of ecstasy—the safer and faster the transaction, ending with both parties getting what result they sought.

Betsy looked at young Lucy's frown. "That won't get you much business tonight, honey."

The frown stayed firmly in place.

Dottie showed more concern. "What's the matter now? Are you feeling poorly, or are you still thinking of that fellow some months ago? What was his name?

"Patrick," Betsy answered with disgust.

Lucy took exception to her tone. "He'll come back for me. He said he'd send for me from San Francisco."

"The day after Preacher Brown asks me to lead the choir in 'Amazing Grace.' There ain't but one thing men come in here for, and you're sitting on it."

"Hush, Betsy," Dottie ordered. "We can all have our dreams."

"It's better she get over him now. It took five years for me to stop listening to those drovers in Wichita. All the promises of being taken to Kansas City, St. Louis. I was humping them for nothing just like she did, waiting for them to come back. Miserable bastards."

"Patrick isn't a filthy cowboy," said Lucy, pausing in thought. "It was different with him. He was a gentleman. He treated me with sweetness, dignity, as it should be. Two people who care for each other in each's arms. We shared true passion."

"Oh, please. You're not the first to squat over a man. All he did was say some pretty words and you gave it to him for free. I don't see him walking around now. Just another carpetbagger."

"You know what Jo said about giving up the profit," Dottie said with motherly eyes. "No owner can stay in business that way. Curly collects for every drop poured."

Lucy sighed. "All right, then. You're right. If whoring my virtue is what it takes to leave this place, then I will be the best that a man can buy." Her lips formed a confident smirk. "I'll flop my top and swing my rear, and when I've enough money for a ticket to San Francisco, I'll leave this town to you two hens and the rest of my second-story sisters, while I enjoy the life of a lady."

The two queens wrinkled their noses at each other in false amazement.

The room fell silent. All eyes turned to the front.

Lucy looked to the swinging doors. She saw a black curled brim moving above the smoky haze. The man wearing it passed the tables to stop at the bar. The poor light showed his shirt to be black or green and a bit too large. Dark hide was laced up to his knees. He slapped a shiny dollar on the oak bar and barked a loud order to Curly.

"Whiskey."

The bald bartender brought the bottle to the top of the bar.

"Don't try it on me, old man. I ain't no kid. I want the sour mash from Tennessee. I know you got it."

A complying grin cracked Curly's face, and he reached down.

The stranger sent a hardened glance back at the staring cardplayers, and the betting quickly resumed.

Curly yanked the cork from a square bottle, poured the amber liquid into the shot glass, and swiped the dollar off the bar.

"Good to serve a man who knows his drink."

The man threw the shot down his throat, wheezed out his satisfaction, and wiped an errant drop off his chin with his sleeve. Another pristine piece of silver came from his vest pocket and wobbled to rest on the bar. "One more."

Betsy peered back at Lucy and Dottie. "Could be a ticket

Tim McGuire

to San Francisco waiting in that one's dungarees," she cackled at the two of them.

"Can a man get something to eat in this town?" boomed the stranger's voice.

Curly smiled as he answered. "You can get anything you want in Nobility. The best steak in New Mexico is at Donovan's down the street. If you like home cooking, Emma Brantley runs a boardinghouse on Mason Street, and she always serves supper at six o'clock sharp."

The stranger swigged the shot, and Curly quickly refilled the glass.

"Livery is at the end of town on Main. Six bits buys a stall and oats for the night. Clyde Sullivan's boy will take him there for you and rub the animal down for a nickel. Chinese have the laundry business here. There are three shops in their part of town. Wong's gets them the cleanest and delivers them back to you. I'd be happy to send for them."

The stranger downed the shot, exhaled, and put the glass back on the bar. "How does a man go about getting a hot bath and a warm whore?"

Curly grinned. "Like I said, you can get anything you want in Nobility." He curled his knuckles and knocked twice on the bar.

"There's the signal, honey," Betsy said with a wink to Lucy. "Remember what I taught you."

Lucy rose and caught the eye of the stranger as he turned toward her. She tossed her auburn hair over her shoulder in order to show her sprouting chest.

"This's Little Lucy," Curly whispered to the stranger.

Her prance to the bar brought a smile to his face. "Buy a lady a drink?" she said, rubbing her palm on the back of his hand.

They found two freshly poured shots on the bar.

Lucy picked up a glass and sipped the whiskey, while her

mark gulped the liquor down. "My name is Lucy. What's yours?"

The stranger smiled wide. "Billy Mansfield. You may have heard of me?"

Lucy shook her head. "No. Should I have?"

Mansfield's grin shrank. "Well, I guess if you didn't know it before, I should give you a good reason never to forget it now." He slammed the shot glass on the bar.

Lucy flinched at the smack of glass against wood, then quickly resumed her enticing smile. "What did you have in mind?"

"Barkeep here says I can have anything I want in this town." He took a false step backward, caught himself, and grinned again. "I just spent two days' ride gettin' here. I've found the mash to wash out the dust, now I'm looking for a hot bath and warm . . . company to get all the kinks out of my bones."

Lucy peered at him from the boots up, pausing a moment on the holstered revolver at his waist, then brought her eyes to meet his. "You get right to it, don't you?" She shook her head once. "Can't argue with a man who knows what he wants. A bath is two dollars."

"And what about the company?"

She gazed quickly at the sweat-stained shirt, soiled pants, and whisker-stubbled face. "The bath is first. Then we'll see how much company you're willing to pay for." She took his hand.

His wide grin returned as he sank his other hand into his pants pocket, threw a double eagle onto the bar, and grabbed the square bottle. "Send for the Chinaman. I reckon I won't have need of clothes for a while. That should cover the room, too."

Curly nodded.

Lucy led him like a pony around the tables and up the stairs. At the top, she glanced at the queens smiling below.

"The next train west leaves at noon, honey," Dottie called, and they both laughed.

Lucy lifted the bucket from the potbellied stove and stumbled while approaching the porcelain tub. The weight made her slosh the scalding water on the wooden floor. Her cloth-covered hand tipped the bucket into the tub. The sound of the splash was drowned out by Mansfield's shout.

"Goddamn, you're going to boil me, woman!"

"Just a little warm water to get the smell off you," she said in her most southern accent.

"You don't have to melt the skin off with it." He grabbed the bottle of mash and took two long gulps. "I ain't that drunk enough not to feel it."

She knelt by the side of the tub and scrubbed the soap into a pink washcloth. After dipping it into the water, she wrung the cloth over the front of her thin chemise. The drops soaked the fabric, leaving a glistening shine on her modest cleavage. She glimpsed his notice of her. His smile signaled the success of her intended accident. She forced her most embarrassed smile across her face.

Three quick knocks came from the door. Mansfield motioned her to answer. Lucy rose and opened the door a crack. A Chinese girl stood in the hall. She recognized the girl's stringy unbound black hair, worn brown shirt, and black pants that stopped knee high above her sandaled feet.

"Laundry, please," the girl said.

"That be that Chinaman come to get my clothes," Mansfield said without looking at the door.

Lucy held up one finger and shut the door. "He sent his daughter," she muttered. "I can't believe he sent that little girl up here." She walked to the bed and picked up the dark-green shirt and dust-colored pants. Coins spilled from the pockets and chattered on the floor.

"Hell, girl. Watch what you're doing," Mansfield scolded.

Lucy picked up the coins. "I'm sorry." With his eyes

turned away, she slipped two silver dollars between her breasts. She went back and opened the door. She gave the girl the clothes but clutched her hand. The girl looked confused bordering on fright. Lucy removed the dollars and forced them into the girl's palm. She put a finger to her lips and winked.

The girl smiled and nodded.

She closed the door and scurried back to the side of the tub. "Where were we? Oh, I remember," Lucy said with a sly grin as she sank her hands into the water.

He took another swig from the bottle and exhaled the bite of the whiskey. Streams of the amber liquid rolled down to his chin. "Where did you learn to talk like that? Where are you from, girl?"

"Louisiana."

"What part?"

She continued rubbing the washcloth against his hairy legs. "Alexandria."

His smile widened when she began soaping his thin-haired chest. "I'm from the South too. I was born in the capital of the Confederacy. Montgomery, Alabama. Some folks think the capital was in Richmond, but they are mistaken." He burped. "Long live Dixie," he shouted, and took another swig from the bottle. "That bastard Lincoln, whipping his dog Grant down our throats—" Two long gulps later he paused, then smiled. "But the South was avenged. Long live John Wilkes Booth," he cried again, then started laughing.

A cynical grin creased Lucy's face. "He's dead. I heard they shot him."

Mansfield quickly scowled, and he lunged forward and gripped her arm. The bathwater's wave lapped into her face. His brow furled and his eyes had a maniacal squint. "Show your respect as a southern woman. Never mock the cause."

She took a long slow breath, trying to slow her rapid heart. It had been a long time since she had been afraid to be alone in a room with a man. Betsy's advice rang in her head; she needed to conclude this interlude as soon possible. "Forgive me." Her voice was laced with the most regret she could muster. "I meant no disrespect."

Her lips parted in a sweet smile. She renewed the swabbing of his chest, sinking the soaping circle lower from his belly to other parts of his body under the water's surface.

Mansfield's scowl slackened to a look of drunken disinterest.

She rubbed the cloth under his knee and moved to his inner thigh. "A southern woman prides herself on how well she can entertain her guest."

She watched his grin broaden with each stroke of her arm. When she felt the objective of her intentions obstruct her motion, she released the cloth and wrapped her fingers around it.

His eyes opened.

She slightly tightened her grip. "Should we discuss the price of my company now?"

His tongue flopped through his open jaws. He clutched her breasts, ripping the chemise to lap at her flesh. He rose from the water. Muscles bulged from his bony arms. Her free hand pushed against his chest, but she couldn't stop him from lifting her. Like a hungry animal, he bit her skin.

She clung on top of his shoulders as he stepped from the tub. Her sucked her nipples like beer foam. His hands wrapped under her thighs, gripping the garter straps and shredding the satin.

She grasped his hair to gain balance on top of this bucking bronco. As she felt a fleshy prod between her legs, she remembered her lessons from Bellowing Betsy and envisioned the sites of San Francisco, which seemed closer than she had ever imagined them.

He slobbered kisses up her neck and over her chin, touching her lips. The stench of his whiskey-stained breath inflamed her nose. She had sold her body, but not her heart.

"Don't kiss me."

The rocking motion stopped. She looked down to see his furrowing face. The impact of his hand against her cheek dropped her to the floor.

"You whore!" His nails dug into her arm and yanked her to her feet. "You want me to treat you like a whore?"

She screamed. Her tightened chest squeezed away her breath as his enraged face flashed by her view. She clawed his cheek. He took hold of her auburn hair.

Her heart pounded, terrified he would kill her.

A fist slammed into her stomach bent her over. He pulled her to the bed. His strength mashed her face into the carefully spread blanket. Her delicate bottom burned from his lancing presence.

"Whore!"

Knuckles crashed against her jaw.

"Lucy. Lucy. Are you okay, honey?" Dottie cried through the door. She kicked at the handle, and the door flew open.

Mansfield stood naked in the center of the room. Behind him was Little Lucy, her knees on the floor, her bare top bent over onto the bed. She didn't move.

"Get the hell out of here. I paid twenty dollars for this room," he declared.

"You son of a bitch. What have you done?" Dottie yelled as she and Betsy entered. "What did you do to her? Jo will have your hide—"

Mansfield reached down and gripped the forty-five from the holster on the floor. The click of the pulled hammer, muzzle aimed at their heads, stopped them both.

"I said I paid for the room. Now get out."

They retreated to the hall. The door crashing shut sent them running down the stairs. "Go to get the marshal. He's hit Little Lucy," Dottie screamed at Curly.

"There's no law against that," said the confused bartender.

"Bastard. You're no better than him," Betsy shouted. The two queens ran past the tables and out the batwing doors.

Marshal Clement C. Thomas carefully poured his first coffee of the evening into his favorite cup. The cup had been given to him three years before by the town fathers upon his sixth-month anniversary as the presiding peace officer of Nobility. As he sipped the steaming brew, he reflected on his success in making the once raucous mining settlement the law-abiding city that it had become. It was the biggest pride of his fifty-two years.

The office door burst open. His reflex made the hot coffee singe his lip.

"What the—" He stopped as he saw the two most famous attractions in all of Nobility standing in his door. "What are you two doing here?"

"Marshal, we need you to come quick. There's a stranger at the Shipwreck and I think he's killed Little Lucy," Dottie panted out. The door became crowded with arriving gawkers.

"Little Lucy? That little girl from Louisiana?"

Both women nodded. "He pulled a gun on us. With Jo out of town, we got no one but you to get her out of there to see if she is alive," Betsy said.

"Just wait a minute."

"You've got to hurry, Marshal. He looks mean, like a gunman, a man-killer. I've seen the type in Wichita before."

"I said wait a damn minute," Thomas shouted.

A tear rolled down Dottie's cheek. "He's hurt her bad, Clement."

"Do we need to go get Vance for you, Marshal?" came a cry from the crowd.

"No. Vance MacGregor is the last thing I need. This town has enough holes in it as it is." Thomas swung around in his chair and stood. "Do we even know who this fellow is?"

"He knows," shouted a voice. A small man in a gray wool coat emerged from the mass.

"Well, who is he?" Thomas asked.

The small man cleared his throat. "I saw him when I was in Colorado about two weeks ago. A town named Platte Falls." He stopped talking due to the shouts from the increasing crowd outside of the door.

"Wait," Thomas ordered. The shouts quieted. "Go on."

"I saw him there. Killed three men in a gunfight."

"What's his name?"

"I don't know that. But it's the same man. The hat, leggings up to the knee. No two men can be mistaken like that."

The shouts for justice rose, then fell when the marshal raised his hand. "But you don't know his name?"

The small man nodded. "I know he was called the Rainmaker."

"What? Like some dowser?"

"Don't know. All I heard him called was that name. After the shooting was over, he took a woman that had just come from the train."

"Took a woman? Took her where? What happened to her?"

"He took her right out of town up into the mountains. I never heard what became of her. My business was done in Platte Falls the next day."

"Oh no," said Dottie as she closed her eyes. "Clement, you got to do something about him."

The distinct brogue of one of Thomas's biggest irritants pierced the crowd's muttering. "Sounds as if we have a celebrity in town, Marshal."

Thomas bit his lip so as not to say what he thought of the foreigner who pushed through to the front, dressed in a buttoned vest, starched-collar white shirt, bow tie, a plaid coat, and a cap.

"Didn't take you long. Is the smell of blood that strong, Kennemer?"

"Someone has to report the truth of what happened before it becomes fiction. I believe the citizens of Nobility have the

37

right to know what they are paying taxes for. Anything to say for the paper?''

''Nothing you could print.'' The marshal took a deep breath and turned to take his gun belt and forty-four from the hook on the wall. He pulled the revolver and checked all six chambers. They were full. He placed it back in the holster.

A year had passed since he'd spent a cartridge in the line of duty. An old miner full of liquor and empty of money and aces wouldn't part with his greener aimed at the dealer at the Shipwreck. After having counted to three, firing a bullet into that crusty bastard's chest was the only choice he had left himself. It was a good idea at the time; most men died instantly when shot in the heart. Although his aim didn't fail him, he didn't feel like a lawman when that scattergun painted the wall with the dealer's face. He swore then he wouldn't put himself in a corner again.

He exhaled and strapped on the gun belt. ''I best go get him before I lose another voter.''

The crowd parted as the marshal passed.

''Some more coffee, Marshal?''

Vance MacGregor stopped slicing into the steak on his plate to peek up at Libby Tidwell's shining face. He had known her since she became orphaned in an Apache raid on a wagon train from Missouri. His father had told him then that if she had been a boy the Apache would have kept her to become one of the warring bucks. Being a baby girl in a basket, she would need too much care before she could serve as a slave to the tribe, and at least twelve years before she would be useful bearing young. She had been left to die in the desert as a symbol of the white man's fate in Apache land.

It was his parents who took Libby from the soldiers and provided her with a roof, food, and clothes. Vance was made a big brother for the infant, but after four years he didn't feel right as a man to be saddled with a little sister, especially one not from his own mother. He made that known with frequent protests. Libby turned five the day his mother left this world after being thrown from her favorite gelding. With his mother gone, her loss coupled with his father's plans for him didn't leave room for Libby's needs. His father arranged for Big Jim Donovan to take her in with his three girls. Once her older stepsisters left, Libby was like an only child. Everyone in town knew her story. She had followed Vance around the last eleven years, eager to finally gain the MacGregor name.

Vance resumed cutting into the beef. "Libby, you know I'm only a deputy."

She placed the steaming pitcher on the table and sat in a chair across from him. "And you know it's you that everyone thinks of as the real marshal of Nobility. Why, Clement Thomas is just an old man who's in your way."

"Don't be saying things like that."

"It's true. People here don't mind their business because of him. If anyone were to cross the law, they know they'd have to face the gun of Vance MacGregor." Her fingers brushed the back of his hand. "That's the kind of thing a man is to be admired for. A thing a woman could take pride in, knowing how everyone thinks of her man."

Vance slowly moved his hand away. "Libby . . ." He stopped once her smile was gone and her head dipped to view the floor. He always figured he'd have to set her straight on how he felt, but every time he started, his will to talk crumbled with that shattered look on her face. "Someone could see you. It's not good for a girl to chase after a man."

"A girl!"

"You know what I mean. I've known you since you were a little baby. I mean, well, you know what I mean." She raised her head to show her tear-welled eyes, a sight he never became comfortable seeing. "Ah, Libby, don't go to crying. People here will think I called you a name."

"I guess they'd be right."

His chest sunk a bit, but it seemed the right time to rid himself of the burden he had kept inside all these years. "Libby, I like you, I like you a lot. You're already like family to me. Can't you see? It's as if you're my little sister. And it ain't right for a brother to court a sister. You can understand that, can't you?"

Loose strands of hair dangled in front of her tear-streamed face. She brushed the hairs behind her ear, failing to match her long single braid. A tear dripped from her chin and darkened one of the blue dots on her red blouse. "I guess you're right," she said, blankly staring at the wall. "I'll try not to shame you anymore."

Vance rolled his eyes. "Why is it when I talk to you I feel like I'm in a mudhole sinking deeper with each step?"

"Maybe it's 'cause you can't bring yourself to tell me what you really want to say. Well, I've got something to say, Deputy Vance MacGregor. Something I don't know if you want to hear."

A blur of someone running past the front window tore his eyes from her.

"I don't care if the whole town knows," she continued, but Vance's attention was fixed on the scurrying townspeople outside.

"Hold up, Libby," he said, rising from his chair, taking his six-gun off the table, and snugging it into the holster. He planted his brown hat over his black hair. He was quickly outside Donovan's, and despite Libby's shouts behind him, he didn't hear a word.

He sought anyone who could tell him what all the fuss was about. A plaid wool cap caught his eye. It belonged to the man whose business it was to know such things.

"Kennemer." His call slowed the newsman to only a brisk gait. "Why is everyone running?"

"I suppose it's to see the show the marshal's soon to put on over at the Shipwreck."

40

"Who's there?"

"Don't know that meself. That's part the reason for the interest. Seems there's an outlaw that fancies beating up women. He may have already killed one of them."

"Killed one? Which one?"

"Lucy Fontenot. The little tart from the South. You'll excuse me, Deputy, but there are a few facts I need to gather for me own."

Vance resumed a quick pace toward the Shipwreck saloon.

Marshal Thomas entered the batwings of the Shipwreck. All exchange of cards and coins stopped as he strode to the stairs. He turned and halted the procession behind him with a point of his finger.

"You people stay down here. This is the law's business, and I don't need any more work keeping any of you from getting killed."

He pulled his gun and stepped up to the second floor. He cocked the hammer and turned the knob on the door to Lucy's room. The force of a rammed boot heel swung it wide open within an instant. Entering, he centered the forty-four on a man sitting on the edge of the bed and wearing only the whisker stubble on his stupefied face.

"Hold it there, mister. Get them hands in the air."

The drunk slowly complied with the order.

Thomas walked in with his gaze drawn to the still woman on her knees, stripped to the waist, her bloodied face nosed into the sheets. True enough, it looked to be Lucy.

"Who the hell are you?" asked the drunk, squinting at Thomas.

"I'm the one that sees you get to a fair trial and no one kills you before you're hung." Thomas turned his head away a moment and breathed deeply. While staring at his prisoner, he called for Dottie to come up. The clomping of shoes on the wooden stairs was quickly followed by horrified shrieks.

Tim McGuire

Dottie and Betsy ran past the marshal to Lucy. Thomas motioned with his gun. "Get away from them."

The drunk stood and stumbled over to the wall.

Moments later, Dottie spoke. "Clement, I think she may still be alive. We got to get her to Doc Fuller's, but we got to hurry."

"Get going. Have some of them downstairs help you if need be."

The two women wrapped the bed blanket around Lucy and carried her out of the room.

Thomas shook his head. "You son of a bitch. Why did you come to my town? Killing men in Colorado wasn't enough for you, so you had to come here to punch women?"

The drunk looked confused. "Colorado? What are you talking about?"

"I know about you."

"You heard of me?" A slight grin grew on the drunk's face.

"Yeah, I heard stories of you shooting three men in Platte Falls and taking a woman to shield your escape. But you came to the wrong town. Here we don't fear the lawless. We do with your kind as the law says, you 'Rainmaker.'"

"What did you call me?"

"I'll not play games with you." Thomas heard hateful shouts from downstairs, probably caused by the sight of Little Lucy's passing. He sensed a lynch mob building like brushfire, but his pride as peace officer couldn't let that happen. The faster he got this man behind iron bars, the easier it would be to put out those flames. Though marching a naked man before a crowd could make for trouble.

"Get your clothes on."

The drunk searched the floor a moment. "I got none. The Chinaman got them."

"Well, pull those sheets around you, then."

The drunk complied again with the marshal's orders. He lifted the bedsheet around his body.

Thomas glanced behind him to see that the stairs would be clear.

"Marshal," the drunk said.

Thomas looked back at him.

"You really heard of me?" he said, only a single hand holding the cloaking sheet.

As Thomas raised his drooped forty-four, hot lead ripped through his chest. His gun fired before he hit the floor. Heat filled him inside. He spat blood from his mouth and gurgled in air. He rolled his shoulders from side to side, trying to get to his feet. Only his arms would move. His hands pressed against his bloody shirt. He had to get up before the drunk could shoot again.

Bells clamored in his head. As he looked around, Vance MacGregor was at his side. The deputy's mouth moved like he was talking, but Thomas could hear only the bells. The marshal pointed toward where he thought the drunk was standing. Vance shook his head, and his faint voice matched his lips.

"He's dead. You hold on, Clement."

Thomas smiled, but there was one more thing to do. He stretched out his shaking finger and touched the tin star on Vance's shirt. With all his force he jabbed his finger into his deputy's chest. The bells fell distantly silent, and a black shroud blotched away Vance's face.

Chapter Four

The grin slackened, the eyelids quivered and closed. Vance felt the body's weight sag into his arms. Despite calling out his friend's name, there was nothing he could do except watch the last few moments of Marshal Clement C. Thomas's life.

The man who had first taught him respect for the law before allowing Vance to pin on a deputy badge lay dead from a bullet in the gut. If Vance had been a step faster up the stairs it was likely his quick gun could have made the difference between Clement breathing or not. That chance was gone forever.

Vance carefully laid Clement's head on the floor. The gasps and shrieks from people downstairs upon sight of the dead marshal dug into his spine like a hundred cactus needles.

He rose and turned to the motionless gunman on the bed. The man lay naked, a forty-five-caliber Colt resting in his open palm. As Vance walked toward him, he heard a low buzzing. As he came nearer, he spotted a slight movement of the man's chest. There was no blood, no holes in his body or the wall.

"You ain't dead. You son of a bitch, you're just passed out." Vance drew his gun. "A no-good tramp, you don't deserve to still be alive." He pointed the muzzle at the man's forehead and cocked the hammer. "Maybe this is what you came for?"

"Do you think so, Deputy?"

Kennemer's voice stopped Vance's finger from squeezing the trigger. "Go back downstairs, Irish."

"I think I'll stay. It seems there's soon to be something happening which people will want to know about. It wouldn't do for me to miss it."

There were times when Vance wanted to shoot that pesky newspaperman. It occurred to him he may get the chance someday with less reason than what he had now. Clement had hated that Irishman with a passion, but he had never broken the law.

Clement was the law, and there was no reason for the law to kill somebody if it could be helped, not even the low-down filth that had killed him. Vance felt the spot in his chest where Clement's finger had jabbed him.

He slowly reset the hammer and took the forty-five Colt.

Ann Hayes watched her son pick at the food on the plate in front of him. It was the way he acted when something was on his mind but he didn't want to tell her. Usually, it was about matters she couldn't answer to a young boy's satisfaction; matters that a boy needed a father for.

"May I be excused?" Noah asked.

"You haven't finished your plate, son. We don't have food to waste. You know that."

Noah pointed his disappointed face back to the stew and took a reluctant bite.

She wanted to ask what troubled him, but felt she knew

and didn't feel a need to discuss it at the dinner table. A glimpse at Evie happily eating her meal brightened the moment.

"I told Lorna Clendenon that you would be starting school this year," Ann said. "She said it would be nice to have another girl in the class."

Evie smiled.

Ann turned to Noah. "How many girls were in the school last year?"

His eyes peered up from the plate. "I don't know. Who cares about stupid girls?"

"Noah, I won't have you talk that way. Not in my house."

"Yes, ma'am."

Evie finished her stew.

"Do you want more?" her mother asked.

The young girl shook her head.

"Then put up your dishes." Evie got up from the table and placed her plate and spoon in a large bucket next to the stove. Ann's attention returned to Noah. He continued to push the spoon through the pile of stew, with most of the serving still on the plate.

"If you don't want my cooking, then you can see that Bender has enough to eat, the hogs too, and get into bed."

She met his look of protest with one of firm resolve he wouldn't challenge. He rose from the table, cleared his dishes, and headed outside for the barn.

A pain twinged inside her as he slammed the door behind him. It was the same pain she often felt after talking with her son.

Her concern was interrupted by Evie's loving arms wrapping around her neck. "It's getting near your bedtime, too."

"Will you read to me?"

Ann smiled and nodded.

Noah returned to the house as Ann closed her Bible. She rose from her chair and leaned over the top bunk bed, kissed her slumbering daughter's cheek, and pulled the blanket over the girl's shoulders.

Noah's face was the same as when he had left, one of resentment from being cheated out of something he wanted, something a mother knew nothing about.

"Are you done feeding all the stock?"

He nodded his head without looking at her. She felt an urge to go and hug her dejected son, but he was at an age when boys didn't want or need a mother's embrace.

"Get in your bed clothes and go to sleep."

Ann swept the floor and washed the dishes as Noah changed into a long bed shirt and climbed onto the lower bunk.

She slowly came to the bed and knelt next to him. Her fingers combed through his hair, brushing his bangs back from his forehead for her to plant a kiss—a maternal reflex when her children hurt in any way.

"Is this all because of that drifter today?"

Noah nodded. "His name is Clay."

"I'm sorry, son, you feel the way you do. But we talked before how we've got to be a lot more careful about strangers coming around. I've said before that I need your help to protect us."

Noah rolled onto his side and closed his eyes. Ann continued touching his hair, remarking how her son looked so much like his father. His blond locks had all turned brown now. Noah had kept his blue eyes since the day he came into the world ten years before. That was the happiest day of her life. She cherished the memory of Robert's blue eyes welled with tears when the boy was born, clutching her hand just as tight as he did on their wedding day. She had the family she'd dreamed of since she was a young girl in Missouri.

News of free land brought them west. While traveling to this new home, she learned they'd left Missouri with another child on the way. When she first saw the land at the end of the Rockies, it scared her. Robert reassured her that he could make good of it and soon made it a home with a house and a farm.

Just as with Noah, he stayed with her the whole time she birthed Evie. He kissed her gently and whispered his love while holding their baby girl. It was Robert's wish to have eight more children, the same-size family in which he was raised. Although it wasn't her desire to mother so many, she would have done so to fulfill her husband's desires. There was plenty of time to build a bigger house and fill it with children, or so she was confident at the time.

While staring at Noah's hair, a knifing scent stabbed her nose. Smoke!

The stove showed no signs of it, nor the kindling either. The lantern hooked to the wall was dark, and the table candle flickered peacefully.

Her silhouette flashed on the wall. She turned around to the window, and there she saw giant flames leaping skyward from the barn.

"Noah!" Ann screamed, shaking her son once as she rushed to the door. "The barn's on fire. Get Evie out of the house." As she came off the porch steps, the light revealed a red bandanna snagged in the front bushes. This was no accident.

She ran to the barn. What little stock they had was inside. Besides their horrible fate, she couldn't afford the loss. The heavy smoke forced her back from the door, but she couldn't stop.

She glanced at the house where her children stood on the porch. She loved them. They were her life. She couldn't just watch their future burn. Ann held her breath, dipped her head, and charged for the barn door.

A fire from the barn lit up the whole farm from the dark of night. Noah saw his mother disappear into the spiraling black smoke. He needed to go after her, but his mind couldn't tell him what to do first. Evie screamed louder and louder, pushing him more toward the fire, but his feet wouldn't run.

Had he dropped a match? Had he left the lantern on the hay? Where was his mama? When would she come out?

Evie screamed, "No, Mama. No, Mama." The fire became blurred by tears. He had to do something. His mama was in there.

He jumped off the porch and with one running step felt his arm snatched from behind, yanking him backward.

When he looked for what had grabbed him, there was Cole, still in his yellow shirt, his face furled like that of a mean dog, the fire dancing on his eyeballs.

Noah shivered as Cole yelled out, "Where's your ma?"

He pointed a shaking finger, unable to swallow the tears fast enough to speak.

Cole released Noah's arm and with one leap was on the porch and quickly inside the house, emerging with a blanket. He was off the porch as quick as a jackrabbit, running to the pump. He cranked the handle faster than he had that morning. Water blew out of the spout. Cole soaked the blanket, then wrapped it over his shoulder as he ran to the barn.

"Fill some buckets," he yelled, and the sight of him shrank behind the wall of smoke.

Noah stood still a moment, not sure he had really seen the man run after his ma, but the pain from where Cole had squeezed his arm was still there. That slight faith made him run inside the house. He took the bucket full of plates and forks and slung out the dishes. He came out of the house and ran just as Cole had, jumping from the porch steps, stopping at the dripping pump. A few cranks of the handle and the water gushed from the spout again. When the water began spilling over the rim, Noah lifted the bucket and trudged toward the fire. He yelled at Evie to fill another bucket, but she still stood frozen to the porch.

A loud crash, such as one from a lightning storm, stopped Noah. He looked at the fiery south-side wall of the barn crumbling to the ground. Another long aching groan came when the roof sank into the center of the collapsing structure. Now nothing stood where the fire swirled.

Water splashed Noah's leg from the bucket hitting the ground. Nobody had left the barn. His mama was under the pile of burning wood. His throat tightened, his knees buckled; he was sure he had seen her for the last time. He took one step, then another, staring at the bleary glowing light.

He wiped away the tears, and when he looked again he saw Bender galloping away from the far side of the flames, and just behind that was a figure coming closer to him. It looked like a man carrying a long log over his shoulder.

He didn't want to fool himself into believing a dream, but it came true. Cole was running at him.

As he ran past, Noah saw it wasn't a log but something rolled inside the blanket.

"Mama!"

Noah ran after Cole, following him inside the house. His mama was lying in his bed. Her cheeks were smudged black, her sleeves burnt through to the skin.

Cole knelt beside the bed. Noah hugged his mother's neck.

"Go get some water!" Cole yelled.

His loud voice brought Noah to his senses. He ran outside and retrieved the bucket. When he returned inside, Cole had his mouth over Mama's mouth.

"What are you doing? Why are you doing that?"

Cole glared at him. "Give me the water." Noah brought the bucket, and Cole dipped his cupped hands into it, then dripped it carefully on his mother's face. He did the same thing three times, then put his mouth over hers again and started blowing. He stopped.

"She ain't breathing."

He turned to Noah. "Go outside."

Noah shook his head.

"Go! Now!"

Noah took only a few steps, then stopped once Cole's head turned back to Mama. He could see only the big man's back, and Mama's head poking past his shoulder. He heard cloth ripping. Then Cole began pushing her chest, the same way he did the pump handle, but not nearly as fast. Mama's head poked farther out from behind Cole's shoulder. Cole pushed at Mama's chest again.

A cough boomed through the silence. Noah saw his mother's cheeks become sucked in, and then she coughed once more. He ran over to the bed, peering over Cole's shoulder to see his mama lying with the blanket slid up under her chin. Her eyes were still closed, but the blanket rose and fell with each breath she took.

Ann's head began throbbing as she squinted from a blinding light. She covered over the light with her hand and focused on the vacant interior of her house. She sat up in Noah's bed, peeking beneath the blanket that covered her. Her breasts showed through her torn blouse and corset. Bringing the blanket back to her chin, she called for her son.

"Noah!"

Instantly, the horrible memory of the barn in flames came to mind. Where were her son and daughter?

"Noah! Evie!"

A long moment passed before her children pierced the western sunshine coming through the open door. She lay back on the bed, hugging and kissing both of their heads pressed against her chest. She didn't want to let go, but the smell of burnt wood lingered.

"Are both of you all right?"

They nodded.

"How are you feeling, Mama?"

"I'm fine, Evie." Ann again sat up in the bed, keeping the blanket taut around her chest.

She glimpsed gray smoke drifting in a light breeze. When she leaned forward, she saw the stranger she had run off the day before. He was standing next to the pump, rinsing that red bandanna and wiping his face with it.

51

"Why is he here?" she asked while getting to her feet. She went quickly through the door next to the stove, which led to her bedroom. Closing the door, she dropped the blanket and put on her winter coat and drew the musket from under her bed. In an instant she returned to the front porch and aimed the rifle at the stranger.

"I told you to get off my land."

The stranger didn't move.

"No, Mama. You don't know."

"Hush, son. It was him that set fire to the barn last night."

"No, Mama. He didn't do it," said Noah. "But he did pull you out of it. I saw him."

The remark made Ann drop the aim of the musket. He still didn't move.

"It's true. He blowed air in you and then punched you to make you cough."

Ann grasped the front of her coat, realizing what this man must have done and seen if her boy was telling the truth. Even though she was alive, just for that moment she wished she were dead.

She stepped down and walked to stand in front of the man, her eyes darting down to the front of her coat. "Did you do this?"

He nodded.

She slapped him before he could speak. "I wish you to hell. I told you to get off my land. Now, go!"

He rubbed his cheek. "I thought you'd appreciate it. I didn't think it right to leave them kids alone. I guess I was wrong." He turned and walked away.

She didn't like him. However, if Noah was telling the truth, she had just slapped the man who saved her life, and her children's as well. Ingratitude wasn't part of her upbringing.

"Wait."

He continued walking.

She aimed the musket at him. "I said wait."

He slowly faced her.

"Did you really do what my son says?"

He nodded.

"I guess I'm beholden to you."

He rubbed his cheek.

"Then I—I have to ask you to forgive me," Ann said, not believing she spoke those words to him. "I guess any man that would set fire to a barn wouldn't be worrying about what got burned up in it."

He walked back to her.

"Can't he stay, Mama? He's got to eat."

She extended her hand. "My name is Ann Hayes. I see you've already met my children. I at least owe you a meal and a place to rest."

"I'll take you up on that. I'm Clay Cole."

"I'm sorry I slapped you," she said as she glanced again at her coat. "But I felt I had to."

"Well, I didn't have much choice last night."

"No, I suppose you didn't." She looked at the smoldering heap that was once her barn.

"Your hogs are dead. I buried them," Cole said. "But there are still some chickens. I'd say you're lucky the fire didn't spread to the cornfield. I didn't see no damage to your buckboard. And that gray gelding is tied to the back of the house."

"Yeah, Mama. Bender saved you too," said an excited Noah. "Ain't that true, Clay?"

"That's the truth. When I got inside the barn, you were on the ground. I wasn't sure how I was going to get you and me out of there, until the horse pawed down the wall and I followed him out."

Ann recalled the flames licking the inside of the barn. The smoke had burned her throat and gagged her breath, and finally she felt the pain against her head. "I'm sorry for what I said to you. There's a man who's been trying to get me off this land. Owen MacGregor is his name. He owns the big

53

ranch just west of those hills. When I saw you with that bandanna, I thought you might be working for him.''

''You think he's the one that did this?''

''I can't prove nothing. I just know he's been wanting this land ever since we got here.'' She stopped talking as if there was more to tell, but not to strangers. Her eyes squinted as she stared at his face. ''What happened to your eye?''

''He got shot!'' Noah clamored. ''A bank robber shot him and I found him. Ain't that right? It looks better now. It's almost gone. You should have seen it when I first saw him. Tell her.''

Ann and Cole turned to the boy. ''That is right,'' Cole answered. ''He does have a gift for using that tongue.''

''From the day he was born,'' Ann finished. She took a long sigh. ''Well, I don't have much to offer you. I don't have room in the house, but should you—''

''I'm used to sleeping outside,'' said Cole.

She nodded, but without smiling, and walked to the house. She was grateful for what he had done, but for a woman alone with two young children, trust wasn't something given to strangers.

Chapter Five

The cool dawn breeze had given way to a hot, still morning. Cole felt the sun's heat on his bare shoulders as he sifted through the charred remnants of the barn. He searched for anything salvageable for rebuilding it but found only scattered nails. They were still as scorching hot as any branding iron, even though it was more than a day since the fire.

He had seen this before.

Lightning had set his own barn ablaze almost twenty years before. The sight the morning after looked much like this one. Building a new barn had seemed a hopeless task at the time, but it also had become one of the few memories of his pa that he welcomed. A rare happy time, even with the loss of the barn.

He remembered how his pa never took the fire as a sign that things were going against him, but more of a challenge to survive it, to overcome whatever might be set in his way.

It was the earliest he remembered using a hammer, a saw, and other tools. His pa was skilled in many trades, as many men were. Soon all the nail-joined planks began to take shape, and before long a new barn was standing. Besides having back what had been lost, they both took pride in knowing they had built it together.

He now viewed the pile of ashen wood for what it could supply him rather than what it had taken. His hands were soon blackened collecting nails, hinges, and braces, and even though he would need more, a vision of what he could do swirled inside his mind.

"What are you doing?" asked a voice from behind him.

He turned around to see the smile on Evie's face change to near shock as she stared at his body. Her mouth fell open. Her eyes scanned him from one side to the other, then locked in the center.

Cole glanced at his chest, surprised by the child's reaction. He quickly put on his shirt to stop further questions. "Ah, I'm just trying to see what might be worth using over to build the barn." His answer brought her attention back to his face. "What are you doing out here?"

"Oh, Mama told me to come call you in for breakfast."

"Breakfast?"

"Yeah. We still got some eggs, and she's almost done with the corncakes." She paused and stared at the soot on his hands. "You better wash your hands, or my mama won't let you in the house."

Cole smiled and nodded. "That's a small price to pay to be fed. You tell your ma that I'll be in shortly."

The girl skipped back into the house.

Cole walked to the pump and cranked the handle, building a surge that rinsed the soot from his hands. He rubbed them against his shirttail and entered the house. The aroma of fresh-baked biscuits stopped him at the door, but Noah's brightened face brought him farther inside.

"Come on in, Clay. You're going to sit by me."

"Noah Joseph," Ann snapped from the stove.

"It's all right, Mama. He told me to call him Clay."

Ann glanced at Cole, then glared back at her son. "I'll not have you act disrespectful in my house."

"Oh, Mama."

Cole felt just as shamed as the boy. "Your ma is right. I shouldn't have told you to call me that. It's my fault." He sat next to Noah.

Ann placed the corncake dish on the table and busily turned back to the stove.

Cole picked up his fork and stabbed one of the cakes, but stopped when he noticed the children's hands in their laps. He shook loose the cake and set his fork down.

Ann put a basket of warm biscuits next to Noah, then brought the skillet of scrambled eggs around the table, scooping a serving onto each plate. She sat down and bowed her head, as did her children. A brief blessing over the meal was said.

Cole's head remained up, and he was embarrassed by his ignorance of the prayer. He took the children's action of placing the cakes on their plates as a sign that it was now time to eat.

As he broke open a biscuit, he couldn't help but admire what surrounded him. Not much more than a day before, this woman lay near death from breathing smoke, her barn burned to the ground. Yet she didn't sulk in tears but continued caring for her family and him, still finding enough strength to be strict about her son's manners. There was something familiar about this as well. Something from his own past. He felt a need, a duty to be paying for the eggs he was eating, but he had no money.

"I was looking at what was left of the barn," he said. "I think I could get another standing in no time without spending too much." He had hoped to get a smile from Ann, but she only glanced at him.

"You know how to build barns?" asked Noah.

Cole nodded. "Helped my pa build one. It's been a good while since then." He stared at Ann until her eyes met his.

"It's been a long time since I was on a farm."

She ducked her head down toward her plate.

"Can I help you?" Noah asked with increasing excitement.

"Me, too?" said Evie.

"Both of you need to finish your breakfast. We can't be late," Ann ordered, still looking at her plate. The children's faces soured upon hearing their mother's command.

Cole took the last bite of his eggs. "I thought I might clear out the debris and the ashes today."

Ann's head shot up with a worried face. "Today is Sunday. I can't ask you to work on Sunday."

Cole snickered. "I've worked every Sunday of my life. Same as every day to me."

"But it's the Lord's day. We're going to church as soon as we finish our meal. You're welcome to join us."

"You're coming, aren't you, Cla—Mr. Cole? Please."

The idea of going to church hadn't appealed to him since he was the boy's age. "I'm not a churchgoer." He forced a smile.

Ann's face still showed her worry. "I hadn't thought of you staying here."

"Please come with us," Noah urged with the desperation of someone set to hang.

"I'll tell you what. I could drive the wagon to church for you. Then I could go into town to get the supplies I'll need for the barn." Although he thought the idea a good one, it didn't show on Ann's face.

"You two clean your plates and go outside and wash up to get ready for church." The boy and girl did as she ordered and were soon out of the house. Ann's pretty face showed a stain of despair. "I don't know how much you would be able to get under my name, Mr. Cole. My credit isn't much good at Jed Farlon's store." She took a quick breath and half laughed. "Too many times like what you've already seen have taken care of that. With the corn stunted or eaten by animals, weeks without rain, and things happening like my barn burning down, it's not hard to see why it's a bad idea to give me a loan.''

"Maybe some of your neighbors?''

"I've already told you most of my neighbors, namely Mr. Owen MacGregor, want me off this land.'' She rose from the table and began clearing the dishes. "No, the only friend I have here is Lorna Clendenon and her family. She teaches at the school, and her family isn't rich either.'' She turned around to face Cole and showed a little smile. "That's one reason I need to be at church today. I've got a lot of praying to do.''

"Well, then, at least let me drive you there.''

She paused, her smile turning to pressed lips. "I should get ready.''

Cole tightened the harness on Bender as Ann and the children emerged from the house. He froze in his steps at the sight of Ann in a dark-blue dress, lace at the front, her blond hair brushed in a bun showing off her young face. Noah wore what looked like his Sunday best, his hair slicked down and neatly parted to one side. Evie's hair was braided in tails with small bows of cloth tied to each end. The bows matched her flower-patterned dress.

Ann appeared surprised that Cole had hitched the horse to the buckboard.

As she approached, something told him to hold out his hand.

She stopped, showing her surprise at the offering of his palm. She placed her hand in his, and he helped her into the seat. Then Cole lifted the girl into the back with her brother.

When Cole climbed into the seat, he noticed that Ann had allowed him most of the space. She didn't look at him or show any sign that she welcomed sitting next to him. As he took the reins, the dirt along his arms and back of his hands caught his eye. His skin felt every thread of the tattered clothes that had been forced upon him. Only then did he feel he would just as soon have stayed on the farm, and he regretted having asked to drive. He shook the reins.

Once the farm sank below the horizon, they got on a smooth road, and before the sun was straight overhead, a white steeple came into view. Cole had a mind to stop a fair way from the church so as not to give people a reason to ask about him, but that would mean having Ann and the children walk too far and would likely lead to more questions.

He slowed Bender at the front of the church. Only a few people still stood on the steps talking with the preacher. Noah and Evie hopped off the back. Before Cole had a chance to climb down and help Ann from the seat, she was already off the buckboard.

She waved at the people on the steps and told her children to go on without her. Turning around, she first glanced at the horse and wagon, then stared at him without a smile.

"The service usually only lasts two hours. You know this is close to all I have now. It's not worth very much."

He had never felt a harder punch in the gut. Anger told him to climb off the buckboard and leave the woman, but it would mean leaving the boy too. It would be a poor way to repay a debt and gain a trust.

"I'll be here when church lets out, Mrs. Hayes."

She turned and walked to the church.

Cole snapped the reins and the wagon pulled away.

He had traveled more than a mile before he allowed himself to peek back at the white steeple. He stopped the wagon to consider what he should do next. He tried to stay angry, but he couldn't blame the woman for feeling the way she did. He would probably feel the same way if he were in her shoes. If there was a way to help, it might make her feel better about him, and he about himself.

Building a barn was what he had set his mind to do at first, but without money he couldn't get the hardware he needed. When he didn't have money before, at least he had something to trade.

The thought made him look into the open desert. There was something he could do.

The horse trudged through the sand, cresting a large dune. Cole reined in and stood to gaze at the desolate plain. Behind him were long ruts that he hoped the wind wouldn't erase. Without them, he could be turning in circles for days.

He glanced down and saw his shadow. A glimpse up told him he'd better find what he was looking for quickly. Just then fate pointed the way.

He hadn't thought of it before, but the sight of buzzards circling give him an idea. He headed Bender straight for the birds. Even though he shook the reins to quicken the horse's gait, he wasn't in a hurry to see what lay ahead.

The wagon came over a small rise. Bender stopped and reared back. The putrid odor Cole had expected wafted around him. No matter which way he turned his head, he couldn't escape it.

A clutch of buzzards was perched atop an object covered by sand. They flew off in panic when Cole stood.

He stepped off the buckboard and headed toward the mound of sand. The flanks and rump showed few open wounds. He was careful to steer his eyes from the head so as not to see what the vultures had done there.

The dark-brown saddle appeared after one swipe of his hand. In little time he had uncovered the bedroll and the empty scabbard.

The choking stench teared his eyes. He hastily fumbled with the cinch and after several attempts finally unfastened it, but the saddle was still pinned under the carcass. He stepped over the horse, squatted, then sat, propping his feet against the neck and rump, trying to push up and free the saddle. His sweat-glazed hands slipped over the saddle horn, slamming him prone onto the ground.

Why was he doing this? Why was he not in Mexico enjoying the only two things he had bothered learning how to ask for in Spanish: *senoritas* and *cervezas*? A good answer didn't come to mind, but a nagging feeling in his gut wasn't going to let him leave. Not yet.

He tried again and succeeded in forcing the carcass high enough to allow him to yank the saddle away. He stood, lifting all his gear over his shoulder, and walked to the buckboard. It would likely be the last time he would ever have a need to be at this spot in the desert, but he had no trouble keeping his eyes aimed straight at the wagon. It was no time for memories.

He tossed the saddle and gear into the buckboard and soon had Bender at a trot.

He followed the lines in the sand. The farther he went, the more sand had filled in the ruts. Finally, the path ahead was without any markers to guide him. The sun had now crested the sky to a point where he couldn't be sure in which direction it would set.

He wiped his sleeve across his sweat-laden brow, and while doing so he glimpsed a distant glint. He had no idea what it was. Once he turned the wagon, his curiosity got the best of him and he pursued the flashing beacon. As he neared the source of the light, it appeared to come from atop a dune. He came upon the dune and jumped from the wagon. He smiled and laughed when he recognized his own canteen and the shine off his Winchester carbine.

If this was where he once stood, then just below the next rise was the pond that had revived him, and where he had been shot and left for dead. He scanned the horizon and placed where Noah and he had walked to the farm.

Shadows growing from under the wagon now showed the way west—and the cost in time lost of retrieving the rifle.

The sun was at Cole's back when the distant buildings of Nobility broke over the horizon. As he neared the edge of town, he recalled what he had heard about this place. It had been said that only Dodge City provided more ways to satisfy a drunk's thirst, the starving man's hunger, and the ugly man's lust, as long as each could pay the price of his needs.

The big horse's gait slowed. Cole didn't mind, since it gave him time to gaze upon what appeared before him.

Tall wooden buildings, some with five and six rows of windows stacked on top of one another, stood on each side of the street. Occasionally, he stopped Bender for the people crossing the dirt street. He hadn't seen so many folks in a town since he was last in El Paso. The traffic of both walkers and riders coming from and turning into other streets looked like the result of a kicked-over anthill.

Loud laughing came from a two-story establishment. A large figure angled out beyond the awning. Chiseled from wood was a bare-bosomed woman with hair flowing over the shoulders and curling back in front to cover what appeared to be unclothed hips. "Saloon," was the only word he recognized on the roof-mounted sign.

He passed by more saloons, a steakhouse with a bull's head mounted over the door, the unmistakable jailhouse, a barbershop with a striped pole in front, another cookhouse fuming the scent of frying bacon out its smokestack, and a place where a man carried heavy canvas sacks out the door. Cole didn't recognize the word painted on the front, but he figured only a general store stocked such goods.

He stopped the wagon in front of the store, tied the reins to a hitch post, and carried the rifle and saddle inside. Bells chimed to signal his entrance. Rows of tall freestanding shelves holding cans and canvas sacks along with wooden barrels full of grain and vegetables lined the room from end to end.

"Is this a store?" asked Cole, instantly feeling a fool.

"It's been one for the last six years. Don't see reason to change now," came a smart reply from between the shelves.

Cole walked toward the voice, careful not to have the saddle crash the shelves down on top of him. When he emerged, he saw a slim bald man dressed with a black apron behind a countertop. Buckets of potatoes, yams, onions, and other vegetables sat on the counter together with small glass jars full of candy. Behind the man were more shelves with more jars clamped shut full of peaches and apricots.

"What can I do for you?"

"I come to trade."

The clerk eyed the saddle and rifle, then peered up at Cole. "Is that thing loaded?"

Cole shook his head.

"Good. I don't trade. This is a cash business."

"But you haven't looked." Cole slammed the saddle onto the counter.

"I don't have to. It's a policy of this business."

"Where's Farlon?"

"You're looking at him."

Cole squinted his eyes at the thin man. "You're him? The meanest, toughest man in this town to deal with?"

Farlon looked surprised. "Is that what you heard? About me?"

"Sure did," Cole answered with a nod. "I reckon I wasted my time." He picked up the belongings and turned for the door.

"Wait a minute," said Farlon. He shrugged his shoulders. "Maybe I could look at what you got. Just look, mind you."

Cole replaced the saddle on the counter. Farlon quickly glanced at the saddle and sneered, then took the rifle from Cole, who had not planned on dickering with his only weapon. Fighting the urge to reclaim it, he watched the storekeeper handle the rifle.

Farlon aimed it at the wall and pulled back the hammer.

"Watch out," Cole shouted as he ripped the rifle from Farlon's grasp. "You nearly blew a hole in the wall."

"I thought you said it wasn't loaded."

"The way you looked at me when I come in, I thought

you would have called the law if I'd told you it was. Maybe think I was going to rob the place.''

"Well?" Farlon asked.

"Well, what?"

"Are you going to rob me?"

"If I was, would I let you handle the gun?"

"No," the storekeeper agreed, then his voice turned caustic. "I guess if you were a robber, you would be smarter."

Cole grimaced. "If you were smart, you'd have a sign saying this was a store."

" 'Emporium' is what it says. It means the same. Can't you read?"

Cole turned his head an instant. "What about the trade?"

Farlon took the rifle from Cole again, admiring the action of the lever. "It is a nice weapon. A bit dusty, but it seems to be kept up good. I have no interest in the saddle, but I'll give you fifty dollars for the Winchester."

"Fifty dollars? That rifle's worth twice that."

"Brand new, could be. But the way it is today, it's fifty dollars."

Cole paused a moment, then shook his head. "No. They sell as a pair."

"You're going to turn down cash money?"

"I told you, they sell as a pair. Are you buying both or not?"

"What would I do with a saddle? The livery sells saddles brand new."

"I don't need it. I haven't got a horse."

"Then how come you have a saddle?"

Cole was stumped for an answer that didn't go into details he didn't care to share. "I guess I'll check and see if the liveryman is buying."

He picked up the saddle and held his hand out for the rifle, but Farlon held it snug. The twitch of his lips showed he thought more of the rifle than he had first admitted. He

65

glanced at the saddle again. "Okay, I'll give you twenty dollars for the saddle."

"Now who is robbing who? I want a hundred fifty for both."

Farlon laughed and shook his head. "There's no way they are over a hundred dollars."

"Fine," Cole said, grinning. "Sold, for a hundred dollars."

Farlon gasped, looking as if the breath had been knocked out of him. After a moment, he offered his hand. "Deal. But I'll not give cash for that price."

More chimes came from the front door. An older lady came to the counter, and Farlon went to her.

Cole took a long breath. He thought he had made a good settlement, but trading for supplies on the whole amount was unfair.

He overheard Farlon's conversation with the lady, learning the price of onions at three cents a peck. When the sale was done, Cole noticed a casual nod from the woman as she left without showing so much as a nickel. Farlon took a sheet of paper and made quick scratches upon it with a pencil.

"Did you decide what you want?"

"How much are nails?" asked Cole.

"A half cent per pound," Farlon answered with a curious look.

Cole spotted one of the candy jars and chuckled. "How about the licorice?"

"A penny for five sticks." Farlon walked back and stood in front of Cole. "You set your sights low, don't you?"

A smirk creased Cole's face but quickly vanished. "I need about twenty pounds of nails, box of hinges, a hammer, saw, ax, all the licorice you got, four sacks of flour, a jar of peaches, and five of them potatoes. I'll take a new shirt—that checkered one on the wall will do—along with those blue overall britches next to them. And twenty dollars in silver."

Farlon seemed perplexed by the order. "That's all? What about the rest?"

"Are you keeping a bill on Mrs. Ann Hayes?"

Farlon nodded and flipped through the pages of paper. "If I remember correctly, she's past due making a payment and has been for the last four weeks. Here it is. One hundred and fifty-eight dollars."

"Put what's left toward that. What'll it make it, then?"

"I'd have to add it up, but that would bring it down close to an even hundred."

Cole nodded. "And give her another thirty days."

Farlon also nodded, showing his agreement with Cole. The sutler placed a metal box on the counter and counted out two stacks of ten silver dollars.

"While you're collecting all that stuff, I need to take care of some quick business. Where's the telegraph office?"

"Far end of town, just on the other side of the Shipwreck Saloon."

"There must be fifty saloons in this town."

"It's the one with Lady Godiva in front."

Cole peeked out the window, then looked back at Farlon with a pained smile. "I'm new in town. Which one is she?"

Farlon raised his head, his eyes squinting and his nose crinkled. "You've been on the trail a long time, haven't you?"

Cole took a deep breath to restrain from cussing. "Just tell me where the telegraph is."

Farlon pointed as he spoke. "Go to the east end of town. It's the last office before you get to the Manor House Hotel."

Cole turned for the door. "I'll be back in no time." He left the store and went in the direction Farlon had pointed. He walked by a marshal's office window. Out of curiosity he looked inside, and glimpsed a man nearly as tall as himself but younger.

Cole continued down the sidewalk, passing all the places

he'd seen on the way into town, stopping at a narrow door that was part of the same building as the hotel. He walked in to find an old gray-haired man with a black visor, sitting at a desk located behind a wooden partition with bars on top.

"This the telegraph office?"

"Does it look like one?" the old man answered.

"What is it about this town?" Cole muttered. "I need to send a wire."

The old man took the pencil from behind his ear. "To where and to who?"

Cole hesitated, not sure he wanted to send the telegraph, but he'd traded all his belongings and would need money for a trip into Mexico. "Jacob Thorsberg. Baltimore."

Noah sat between his sister and mother while the choir sang. His eyes were drawn to Evie, swinging her legs back and forth under the pew. Then he stared at the large round wooden beams at the top of the ceiling, hearing his mother's voice sing the hymn, doing his best to pay attention to what was happening.

The worst part about going to church was the time it took hearing about things that happened to people he didn't know in places he'd never been. His mama had once told him that if he listened to what was being said, time would pass by faster. He didn't understand the words in the song, so he tried thinking of what was good about going to church.

The hymn ended with a long "Amen." Reverend Brown, dressed in a black coat and a stiff-collared shirt, thanked the choir and stepped to the pulpit before Noah could think of an answer.

"It is good to see all of you here today in the house of the Lord," Reverend Brown said. "There are some faces I haven't seen in a long time and some others I don't think I have *ever* seen before. Therefore, I should like to conclude today's service with a brief history of our home here."

Nobility

The Reverend opened a book and cleared his throat.

"This place we call home was once a wild and savage land, inhabited only by the Indian with primitive ways since the Almighty first put the stars in the sky. It was the Spanish conquistador Coronado, while seeking mythical cities of gold, who first left soldiers, settling the land and building missions, bringing the Lord's message to the redskin more than three hundred years ago. Years later, upon the command from the King of Spain, a man named Peralta constructed *La Villa Real de Santa Fe*, as the new capital of the New Mexico. A new land would mean colonization, commerce, bringing new people both common and aristocratic. So Peralta patterned this new society after the old one he knew of in Spain, where the two classes were separated and blood would remain pure. He came here and began the task of building another city where the rich and noble would live. *La Ciudad del Nobleza Real*, the City of the Royal Nobility."

The Reverend paused.

Noah took pride that he had listened to every word, and although he wasn't sure what the man was talking about, the idea of people living long ago where he now lived made him want to listen more.

"Streets were cleared, water trenches were dug, but correspondence to and from Mexico City for the sale of the choice property on which to build castles was slow at best. With more frequent uprisings of the Pueblo Indians and other urgent matters pending, the plans for the city waned, and when the Pueblos vanquished the Spanish out of New Mexico, the vision of the original City of the Royal Nobility was lost forever. It wasn't until Americans came to this newly acquired land—some of you here came with your own family traveling over the Santa Fe Trail, farming this fertile valley— and with the discovery of silver and gold under the dust just outside this door, that the ancient city meant for noble people came to life."

69

The Reverend frowned and shook his head slowly.

"But the riches brought wickedness. You have all seen the decadence displayed in that town down the road. The sloth, drunkenness, deceit, and other unspeakable vices that are going on in their saloons. It was blasphemy to name that town Nobility."

Reverend Brown stared right into Noah's eyes. Sweat rolled down his cheeks and his face turned red.

"Because the true measure of nobility is not only righteousness, but dignity when surrounded by the indignant, strength to offer the weak, charity for the poor, kindness to the angry, and bravery to those needing courage."

Reverend Brown smiled as he put on spectacles and looked down at his book.

"In my desire for an answer to why this was, I sought out the Lord."

The smile left his face and his voice got loud.

"For you see, brothers and sisters, there was another city that had lost its virtue. And that city was the great city of Jerusalem. When the Romans had brought their sinful evils upon the holy land, the Israelites were so infected by the fever of greed that the merchants sold their goods on the steps of the Great Temple on the Sabbath day. But there came one noble man who struck down the infidels, chastised their blasphemy, and chased them away from the temple. That man was the Lord."

Noah leaned forward and scooted to the pew's edge. He had never seen a picture of the Lord that didn't show him nailed to a cross. He couldn't imagine that man chasing people. So an image of another man came into his mind, because his mama once said that a little part of the Lord is inside everybody.

The Reverend continued. "And so it is today that we find ourselves surrounded by infidels. We need not cower away from their shame, because the Lord is with us all. And al-

70

though the law sees fit to condone the actions of our lost brethren, we can go about our lives with the faith that one day the plagues which surround us will be chased away with the coming of one noble man.''

Chapter Six

Reverend Brown stood on the outside steps shaking hands with each member of the congregation. Noah walked behind his mother and sister with the sermon still fresh in his mind.

Lorna Clendenon was the first to shake the Reverend's hand, followed by Morris Taylor, who stayed next to Lorna's skirt like a small child, even though he was near her own age.

When Ann had said her good-byes, Noah put his hand inside Reverend Brown's.

"Thank you for coming to our church today."

Noah looked up at the tall man. "What you said in there, is all that true? I mean, all that about the Lord coming here?"

The Reverend nodded. "I believe it."

"Well, if the Lord was too busy, maybe, might he tell someone else to show up for him?"

"The Lord is never too busy for anyone."

Noah took a few steps, his head dipping a little lower with each slow stride.

"Noah."

The boy turned back to Reverend Brown.

"Sometimes he does send messengers."

Noah grinned and nodded. He went to join his mother and sister, who stood away from the church steps. They spotted Henry Taylor, Morris's big brother, walking toward them. Lorna Clendenon, her mouth and eyes wide open, stood next to his mother as he approached.

"Do you know who did it?"

Ann looked to the ground. "I have a good idea who was behind it."

"Oh, Ann. You've got to do something."

"What can I do?"

"You can report it to the marshal that someone set fire to your barn!"

Noah looked into his mother's eyes. She almost smiled, then took a long breath. "The last time I asked the law to help me . . ." Her arms wrapped around Evie's shoulders. She reached for Noah to come to her, and soon he felt her hand's gentle brush around his head. ". . . was the last time I will ever ask the law to help me."

"Forgive me," Lorna said while touching Ann's hand. "I'm sorry. I didn't mean for you to have to think of that. It's just, I think you ought to do something. Not just turn the other cheek. You can't fight by yourself. At least if you make it known, then it's the law's duty to see who is responsible for the crime. Even if we all know who truly is." Lorna looked at the road in front of the church. "Where's your wagon?"

Noah saw his mother's head dip for only an instant, but he noticed that pained expression she'd show anytime something hurt her inside. When her lips were pressed straight together, that meant she had to tell something she wasn't proud of telling.

As he looked upon the empty road, he knew what pained his mama. A feeling of misplaced trust. Noah hated the look his mother had, and hoped the man he had placed so much faith in was just a little late.

"My uncle Clay has it."

Everybody's mouth fell open, including Mama's.

"Your who?" asked Lorna.

Noah glanced at his mama, waiting to be scolded for lying. She didn't say a word. The absence of a correction fueled his imagination.

"My uncle Clay. He said he might go into town. I guess he's just a little late coming back."

Henry Taylor asked, "Since when do you have an uncle?" He turned to look at Ann. "I never knew you had any kin living out here."

"He's my pa's kin. Uh, he's my pa's brother, I guess." Noah hoped his latest explanation would stop further questions from Henry Taylor. If Henry had the chance to stay close to Ann, he'd find a reason to be at the house and boss Noah like a little brother.

Lorna smiled. "Why haven't I heard anything about a brother-in-law?"

"When did he get here, Ann?" asked Henry.

"You ought not call my mama by her first name. It ain't polite."

"Be quiet, boy. I wasn't talking to you. And grown-ups can call each other by their first name."

"You're no grown-up. You're only eighteen."

"Nineteen." Henry snapped, then softened his tone as he looked at Ann. "I'm going to be twenty years old in a few months."

"That don't matter none."

"Now wait a minute, everybody," Ann said. "Stop all this quarreling." She raised an eyebrow at her son. "I'm still a little shocked to know that my brother-in-law is here myself."

Lorna placed her hand on Ann's shoulder. "How long is he staying?"

"Forever," Noah answered, staring at Henry.

Lorna again showed shock at his answer. "What? He's come to stay with you?"

Noah proudly nodded.

"I don't want to talk about him or this right now. I'd soon talk about my barn burning."

Lorna took a deep breath, glancing at the Taylor brothers, then at the empty dirt road. "Why don't Morris and I give you a ride to town, since your brother-in-law's not here."

Ann nodded. "Thank you, Lorna."

Noah went with his mother and sister to Lorna's buggy. He and Evie hopped in the rear seat. Henry took the chance to help Ann into the buggy while a hesitating Morris, after a quick glare from Lorna, did the same for her.

"Where will I sit?" Morris asked.

Lorna closed her eyes. She squinted hard, as if something pained her.

"You'll ride double with me," Henry said with a smile and a tip of his hat toward the ladies. Lorna shook the reins. The buggy moved down the road toward Nobility.

Noah gazed upon the big buildings of town with awe. It was a rare sight for him, since his mother didn't like taking him or Evie on her infrequent trips here.

"Children, shut your eyes and don't open them until I tell you to," came a stern command from Mama.

Noah closed his eyes. Music and men laughing and shouting drew his head to wander. His quivering eyelids allowed a peek at the source of the noise, along with a glimpse of a big wooden woman with no—

"Noah! You turn your head to your lap."

He complied immediately. He hoped the moment of curiosity hadn't cost him a switching on his bare behind, but the sight of that woman would have been worth it.

The buggy stopped. He knew that didn't give him permission to open his eyes. His mother pulling his hand was a signal to follow her. He stumbled over the raised boardwalk.

"Would you like me to go with you, Ann?"

"No, thank you, Lorna. I'm obliged for your help already."

"It's no trouble."

"There's no need. My business may be long, and I may have some other errands."

"How about if I invite Evie to my place? She can help me fix dinner."

"Oh, please, Mama. Can I go?"

After a moment, Noah heard the clopping of little steps on the wooden planks.

"Ann, I'll come in with you." The voice belonged to Henry.

"No, I don't want to keep you from your dinner."

"Don't be silly. A woman shouldn't be in town by herself. I'd be glad—"

"I'd like to do this by myself, in private, Henry."

Noah could feel a smile broaden his face.

"Well. If that's what you want. I was just making sure you get home safe."

"And I appreciate your thinking that way. But I'll be okay."

A few minutes went by before Noah felt the tug of Ann's hand lead him indoors.

"How do, Mrs. Hayes. Who'd you bring with you today? What's a matter, boy? Something get in your eyes?"

"This is my son, Noah."

He took his mother's introduction as permission to open his eyes. He focused on a metal star pinned to the vest of a man with a big smile across a face not much older than Henry Taylor. Behind the man was a desk, and behind it was a rack of rifles on the wall. A door made of bars led to another room, where there was another barred door off to the side.

The man stuck out his hand. "Pleased to meet you, Noah. I'm Vance MacGregor. What can I do for the two of you?"

Noah shook hands with Vance.

"I'm here to see the marshal. Is he here?"

The smile faded quickly from the deputy's face. "Well, no, ma'am. I guess you haven't heard." He cleared his throat and slowly walked back toward the desk, where he picked up another star just like the one he wore. "Clement ain't here no more. Won't be here ever again."

Ann let go of Noah's hand and covered her mouth. Her eyes were as wide as he had ever seen.

"Yes, ma'am, it is a terrible thing. A drunken tramp gunned him down over at the Shipwreck. Seems the tramp, calling himself the Rainmaker, pistol-whipped a whore."

Ann's eyes darted over at Noah.

"Oh, I beg your pardon, Mrs. Hayes." He paused a moment. "Well, Clement went over there to take that no-good to jail. And when Clement wasn't looking, the filth shot him."

Noah looked at his mother. She had never swallowed so hard without eating anything.

"I'm so sorry. I'm so terribly sorry to hear such a thing."

The man nodded. "Not as sorry as I was to see it firsthand. Don't you worry none, though." He pointed toward the first barred door. "I've got the outlaw locked up tight. He isn't going to cause no hurt to anyone anymore. He'll soon be stretching a rope."

Noah leaned his head in hopes of seeing what might be behind the barred door. He didn't see anyone or anything other than the bars.

Ann gripped his hand once more. "I don't mean to bother you, then. I'll leave you to tend to your duties, Deputy." She turned to the outer door.

"Wait a minute," Vance said. "You came in here for something. What did you come for?"

Ann looked to the floor, then, shaking her head, she said, "It was no matter to trouble you with."

77

"Well, I'm all the marshal you're going to get. Something brought you through that door."

Noah looked up at his mother. "Aren't you going to tell him, Mama? About the barn?"

"Barn?" repeated the deputy.

Ann gave a brief smile to the boy and nodded while turning to Vance. "Yes. Two nights ago, someone set fire to my barn."

Vance looked surprised. "What? Do you know who?"

"Deputy," Ann said with a sullen face. "Who do you think would have reason to burn my barn down, while my children were sleeping in our house just a few feet away?"

"Now, hold on, Mrs. Hayes. I know what you're trying to say. Did you actually see anyone set fire to the barn?"

Ann looked at Noah, then shook her head.

"I thought that might be the case. Well, you sure that there was no match dropped into the straw? Maybe by accident?"

Ann again shook her head. "No. My boy knows how to handle a lamp. It was on the wall when I saw the flames."

"Any strangers been around?"

Ann again peered down at her son. Noah met her gaze with pleading eyes. However, his mother's reassuring smile wasn't there. As she turned again toward Vance MacGregor, Noah felt the urge to tell the same tale that he had to Lorna Clendenon and the Taylor brothers. This time he would be lying to the deputy and wouldn't get away with just a stern frown, and likely get worse than a switch to his bare backside. The barred door seemed a bit closer, and a vision of himself behind that door flashed before him.

"No," said Ann.

Noah awoke from his daydream and quickly looked at her.

"There hasn't been anyone around I don't know about."

Now Noah's mouth fell open. He had never heard his mama tell something that wasn't the pure truth.

"Well, if you didn't see anybody do it, you know I can't do much about it."

"I didn't expect you to, Deputy."

"Now, Mrs. Hayes, I know how you feel about my father. But that's not me. I'm the acting marshal of Nobility now. Clement Thomas himself, as his dying wish, wanted me to act as the law, and that's what I plan on doing until the circuit judge gets here."

"Very well, then, I would be thankful if you'd keep it on your mind. Should you find out who might have done it, I'd appreciate the law punishing whoever that might be."

"Yes, ma'am," Vance said, tipping his cap. "I'll look into it."

She led Noah outside, and they stood at the edge of the wooden sidewalk. "Noah."

"Yes, Mama," he answered, looking up at her.

"Don't ever let me catch you doing what I just did in there."

"Yes, ma'am. Can I ask something without you being mad?" Her nod gave him the courage to continue. "How come you lied?"

"It's a hard thing to say." She paused. "I guess I'd rather it be thought that man was part family than have folks think me a big fool for letting a stranger stay at my house." A small grin creased her face. "That's what I get for lying. What are we going to do now? How are we going to get home?" she muttered, staring at the street.

"Don't worry. I know he didn't run off."

"Mrs. Hayes," came the deputy's voice from behind. He walked toward them again, tipping his hat. "Beg your pardon, but I forgot to tell you to be watching for strangers, drifters, and the like. You said you hadn't seen nobody, and that's good, because a lot of times killers like what I got in there tend to have friends they ride with. You know, someone may try busting him out of jail."

Ann stood still and spoke slowly. "What would they look like? A killer, I mean?"

"Hard to say. Just like anybody you'd not seen before."

Noah's eyes drifted away from his mother and the deputy, through the passing townspeople, and fixed on a familiar figure next to the family horse and wagon. Although he didn't recognize the new shirt, he waved gladly and gently tugged his mother's skirt.

"There he is, Mama."

Ann and Vance stopped talking and turned to the object Noah pointed at. Once all eyes were looking in the same direction, Cole spun around.

Noah ran to him. "Where you been? Mama thought you'd run off."

"Oh," Cole mumbled, "I had some things to take care of."

Upon the approach of Ann and the deputy, Noah proudly proclaimed, "This is my uncle Clay."

Cole jerked his head first to the boy, then at Ann, who only dipped her head to the street for that moment.

"Why, I didn't know you had an uncle," Vance said as he offered his hand.

Cole acted like a frightened cat.

"Yup, I sure do," Noah continued. "He's my pa's brother, come to live with us."

Cole's eyes widened looking at the smiling boy. Slowly he took the deputy's hand.

"I'm Vance MacGregor, city deputy marshal. Nice to meet you, Mr. Hayes." The two men shook hands. "You feeling all right, Mr. Hayes? You look a mite pale."

Cole grinned an instant. "I'm fine. Just not used to being called that."

"Well, I guess I'll leave you all to your business." Vance tipped his hat once more. "Good day, Mrs. Hayes. And don't forget what I told you."

Ann nodded as he walked away, then looked at Cole as she would Noah just before she'd cut a switch. "You lied to me. You said you'd be at the church."

Cole shook his head. "I didn't lie. I just . . . well, I got slowed up."

His explanation didn't change one thing about the way she looked at him. She slowly turned away from Cole and opened her mouth, taking a breath as if to shout to the deputy, but just as instantly, she exhaled as if hesitant to call.

"Wow!" shouted Noah. He clung to the side of the buckboard, gazing at the supplies lying inside. "Look, Mama, at what he got. Where'd you get all this stuff? And where did you get them clothes?"

Ann also peered at the tools and hardware in the wagon. Her face softened for only a moment. "How did you come by these things?"

Cole pointed toward the store. "I dickered with Farlon for them."

Ann appeared confused. "And what did you give him?"

Cole answered, "Some personal things." His eyes turned away from her.

She shook her head but didn't smile while looking into the wagon again. "Why are you doing this?"

"He's going to build a barn, Mama. Aren't you, Uncle Clay?"

"Noah," she snapped. "Don't call him that."

"The boy's right," said Cole. "Things just keep pointing to a barn needing building. I guess I'm the one picked to do it."

She continued shaking her head. "I want to go home. We'll talk about this when I don't have all of creation gawking at me."

She prepared her skirt for the climb onto the seat. Cole began walking around Bender to help her, but she quickly gripped the side of the seat and sat atop it before Cole could get there.

With Noah standing in the back of the wagon, Cole climbed into the driver's seat, took the reins, and pointed Bender on the road out of town.

81

Tim McGuire

Halfway home, the silence was broken by Noah's anxious voice. "Did you know there's an outlaw in jail?"

Cole shook his head. Ann kept looking straight ahead.

"Some man that shot Marshal Thomas."

Cole turned with a quizzical look. "Really?"

"Yeah, the deputy said he was a tramp named the Rainmaker."

Cole twisted around to the boy. His face showed an anger like a stick had been jabbed into his side. "What? Who did you say?"

The young boy backed away from Cole's reaction. Ann also was surprised by his sudden change.

"He said he was named the Rainmaker. That's what Deputy MacGregor said," Noah meekly answered. "I didn't mean to make you mad."

Cole's furrowed brow shrank. "I'm sorry, boy. It weren't aimed at you." Cole drew two licorice sticks from his chest pocket. "Here, make sure your sister gets one."

"Is that somebody you know?" Ann asked.

"No," said Cole, settling straight in the seat. "At first I thought so, but I guess I don't. Can't be the same man I know."

He shook the reins to hurry Bender's stride. Not another word was spoken the rest of the ride home.

Chapter Seven

When the door opened, Cyril Walker jumped back from the barred hallway door. The whiskered old-timer flashed his ever-present grin and greeted the man in the doorway.

"Howdy, Vance." He finished with a chuckle, as he did every sentence.

"What are you doing in here?"

"Oh, just thought I'd come grab a look at who you got in here. Heard the news yesterday. Shame 'bout Clement. I always liked him."

Vance slammed the door and walked to stand by Cyril.

"Do you know who he is?"

Vance shook his head. "All I know is he goes by reputation as the Rainmaker." He stared at the prisoner lying on a narrow cot in the first cell. "He's been passed out since it happened."

"No, I seen him move. He's coming to," said Cyril, nodding.

"Hey you," Vance called to the prisoner. He took the

large circular key ring off the wall and unlocked the hallway door. Standing in front of the cell, he yelled again. "Wake up!"

A shake of the head was the first sign of life from the slim young man inside. He sat up in the cot and squinted his eyes at Vance. "Where the hell am I? Who the hell are you?" he said, appearing confused at wearing oversize trousers.

"I'm Deputy Marshal Vance MacGregor. You met the marshal Friday night just as you were shooting him."

"Rainmaker, huh?" said Cyril.

The dazed look quickly faded. "What did you call me?"

"I've been calling you every miserable thing I can think of since I dragged you here. You killed the town marshal, and a little whore's been near dead since you punched her senseless. I'd say that calls for me to name you everything that describes the piece of horseshit that you are."

Cyril guffawed with delight.

"I don't remember nothing," said the prisoner, shaking his head.

"And that ain't no wonder, either. There was an empty whiskey bottle in that room wasn't sold to you for more than an hour. I wired for the circuit judge to come from Santa Fe, and when he gets here, he's going to make an example of drunken gunslingers like you. We don't cotton to your kind. According to people, your reputation is you like taking women. Hell, if that girl dies, we just might hang you twice."

"What reputation?"

"Your reputation. The Rainmaker."

The prisoner stood and slowly walked to the bars. "What are you talking about? I never heard that name. That man in the saloon, he said something, I can't remember—"

"You can't remember because you shot him and passed out right after. Are you denying that, too?"

"I don't know. . . . My head hurts so bad, I can't remember anything. But my name's Billy Mansfield and I'm from Alabama."

"Billy?" Vance questioned. "Are you the same Billy that's been raising so much hell down in Lincoln County?"

"What? No. Lincoln County? I don't know anything about Lincoln County."

"Sounds like lies to me," Cyril said.

"No. You gotta listen to me."

"No, I don't," Vance answered. "Whatever your name is—Billy Mansfield? the Rainmaker?—enough people around here are buzzing about what you did, they'd just as soon have you hang without knowing who you are."

"Rainmaker?" Mansfield said. "Why do you keep calling me that?"

"That's who you are, ain't it?"

"I told you, I don't know that name. I ain't whoever that is."

"Is that right?" Vance smiled. "There's at least twenty people told me that a man of your description, wearing leggings such as the ones you had on, was seen in Colorado not more than a month ago. They said you took a woman up into the mountains that hadn't been seen or heard of since. They said they saw you take her. A man called the Rainmaker. That ain't you?"

"Colorado? You got me mixed up. There was another man I saw outside town here. He took my clothes and—"

"Lies," Cyril said as he and Vance enjoyed laughing at the panic in Mansfield's face. "I said he'd lie to save his neck from a noose."

"Yeah, and I don't have time to listen to all of them he's got to tell. I'll let the judge figure that all out."

Vance led Cyril out of the hallway and relocked the barred door amid Mansfield's pleas for them to listen. Vance hung the key ring back on the wall and turned to the whiskered old man. "I need to take care of personal business. With being by myself, I don't have anyone—"

"I'll watch him for you, Vance. Be glad to help the law where I'm needed. You know that."

Vance nodded and gave a slight grin. "I appreciate your help, Cyril. Don't let him get you riled. Stay away from him, keep the door locked, and I don't want anyone coming in here looking at him."

"Yes, sir, Vance—I mean Marshal."

Vance grinned again and put his hand on Cyril's shoulder. "I'm still just the deputy."

He walked outside, only to stop dead in his tracks to keep from hitting the supper tray carried by Libby Tidwell. "Beg pardon, Libby."

She didn't smile, appearing surprised or embarrassed at meeting him on his way out of the jailhouse. "That's okay. No harm done. I was just going to leave this for your prisoner for whenever he wakes up."

"He's up now." Vance stood, thoughtless for a moment as to what to do next. "I was just on my way to see to something out of town," he said while opening the door. "But Cyril's in there, and you can give it to him."

After a moment, she dipped her head to the tray and slowly stepped inside.

"Cyril," Vance called, bringing the old man out of the office chair. "Libby's got food for the prisoner. See to it she gets back to Donovan's all right."

"Yessir, Vance. I'll see to it," Cyril replied.

With a tip of his hat to her, Vance closed the door.

Libby watched him through the window. He climbed onto his sorrel and rode south.

The only reason she had pestered Big Jim Donovan into providing a meal for Clement Thomas's murderer was so she could have a reason to come to the jailhouse and have Vance to herself. Now abandoned, she had a mind to drop the strip of beef, mashed potatoes, and apple cobbler.

She turned to the ever-grinning Cyril. Word of her spoiling the food would likely arrive across the street before she would.

"I'll take that for you, Libby."

With Cyril appearing like a hungry dog and eyeing scraps on the table, she proceeded with her intent to give the food to the prisoner. At least she could tell Big Jim she'd truly accomplished the deed. "No, that's okay. I can give it to him. I'd like to get a look at him anyway." She started toward the barred hall door, only to have Cyril step in front of her.

"You can't go back there. He's only got pants on. It ain't right for you to see him."

"Mr. Walker, I've seen plenty of men with only pants on, and some with only their underdrawers coming out of the Shipwreck and walking down the street. Step aside. Let me have a look."

"No. It ain't right. I can't have people talking about how I let a young girl near a killer like him."

What was once only the excuse for her coming here was now a challenge. "I'll let you have the cobbler if you let me pass," she whispered.

The old man peeked under the tray's cloth cover. Slipping the dessert bowl into his hand, he forced a serious frown to warn her. "Maybe a minute won't hurt." He reached for the key ring and opened the hallway door. "Don't get too close."

She nodded her understanding and went to the door of the first cell. She gazed upon the man inside, who looked not much older than she. A bit of fright shot through her when he first raised his head. He rose from his cot and came to the bars. She stepped back.

"Who are you? What's this?"

"I'm food for you, er, I mean, this is food for you." She carefully placed the tray on the floor and slid it under the cell door. He knelt to remove the cover, then, rising with the tray, gave her an appreciative look. "This is very kind of you. And who might you be, miss?"

"Libby," she answered, trying not to blush.

"I thank you most kindly, Miss Libby. My name is Billy

Mansfield.'' His southern gentlemanly tone was appealing. He took the tray to the cot. ''I wish I could invite you in to enjoy these treats with me, but you have been warned to keep your distance, I'm sure.'' He returned to lean against the bars. ''Forgive me if I stare. I haven't observed a young beauty such as yours since I left Alabama.''

''You're from Alabama?''

''Yes, ma'am. Montgomery. The Heart of Dixie.'' He glanced down at his bare chest. ''I beg your pardon for my appearance. At home, they at least provide proper clothes for jailed men, nor would we allow a delicate flower into a place such as this.'' He lowered his voice and propped his face between the bars, compelling her to come nearer. ''Where I come from, we know how to nurture flowers.''

She couldn't speak, but preferred rather to bathe in his warm complimentary breath.

''I wish I could take you home to show you off to all my friends. They would be so jealous of me with you on my arm. And I would do so, if only I wasn't unjustly detained in this town.''

She peered at the bars, which stretched from the ceiling to the floor, and then at the keyholed latch on the door.

''You would enjoy it so much.''

''Libby,'' Cyril whined from the front office, shattering her trance. ''It's time I took you back across the street.''

''I've got to go,'' she said, regretting the words.

He stuck out his hand to shake hers. Feeling no harm could be done, she gave him her hand, which he slowly drew, toward him, bringing her face to press between the bars. ''Please, Miss Libby. Don't let this be the last time I see you.'' He closed his eyes while holding her hand firm. He gently kissed her lips, her first touch of a man's mouth other than a paternal smooch from Big Jim. She, too, closed her eyes. His warmth sent a shrill to her toes.

''Libby,'' came another whine from Cyril, his stumbling footsteps sounding louder.

"I've got to leave," she said, pulling away from his slacking grasp.

"Promise me, Miss Libby."

She hesitated, not knowing what to say. Cyril's presence behind her made her turn away from Billy and walk out of the hall. While she waited for Cyril to lock the hallway door, the thrill from Billy's kiss settled as a tingle beneath her blouse and skirt. She had never felt it before, and she yearned to have it again.

Vance guided his horse through the gated archway of the OKM ranch. It had been some time since he had last paid a visit to the place of his birth. It had been an even longer time since he held any fondness for these surroundings with which he was so familiar.

He dismounted the sorrel in front of the three-story mansion and tied the reins to a hitch post. The door was open as he approached up the steps. People he had known since boyhood milled around in the hallway, all of them eagerly greeting him with smiles and handshakes, which he graciously returned.

Threading his way through the crowd, he spotted the man he had made the hour's ride to see. As expected, he saw the boastful host glad-handing the men while charming the ladies, continuing a long practice of keeping his guests aware of just who he was and what control he had over them.

Vance reluctantly walked over to the man, noticing that the once full head of red hair had thinned to light gray. Wrinkles showed around the twinkling green eyes with every wide smile. A string tie was neatly knotted around a new white shirt that peeked out above a wool tweed waistcoat.

A look of surprise came over the man when he saw Vance, one meant to impress the visitors that he now had a famous son.

"Well, it's like I say, you never know who might come in if you leave the door open, especially if you're giving away food." People laughed. The two men shook hands. "Everyone, let me introduce to those of you who have never seen him—and I know most of you have—my son the lawman, Vance."

Always a respectful son, Vance smiled and nodded to the appreciative applause.

"Hello, Dad."

Owen MacGregor firmly slapped a grip on his son's shoulder. "It's good to see you. It's been a while. You're just in time, we're about to cut the brisket. Do you want a drink?"

Vance shook his head. "I didn't come to eat."

"Hell, I know you must be hungry for some good food, after all the slop they serve in town." He turned and called to a servant. "Fix my son a plate. He'll eat it. And he'll have a snort of brandy, too."

Vance again shook his head. "I'm not staying, Dad. I need to get back before sundown."

"Nonsense. You can stay long enough to eat, can't you?"

The persuasive expression was in place. Vance felt compelled to nod. Another slap on his shoulder signaled another small battle lost in a long-smoldering conflict.

They both walked toward the linen-draped table.

"I'm out here on business," Vance whispered.

"What business? The last I knew you didn't have a business. You were working on the city payroll."

The jab to his pride didn't bother Vance as much as it would have in the past. He took the prepared plate of sliced beef. "That is my business. And right now, it concerns you."

His father's smile quickly turned sour. "What do you mean it concerns me?"

After swallowing a bite, Vance said, "I got a visit from a neighbor of yours. Ann Hayes."

"What did she want?

He sunk his fork into another slice. "It seems someone burned down her barn two nights ago."

"Let's not talk about her here."

"That's why I came. She asked me some questions, and I need to give her some answers."

MacGregor nodded. "Follow me." Relighting a smile to his face as quickly as flame to a struck match, he excused himself from his guests as Vance followed him around the twin staircases into the study. The walnut panels and drawn drapes still provided a gloomy presence. The only light was provided by a lamp on the corner of a large oak desk where the older MacGregor soon took his normal imposing stance.

"Now, what is so important that it would be the sole reason for a son to visit his father?"

Vance smirked for an instant. "Well, first I better tell you. Clement got shot. He's dead."

"I mention 'father' and you bring up his name," MacGregor muttered.

"This isn't about him."

"Yes, I heard the news. I heard he was shot in a whorehouse by some cowboy that rode into town. I never heard if he had his pants on or not."

"It wasn't like that. That 'cowboy' is a drifter that got drunk and beat one of O'Malley's girls near death. Clement went over to take him in, and the drifter shot him."

MacGregor's face showed little remorse. "So, what does this have to do with me? Are you collecting money for the good marshal's funeral?"

The snipe wasn't meant at Clement Thomas, but rather at Vance for his decision to leave the ranch five years before. After a few moments had passed, Vance cleared his mind to focus on why he had come.

"No, I was just telling you why I'm here and he's not."

Owen MacGregor ducked his head, then sat in his padded leather chair. "Well, then go on."

"Sometime night before last, somebody set fire to Ann Hayes's barn."

"That's a pity."

"She said she didn't see who did it, but she made it plain who she thought was behind it."

"She thinks I had something to do with it."

"I said I'd come find out what I could."

"Well, now you've come. And you can tell her that I did not burn her barn down."

Vance paused a moment, careful not to question his father's word, which would surely spark another fight. "You sure none of your boys might have done it, just to get on your good side?"

"I don't think they would do such a thing," MacGregor answered with a grin. "But we can ask them if you like."

A nod from Vance brought MacGregor out from his chair and over to the door, where he ordered, "Tell Brice I need him in here, pronto." Within a minute, he was back in his chair. "Why are you so concerned about this woman's troubles?"

"It's the law's concern. That makes it mine."

The snide grin his father wore anytime he held an ace to play began to show.

"Well, let me tell you about the law, son." He leaned back in his chair. "The law says that a woman cannot own land that she inherited by marriage. Without an heir of legal age, that land must sold at auction. So, you see, that Hayes woman is trespassing." The snide grin grew even bigger. "Now, Clement was too softhearted to throw a widow woman with two kids off her farm. He was delaying what he knew he had to do. But now that he's gone, that job falls to you."

Vance's jaw clenched. "Why is that so important to you?"

MacGregor stood and turned to open the cabinet behind him. He pulled out a rolled document, which he spread out over the desk. It was a map.

"You see, son, it's okay to be softhearted, until it gets in the way of business." He pointed on the map to a dotted line across a boundary. "This is the property in question, and here are the plans for the new railroad. The Atchison, Topeka, and

Santa Fe has already started laying track across this land on their way right through the middle of Nobility. It'll bring people, business, opportunities for everyone.''

Vance had to grin. ''Especially you.''

''I am a businessman. Didn't hurt when I was raising you. Once the railroad gets here, this territory will change overnight. Opera houses, fancy restaurants, and banks will be on the street instead of those dance halls and cathouses. I saw it happen in California. Nobility will be the San Francisco of the Southwest.''

''You haven't told me what I asked.''

''Don't you see? The Hayes farm leads right up to the edge of town. Places for more new people to live. New businesses to be built.''

''With you being the landlord holding the deed.''

MacGregor's prideful smile returned. ''I knew my side of you would show sooner or later.'' He laughed.

''What if there were an heir of legal age?''

''Like who?''

''A brother.''

''Robert Hayes didn't have a brother,'' MacGregor said, rolling up the map.

''I met him today.''

''What?'' The smile was wiped away.

''I don't know when he got here. But that's what the woman said.''

MacGregor slowly sank in his seat. ''Hellfire.''

A knock at the door and a call to enter brought in the dusty presence of Brice Canton. The stocky foreman walked in with each click of his spurs dropping chips of dirt-covered dung onto the carpet. His scruffy beard covered his face up to the brim of his sweat-stained Stetson. His chaw-stuffed mouth was ballooned to one side as a remnant line of his last spittle ran down his jaw.

''Do you want me, Mr. MacGregor?''

93

"Do you know anything about the Hayes widow's barn being burned?"

A slow shake of Brice's head was the response. "No, sir."

Vance looked at his father, who wore a satisfied smirk. "You see, nobody here knows anything about it."

"Is that all you need me for?"

MacGregor nodded with momentary disgust. "That's all, Brice. And clean yourself up next time you're in here. What happened to that red spit rag I gave you? You look like one of those broken-down drovers you're supposed to be bossing."

The foreman shook his head and wiped his lips with his brown-streaked sleeve. "I don't know. I been tracking wolves that look to come down from the hills. They took two calves. I guess I lost it somewheres while I was hunting them."

"Well, get yourself another one."

A quick nod from Brice showed his understanding. He walked out of the study on his toes so as not to add to his dirt trail.

"Now that your business is done, maybe you can see fit to stay and talk about old times with this old man."

Vance shook his head. "I got to be getting back. I've got the man who shot Clement as a prisoner. I left old Cyril with him, and I imagine he's giving tours of the jail for a nickel apiece."

"Who is he?"

"A kid saying his name is Billy Mansfield. But there are others who recognize him as some gunslinger called the Rainmaker. I asked to know if there's any paper under that name when I wired for the circuit judge. Talk is he may have killed a woman in Colorado."

MacGregor responded with a pleased nod. "A hanging is always good for business. It shows a town's social responsibility to punish the lawless."

Vance nodded, and turned for the door.

Nobility

"Vance."

He looked back at his father, whose expression was firm.

"I know you never had much of a chance to know your own mother, but listen to me when I tell you that those that give us children have no head for business. The railroad will be in Nobility in a short time, and brother or not, it's now your duty to enforce the law."

Chapter Eight

Ann began cleaning the dishes. She glanced out the window and saw that the orange glow was all but gone from the sky. The dim light was barely enough to make out the figure of the man outside. He continued to work at the pile of charred wood and ashes where her barn once stood, making smaller piles out of the larger one. Her attempt to ignore his presence worked even less well than her meager swipes across the plates.

Noah had already swept the floor, as was his nightly duty, and just as quickly burst out the door. Her young boy's excitement over the man was troubling. The absence of a father in Noah's life was a matter that had always troubled her.

Thoughts of remarriage had once been considered, but she hadn't found someone with whom she could spend the rest of her life. Henry Taylor had all but asked her to marry him. He had been sweet on Lorna Clendenon but pushed Morris on Lorna once Ann's wedding band was gone from her finger.

Although Henry Taylor had spent the last eight years without any parents and had raised a younger brother, he was still a boy, one she would have to teach what grown men already knew.

Ann finished the dishes and tucked Evie in. She walked outside to the corner of the porch. Noah stood next to the man, as it seemed he always would.

"When are we leaving?" Noah eagerly asked. "Let's go now."

"I don't think we'd get far in the dark."

"We could take lanterns."

"No. We'll leave at sunup."

"Noah," called Ann. "It's time for you to be in bed."

"I don't want to go to bed, Mama. I'm going to stay up with my uncle Clay."

"You best do as your ma says, boy. We'll have to have an early start tomorrow, and if you're still sleeping 'cause you stayed up late, I'll be gone without you."

"Uh, ah, you wouldn't leave without me, would you?"

"Do you want to find that out in the morning?"

After a moment's hesitation, Noah hopped onto the porch and turned around on his way inside. "I'm going to bed right now. You better not leave without me." In five steps, the boy shed his clothes and crawled under his blanket.

Ann shook her head. "I have to say I've never seen that before."

Cole laughed. "Threaten a boy's chance to do something he wants to do, and you can likely get most anything out of him."

"What did you tell him he could do?"

His smile from laughing quickly became an openmouthed stare. "Well, I hope I didn't offer nothing I ought not have, but I told him I was going to head out tomorrow to cut timber, uh, for the barn."

Ann nodded. "I see. So you're planning on really doing this?"

"Yup, I guess I'm kinda stuck to doing it now," he said while organizing the piles. "Being I have all the hardware for one."

"And you were going to take Noah, without asking me?"

His blank stare returned. "I guess I was."

"Let me tell you, Mr. Cole. He may enjoy the notion that you are his uncle, but let me make it clear that you are not."

Cole nodded. "Yes, ma'am."

His quick answer showed respect, something she hadn't expected. She lost the target of her anger. "So, what will you do?"

"If you don't want him going, I'll tell him it weren't my place to tell him he could."

"He'll be mad."

He nodded again. "I know. But I bet it won't be the first time."

His acceptance of blame also surprised her. While she looked into the house at her resting children she reflected how there were many things about this man she hadn't come to expect. There were also other things she didn't know.

"I asked you before. Why are you doing this?"

He stopped once more and took a deep breath. "What?"

"Telling me and him this foolishness about building a barn by yourself. I figured you to be a smarter man than that. And if you are, why are you teasing the boy?"

"I ain't teasing. I can't say why, but like I told you, things keep pointing to me building this barn."

She didn't understand his excuse and wanted some answers. "Why did you act that way when my boy told you about that man they got in jail? Do you know him? Do you know the Rainmaker?"

He stopped again, and this time walked slowly to stand in front of her. "I know the Rainmaker, and that man in jail can't be him. But he may be the one that shot me." He turned away from her, then quickly twisted around. "A few days ago I was shot and left for dead, Mrs. Hayes. If it hadn't been for your boy, I might have drowned in less than a foot a water. Now, there's things I done like any man that I don't go shouting for every soul to hear. But one habit I tried to keep was paying those I was beholden to." He gulped a breath. His voice had a tone of anger, but it didn't seem aimed at her. "Like I said, you have a barn needs building, and I'll say it's been a while since I was the boy's age, but I built one before with my pa. I'm willing to do it. But if me being here troubles your mind, then tell me so, and when you wake up I'll be gone."

Ann was surprised once more, but she had gotten what she wanted, or so she first thought. She had no knowledge of how desperate men acted, but he had some traits that might befit one. He had always appeared as a drifter, someone with a past she didn't want to get close to. Although Noah was fond of him, she had to protect her family from the likes of outlaws, which he easily could be. The deputy's caution to be wary weighed heavily on her mind. Though, if she asked him to go, she believed he would, instead of forcing his presence on her and the children.

As she looked into his blue eyes, she sensed a softness she hadn't noticed before. If he did leave as asked, what kind of outlaw would do as a woman told him? A woman alone, at that.

"No, Mr. Cole. I won't ask you to leave. I guess I should thank you for your helping me in my time of need. The tools you brought show a sign of good faith, and I'd be ungrateful if I didn't let you do as you have offered. Ingratitude wasn't something I was taught to practice, either. I'm sorry." She felt some shame, but not enough to add a smile to her apology.

He nodded. "Well, then I guess I'll be leaving in the morning. To cut the wood, that is. Just me."

"Oh, no. I'll not have that boy pester me about being left behind. I'll have him ready at sunrise."

Cole smiled at her remark and nodded. "Yes, ma'am."

Tim McGuire

The lush green of firs reflected the midmorning sunlight. As the incline continued to steepen, Cole began to feel the heat of the desert floor give way to the light cool air. A sharp scent of pine filled his nose. A glance behind him showed the mixed shades of brown, red, and green sculpted into the valley below.

As he looked back to the front, a slumbering Noah caught his eye. According to his mother, the boy hadn't slept much during the night for fear of missing the day's trip.

Once surrounded by piñon pines, Cole halted Bender's stride and tied off the reins to the brake. He hopped off the buckboard and reached to shake Noah, but thought better of it. He lacked the heart to disrupt such a peaceful picture. The boy's angelic features favored his ma. Had she been a boy, this is surely how she would have appeared.

The hesitation allowed him a moment to ponder his own boyhood and his present life. At the same age as Noah he had lost his mother. The time when the wonder of life ended and the pain of its reality began. There never came the chance to live that simple a life again.

At one time, the idea of a wife and kids with a house as a home seemed as close as the next day. But tomorrows never do come around.

How would it have been different if he had had a fine son such as this one? A family might have given him a life in one place, replacing the one he had on the run.

It would be hard not to be proud of this respectful young man. He saw a lot of himself in the boy.

Staring at Noah brought to mind one of the few solid truths he had come to remember. Though the name is passed on to honor the father's tradition, sons are raised by their mothers.

He nudged Noah's shoulder, but the boy didn't awaken. After two firmer pokes didn't work either, a shove off the seat and a crash onto the dirt did the trick.

Noah's eyes opened wide and snapped around in search

of an answer to how he got there, finally locking on Cole standing above him.

"You weren't sleeping, were you?"

Noah shook his groggy head as he rose off the ground.

Cole smiled at him and picked up the ax from the bed.

"Are we going to cut down all these trees?" asked Noah as they approached a tall pine.

"Two or three at most is more like it. We'll have to cut them up in halves or smaller to get them all in the wagon."

Cole brushed the dust off the bark, and when he took back the ax, he grabbed at his ribs and winced.

"Are you hurting?"

Cole nodded. "Still feeling a little sore there."

"Can I do it?" the boy asked with a bright smile.

A pause in thought by Cole was all the opening Noah needed to seize the ax handle.

"Please. I can cut down this tree in no time."

"Are you sure you know how?"

"Sure," the confident boy answered. He spread his hands to each end of the wooden handle, stepped back, and butted the edge against the trunk. The bark was dented but didn't split. Noah repeated the motion and landed the ax at a different spot. Again he rocked back on his heels, straining to keep from falling, and rammed the ax into a new mark below the previous two.

"See, I told you I could do it."

Cole nodded with a wink. "Yup, you're sure enough a woodsman. But we might be done before supper if you hit the same cut more than once."

Noah looked at the several slits in the bark. "Oh. You're probably right."

Cole reached for the ax, only to have Noah yank it away. "I ain't done yet."

After a long exhale, Cole said, "You need to watch me so you see how it's done. You ain't going to get anywhere with your hands as spread as they are."

101

"Well," the boy answered with defiance. "This is how I hold it. This is how I cut down trees."

Cole put his hands on his hips. "Well, excuse me for not knowing how a man ten years old can get set in his way of doing something he ain't never done in just two minutes after he ever done it."

"What did you say?" Noah asked with a puzzled face.

"Never you mind." Cole shook his head. "Why don't you rest a minute, and I'll show you how I was taught. Maybe you can show me what I'm doing wrong."

Cole took the ax, resting the handle against his leg long enough to spit into each hand, then lifted the ax, slowly sawing a mark in the trunk. With a deep breath, he raised the ax behind his head and swung it at the tree. Bark splintered into the air. The edge sank deep into the trunk. He yanked the ax free and chopped out another horseshoe-size piece of the pine, then another and another, continuing until half the trunk was missing.

Noah stood awed by the sight. "Wow."

"You better get hold of Bender. I'm going to cut on the other side now, and it won't take much more before it comes down. It might spook him. Take him out a good ways."

Noah started for the wagon and turned to face Cole. "All right. But I get to cut down the next one. Okay?"

Cole smiled at him. "Okay."

The Rocky Mountain Line stagecoach rumbled through the town's streets. The driver reined the four horses to a stop in front of the depot. A soldier emerged from the coach amid dirt kicked up in the stage's wake.

He caught a glance of himself in a depot window. The shroud of dust on his blue uniform looked more befitting a defeated confederate. A once neatly trimmed black beard had sprawled all about his cheeks, making his condition appear no more lofty than that of a common destitute.

His zeal in pursuit of a traitor had betrayed his judgment.

His squad was gone, half of which he'd seen die before his eyes. He alone survived, without a mount or weapon on which to rely. Seventeen days on his own, with only his instincts on which to exist.

His image still in view, he straightened the sling strapped over his right shoulder that obscured the adorning gold leaf. There were certain standards he could maintain. He remained an officer.

He peered up at the driver. "I'm grateful for the transport. I don't know what I would have done if not for you picking me up on the road. You've done a good service to your country."

The driver chuckled and shook his head as he began unstrapping the baggage.

A young man was next out of the coach. He brushed off the dust from his pin-striped suit and derby. "Excuse me," the young man said while squinting through spectacles and dodging the falling baggage. "It's been some time since I was here last, but I'm looking for the Shipwreck. Can you tell me where it is?"

The driver chuckled again as he pointed. "It must have been a hell of a long time ago, 'cause it's hard to forget that place. Head down this street and it will take you to the middle of town. You'll see it to the left. A woman stands out front; if you've seen it before, you'll recognize her."

"Thank you," said the young man. He picked up his bags and began walking in the direction the driver had pointed.

"Where can I find the nearest lawman?" the soldier asked.

"Follow that fellow. It's just down the street from where I sent him."

The soldier nodded his appreciation. A few steps had him at the side of the young man, who tussled over his bags with small Mexican children in peasant dress. After a moment, the young man relented and let the children carry his bags, then looked at the soldier.

"I guess I can add a few pennies to the local commerce."

They both resumed walking, and the children followed. "I saw you sleeping in the stagecoach and didn't want to disturb you." He offered first his right, then his left hand. "I'm Patrick Franklin."

"Miles Perry."

Franklin nodded at the sling. "Indian wars?"

Perry shook his head. "Another encounter."

"Really," said Franklin with a curious grin. "Who else?"

Perry glared at him. "I'm not at liberty to remark."

"Oh, I see. So, have you've been in this town before?"

"I'm unsure of what town this is."

The two men stepped up on the wooden sidewalk that led around the corner of a hotel. They stopped to step over a sleeping man who reeked of whiskey.

Franklin announced, "This is Nobility. New Mexico Territory."

With the main street in full view, the town seemed quiet for this time of day. Sunlight had only crested to one side of the street. Most of the citizenry were likely sleeping off the previous night's frolic. Much like Dodge City and Abilene, this fit the image of a town built on quick greed and low morals.

"Are you looking for someone here?" Franklin asked.

"Not particularly. At the moment, I'm seeking whoever is responsible for upholding law and order."

Perry took notice of a telegraph office and other normal sites of a boomtown. Along with the window-painted shops and various assay offices were the sun-bleached signs of saloons, gambling parlors, dance halls, and vainly disguised brothels.

While continuing down the sidewalk, Franklin's urge to discuss why he had traveled here was equally hard not to notice.

"Actually, I'm here to see a girl."

Perry smirked at the young man. "You should have little trouble finding one here."

"No, I mean a particular girl. I met her some months ago while on the way to San Francisco. But my enthusiasm for fortune began to leave me, as did most of my fortune at hand, when I was about to cross Utah. I felt, should I go on, it should be with a woman on my arm. So I turned around and came back for her. Her name is Lucy."

Franklin stopped in front of a saloon. The figure of a nude woman jutted out from the awning. It appeared in the style seen on the front of ships.

"She's in there?" Perry asked, surprised.

Franklin replied with a nodding smile. "Yes. I know what you must think. But she really isn't that type of woman."

Perry extended his left hand, which Franklin accepted. "Good luck, son. It appears you'll need a great deal of it."

Franklin's smile never cracked as he collected his bags from the children and flipped them a coin, which they received with collective cheer. He proceeded through the swinging doors.

Perry continued down the street and within a short distance found a building with barred windows. The sign above the door read "Nobility Town Marshal." The door was locked, and a peek around the drawn shades showed no one inside. After repeated knocks and no answers, the increasing heat outside reminded him of the dryness of this area.

He looked back at the nude figure.

He considered himself an officer on duty, and liquor wasn't allowed, no matter his thirst. However, most saloons kept water to thin their whiskey to drunken cowboys. He walked back to the place where he had left Franklin and entered through the same swinging doors.

Smoke hung throughout the room, slowly revealing men at card tables with few chairs unfilled. The absence of women seemed normal for the early hour. Like bats, they would be resting after the night's work of consuming their bounty of victims. Another thing he noticed was the absence of drunks sleeping on the floor—an unusual and pleasant surprise for a bawdy house.

Perry slowly stepped to the bar. A short bald man without benefit of tie or apron emerged from the haze on the other side and seemed unhurried to serve him.

"I was wondering if I could trouble you for some water?" Perry asked.

The short man walked to the far end of the bar and returned with a drawing bucket and a ladle. "Four bits."

Perry's surprise showed in his voice. "For water?"

An instant nod was the answer.

"I was hoping for an extension of courtesy. I'm a major in the cavalry."

"And I'm the bartender at the Shipwreck Saloon, and every drink gets paid for. If you wanted it free, there's a trough outside. Water is harder to get here than whiskey."

"I just arrived by stage. I'm afraid I've no means of currency."

The bartender frowned and began removing the bucket from the bar.

"Now, hold on, Curly," said a voice from the haze, followed by the slap of a coin atop the wooden bar. A tall man with a friendly smile walked toward Perry. He wore an unbuttoned black coat and a gold shimmering vest that covered a protruding girth. "I would be proud to buy any soldier a drink of his choice. Can't you see he's wounded, no doubt from killing Apaches or some other redskins? Isn't that true, sir?"

Perry found it hard to observe the code of an officer for honesty. His thirst won out over the truth. "No doubt."

"I thought so. Leave the bucket, Curly," the gentleman said with a chuckle, and the bartender complied. "I'm Big Jim Donovan. I own the steakhouse and a few other businesses in town. If you're wanting something to eat, just go across the street and tell them Big Jim said it was on the house."

Perry removed his left glove. The men shook hands.

"I'm Major Miles Perry. And I'm in your debt, Mr. Donovan."

"Think nothing of it. Always glad to help a killer of Apaches. What brings the army to Nobility?"

"I'm afraid I'm by myself. I became separated from my men. . . . Well, that's a long story I don't wish to bore you with. I'm looking for the marshal of this town to ask for some assistance."

Donovan's head dipped just a moment, and he pushed his hat back. The smile that seemed forever etched on his face faded.

"Well, I'm afraid you're too late for that. It's the reason most of us are in here right now. You see, the marshal was a friend of mine and . . . well, to just say it, a son of a bitch killed him a few nights back. He was buried this morning. We're all here drinking to his memory."

"Oh," Perry remarked with the due respect. "My condolences for the loss of your friend."

"Yup," Donovan sighed. "Ol' Clement Thomas will be a hard man to replace. But if you're looking for the law here, you need to see Clement's deputy, Vance MacGregor."

Perry slurped water from the ladle and wiped his mouth with his sleeve. "Where might I find him?"

"He's down at the marshal's office."

Perry shook his head. "I just came from there. The door was locked and there wasn't anyone inside."

"Oh," Donovan said with a smile, as if he had just remembered something. "He must still be at the cemetery. Probably saying his last good-byes, you know. He'll be along anytime soon. The reason the door's locked is the prisoner they got in there."

Perry's eyebrows rose with interest while he drank another ladle of water.

"The son of a bitch that shot Clement." Donovan raised

107

his shot glass to his lips. "Some young snapper calling himself the Rainmaker."

Perry dropped the ladle, letting it bounce to the floor. As the bounding echo shot through the room, all eyes turned to the two men only for a moment. The major's left hand froze in the same position upon hearing the news. Slowly he leaned closer to Donovan and whispered, careful to clearly pronounce each word. "Say that name again."

Donovan appeared puzzled from Perry's reaction. "The Rainmaker. Is that someone you know?"

Perry's right arm tingled, and he glanced at the sling. "Very well."

"Oh, I see, maybe better than you'd like to have known him," Donovan said with a chuckle, then quickly squelched his levity. "You know, the man you ought to be talking to is ol' Cyril Walker, over there." The big man pointed to an old-timer sitting at one of the card tables. "Cyril's been helping out Vance since Clement was shot."

Perry started for the old-timer despite Donovan's continued warning.

"Don't believe everything. Cyril's from Texas. He'd tell you he was at the Alamo for a bottle of rye."

Perry approached the older man, who wore a dusty old coat and a tethered Panama hat. Scraggly whiskers were visible below the brim.

"I heard you know about the prisoner called the Rainmaker."

The old-timer looked up over his shoulder, revealing his grinning wrinkled face. "Yes, sir, I do," Cyril answered, rubbing his lips together and taking a grip of his empty shot glass. "I know all about him."

Perry quickly grabbed the glass and tossed it aside. He grasped Cyril's coat and yanked the old man from the chair amid the sound of shattering glass. "Tell me what you know about him. Tell me right now."

Cyril's grin turned to an openmouthed quiver, stammering

to answer the question. "Wait, wait a minute, mister, er, General, sir."

"Major. Major Miles Arthur Perry, Seventh Cavalry, Army of the United States."

"Yes, yes sir, Major."

"I told you to tell me what you knew about the prisoner in the marshal's office. Is it the Rainmaker?"

The old-timer nodded.

"When did he get here?"

"A couple of days, maybe a week, no longer."

Sensing the stillness of the normally rowdy place, Perry eased his grip of Cyril's coat and allowed him to sit down. He reminded himself that orders were best given in a low authoritative voice. "This is army business. I must insist on your cooperation."

Cyril nodded again. "Anything you need."

"I need to get in that jail. Can you unlock the door?"

The old-timer shook his head. "Only Vance MacGregor got a key. He only let me sit in there once, but he don't no more."

"Where is the deputy?"

"Burying Marshal Thomas. Should be back real soon. I'll be glad to run and go see for you. I don't mind, if that's what you need."

Perry shook his head. "I'll get him myself."

He stepped out of the saloon and walked to the marshal's office at a quick pace. As he approached, a rider dismounted in front of the jailhouse. A black armband and a tin star were first to catch Perry's eye.

"Are you Deputy MacGregor?"

The young man nodded with a friendly smile, which reminded Perry that diplomacy would be needed to achieve his goal. He forced a grin.

"I'm Major Perry, Seventh Cavalry. I understand you have a prisoner who calls himself the Rainmaker."

"That's right," Vance said as he stepped onto the sidewalk.

"With your permission, I would like to speak to him."

"What's he to you?" Vance placed the key in the jailhouse door.

"That's an army matter."

Vance snickered. "Army matter? He don't seem the type to do with the army." He turned the key. "I have to keep this locked or I'll have the whole town in here gawking. Old Cyril would be giving nickel tours." He opened the door.

"Yes, I've met the man," Perry said as both men entered.

Vance slowly walked to the back wall to get the cell key ring. He was followed closely by the impatient major. Within a few moments the barred hall door was open, and Perry charged in and stood in front of the first cell. He sighted a thin, unshaven boy, perhaps the age of twenty, lying on the bunk.

"Where is he? Where's the Rainmaker?"

Vance peered into the cell with a quizzical expression. "You got eyes? He's right in front of you."

"This man isn't the Rainmaker."

"See," said the boy behind the bars. "I've been telling you that for two days."

"Shut up," Vance yelled. "What do you mean? That's what he called himself."

Perry shook his head. "I don't care who he says he is. He's not the man I'm looking for. He's not the Rainmaker."

"You tell him, army man," the prisoner said.

"Shut up," Perry and Vance yelled in unison. Vance waved his hand for both of them to leave. Without any words spoken, after the barred door was locked they walked outside onto the sunlit sidewalk.

"Now, what the hell are you talking about?"

"He's not the Rainmaker any more than I'm Abraham Lincoln. The man I'm looking for is named Cole. A man over six feet tall, near thirty years old, maybe older."

"He claims his name is Billy Mansfield. From Alabama."

Perry paused. "Why did he say he was the Rainmaker?"

"I don't know. I guess he came into town spouting it. I heard it from the folks around the Shipwreck. The night he shot Marshal Thomas."

Perry nodded and dipped his head. "His gun?"

"Forty-five Colt," Vance said. "Seven-inch barrel. Like an army model."

The major's head shot up. "Where is it? Do you have it?"

Vance nodded, and the two walked back into the office, where the deputy opened a desk drawer and removed a revolver.

Perry took the weapon and immediately flipped the butt up. "7 CAV" was stamped in the metal. He looked into Vance's eyes.

"This is Cole's. Where'd Mansfield get it?"

Vance shrugged.

"I need to find out," Perry said as he turned for the hallway.

"Wait," Vance said with a firm voice. "I'm not having you talk to him no more. You got that no-good bastard believing he didn't shoot Clement Thomas, and I was there when he did it."

An order from a civilian, one not much older than a cadet, was an unaccustomed experience for Major Perry. However, he was alone and without jurisdiction. He held his tongue and started for the open door outside. "I'm keeping this weapon."

"Like hell you are," Vance answered. Perry stopped. "That's evidence in a trial, Major, and I'll not have it leave this office."

Perry slowly walked toward Vance. "This weapon belongs to Cole, a man who is wanted for treason. Three years ago he betrayed the Seventh Cavalry by warning the Sioux of our advance at the Little Bighorn River. Men were slaughtered, including the greatest leader of men since Washington, George Armstrong Custer." He turned the pistol's butt up for Vance's inspection. "This weapon is an army-issue revolver. Stamped especially for the Seventh." Vance looked back at Perry. "Not more than two weeks ago, I apprehended Cole in Colorado." The major paused and looked at his sling. "But he shot me. With this weapon."

A brogue came from the open door. "He told the men in the Shipwreck he was given that sling due to fighting with Apaches."

The deputy and the major both turned to see a small man in a buttoned vest. Perry then looked at Vance.

"That's Kennemer. He runs the newspaper in town," Vance explained.

"Reporter?" Perry shook his head. "I share General Sherman's view. They should all be shot as spies."

Kennemer smiled. "Don't mind me. Please go on. I'm just here in the people's interest."

Vance nodded and picked up a telegram off the desk. "I got a wire back from a county sheriff in Colorado. He says the Rainmaker shot three men in a place called Platte Falls."

"That's true. I was there, I saw the coffins."

"It also says he took a woman up into the hills. They found the woman's husband shot in a mine shack and his partner at the bottom of a place called Danger Ridge." Vance handed Perry the telegram. "It also says they found soldiers."

Perry looked up and slowly nodded. "Those were my men."

Vance murmured, "Now, I see why you are so interested. It says he wounded two of them in town and rode out on a Palouse."

Perry whispered, "Deputy, I need your help. I don't believe that adolescent outlaw got the drop on the likes of Cole. If he did, we should look for the body, but if Cole's not dead . . ." He looked again at the pistol. "Then I believe Cole will be back for this. He's a killer. It's paramount we find him."

"Hold on," Vance said as he took the pistol from the major. "I got no one here to watch my prisoner while I go on a wild-goose chase looking for some man you don't even know is around here or even alive. I'll just keep the gun here."

"Very well, then," Perry said as he leaned closer to Vance. "Then you'll have the real Rainmaker to deal with. Good day."

He sidestepped Kennemer and marched out of the office, and a fast gait had him inside the telegraph office in little time. The sling hampered his right hand, so he unstrapped it from his arm and threw it to the floor. He wrote on the pad of paper:

> *Have found traitor, the Rainmaker.*
> *Send reinforcements, Nobility, New Mexico.*
> *Maj. M. A. Perry. 7 Cav.*

"Send this at once," he told the clerk. "Fort Abraham Lincoln."

Cole shoved the last of three logs into the buckboard. He had originally counted on being able to take more home, but the sagging wheels of the buckboard forced him to be satisfied with the load he had.

"Are we going to leave the rest of them?" asked Noah.

Cole nodded while glancing at the sun. "Yeah, we have to come tomorrow for the rest. It's time to head in."

"But what if someone comes by and takes them?"

A grin broke Cole's face. "Anyone comes along and picks them up, I don't want to get in their way." He walked back to a stump and bent over to pick up his ax. The jolly mood brought on by a satisfying job done vanished when he saw a small bone protruding from the brush. He picked it up and discovered beneath the brush even smaller bones, these with gouges. Teeth marks. Paw prints in the dry dirt were now easily visible. He stood and scanned the horizon for any presence of what he had just discovered. Sighting no immediate threat, he walked directly to the wagon. "It's time to get a move on. Right now."

The concern in his voice was reflected on the boy's face. "What's wrong?"

"I seen something," Cole answered. "Be nice to have a gun." He snapped the reins like a whip and yelled loudly at the horse.

"You said that we shouldn't go fast."

"That was before. Besides, it's all downhill." The wagon swayed with the heavy load, while Cole rode the brake down the curved and bumpy path. Bender galloped from being pushed by the speeding weight behind. A once-happy Noah now grabbed the seat in panic with both hands. The wagon creaked with the strain, the rear sliding to the side over the dirt and stones with each turn. As the slope gently leveled, Cole pulled in on the reins and slowed the wagon.

He looked over to a wide-eyed Noah. The fright in the boy's rigid body took Cole by surprise. Although Cole thought the risk necessary, the effect on the young one wasn't something he had considered.

"You okay?"

Noah nodded, then looked at the hill behind them.

"We're far enough now. We'll take it easy from here in."

"Far from what? What'd you see back there?"

He didn't want to worry the boy any more than he had, but he didn't want to lie to him. "I saw some tracks and what was left of a fawn or calf." He turned to Noah. "Wolf tracks."

Noah's eyes widened even more. "You sure?"

Cole nodded. "Didn't look fresh, but it's been since the last rain. Anyway, we'll just have to be watching next time."

"Well, let's go back. I want to see them."

"Hell no," Cole blurted, then regretted he'd cussed. "Just bones and some prints."

"But you said it was a fawn or calf."

"It was! Them were small bones of some small young'un."

Noah looked to the front for a moment, then turned his questioning face to Cole. "Why do they kill babies? Not much to eat."

"Because they're easier to catch."

"Don't their mama protect them?"

"Yeah," Cole drawled. While thinking he hadn't answered so many questions in his life, it came to him that this was one of those times he'd wished that day for fate to give him. "But them wolves likely run her off. They gang up on her and chase her away. See, an animal mother ain't like yours. After a while fighting, she wears down, and when the fight's over, she forgets that baby and has another."

"Oh," came the answer from a satisfied-sounding Noah. "You know a lot of things, don't you? Probably everything there is to know."

"I guess I've took notice of a few things," he said with modest pride.

Noah looked to the front, then came that look again.

"What's a whore?"

Cole's mouth fell open. His jerk of the reins snapped Bender's head to the side. "What'd you say?"

"I said, what's a whore. It's okay if you don't know."

"I know what one is. It's just—just that—you aren't supposed to ask someone that. Not someone you don't know good. You ask your ma those kind of things."

"She looked at me like she'd whip my britches for hearing it when the deputy said it. Besides, I thought I knew you good."

The boy's remorseful tone made Cole pause. He could've ignored the question, but he didn't think it fit for his young friend to learn the answer from the same type of people Cole once had. He rubbed his brow and squinted.

"A whore is," he said slowly, trying to think of another

answer than the one he had in mind. "A whore is," he repeated, now with a blank mind, until a memory appeared of his own mother once explaining to him why she had married his father. "A whore is a woman that sells her secret." He turned to the confused Noah.

"Secret? What secret?"

Cole jiggled the reins. "Well, every woman is born with a secret. And she can only share it once."

"What kind of secret?" asked Noah, hanging on each word.

"A real special one. That's why she's real careful to share it with some man . . ." He took a deep breath. ". . . she really likes. Even loves him. It's not something you give up for money. It's something a woman saves up to share with the man she marries."

"How come it's got to be a man?"

Cole jerked his head at Noah. "That's just the way things are, son. Some things can only go a certain way."

The boy sat with a pondering expression. "So you mean Mama shared her secret with my pa?"

"Yup," Cole said with a wink. "I 'spect she did."

"Well, then," Noah said, once more with that look in his eye. "Don't men have secrets? Something they keep to share?"

"Oh yeah," Cole answered, then muttered, "Most of the ones I know were wanting to share it with every woman that come along." He pulled up on the reins, hopped off with canteen in hand, and walked to the horse. He dripped water in his palm and placed it under Bender's nose.

"I told you you'd know most everything."

Cole smirked. "I was told by the smartest man I knew that there ain't no one that knows it all."

The boy hopped off and threw stones down the hill. "Was he your pa?"

"No, I can't say that. No, he was a man I met while in the army, then I rode with him for some years."

"You were soldiers?"

"I was. But he weren't in our outfit . . ." Cole paused, then continued with a reflective tone, " 'cause he was colored. He was a scout, and taught me to be one."

Noah stopped throwing stones and turned with a confident look. "You mean he was a nigger?"

Cole looked at the boy, a bit stunned. "Your ma teach you that word?"

Noah seemed puzzled. "No. But I heard Henry Taylor say it."

Cole twisted the cap back on the canteen, patted the horse, and started for the wagon seat.

"I have to admit, I used to call them that, too. When I was little, like you, everybody in Kansas called them that." He climbed onto the seat and was soon joined by Noah. "But after my ma passed on, I went to be with my pa. He was in the war and had a lot of them as soldiers." He shook the reins, and Bender ambled forward. "But I have to say, I heard a lot of white folks calling them that just to be mean to those men. There were some good ones and bad, just like the white men, but all of the colored were called niggers." He turned to look at Noah. "So I didn't call them that no more. I may have said it toward the ones I didn't like, but I never thought it of the ones that I did. It was shortly after that my pa told me I was named for a colored man he admired. A fellow who fought people for money in Kentucky but was a good man in his heart. His name was Clay."

The squeak of the spokes turning under the weight of the wagon became the only sound for all of a minute.

"Where is he, the smartest man you knew, that taught you to scout?"

"Jenks?" The name brought a slight smile to Cole's face, but it faded quickly. The memory of burying his old friend came to him. The memory of the trouble that followed him and had ended up killing Jenks wasn't something Cole thought Noah could understand, nor was he in the mood to talk on the matter.

"He's in Colorado." Cole again looked at Noah. "You do remind me of him, though."

Noah smiled and giggled. "How come?"

"Because the both of you can't stop flapping your lips once you start. You can wear rock into gravel with all your questions."

The two laughed as the farm appeared in the distance. The squeaky spokes continued until the wagon stopped in front of the house.

Noah jumped off the wagon and headed inside.

The fear of what was about to happen made Cole call to him.

"Hey, boy."

Noah stopped and twisted around.

"You might ought not tell your ma about us talking about a woman's secret."

Noah looked at the door, then turned his smile back at Cole.

"Maybe we should keep it our secret."

Cole smiled too. "Yeah, maybe we should."

Chapter Nine

The eastern sun silhouetted a boy's figure at the edge of the farm. Noah swung the ax at the stack of timber as if cutting the trees down once more. Seeing Cole approach with Bender, he quickly tossed the ax out of view behind the wood.

"Where you been?" asked Noah.

"Were you chopping on those logs?"

Noah looked at the wood and slowly shook his head. His look of curiosity returned. "Where you been?"

"Oh," Cole muttered as he walked toward the stack, leading Bender behind him. "I let the horse chew on the new grass out a ways while I started shaving these of the bark. Next thing I knew, he was heading yonder for Texas."

Two trunks had three gouges each. Cole peered at Noah, who, after meeting Cole's eyes, turned to look at where Cole had just come from.

"How far'd he get?"

"Far enough for me to waste the morning running after

him." Cole rubbed the indentations. Noah avoided his stare. "You know, it was a damn fool thing to do."

Noah jerked his head at Cole with sorrowful surprise at the remark.

"Me, letting the horse wander. It just made more work for me to do with less time to get done what I started. But sometimes I guess we all do things we'd as soon not done after we thought about the trouble it caused. You think so?"

Noah nodded and ducked his head. "I was just practicing for when we went back to the hills today."

Cole rubbed the boy's hair. "It's all right. Let's not do it again. That ax may just as soon chop off your fingers as cut that wood. Then you'd be no help to me at all." A grin broke both their faces, until Noah looked closer at Cole's bare chest.

"Evie was right," he said as he ran his fingers over the creases in Cole's arms. "Where'd you get all them bumps?"

"Doing chores."

Noah followed as Cole picked up the ax and tossed it into the wagon. "I seen Henry Taylor and Mr. Grover do plenty of chores. They don't look like you. Do those hurt?"

"They did at the time." Cole searched the ground. "You seen my shirt?"

"Mama's got it. She said she'd wash it with all the rest." Cole smirked. "She did?"

"Yeah. How come you took it off?"

He shook his head quickly "Ain't nothing like the cool morning air of summer on your skin to make you start working. Learned that when I was your age."

Noah unbuttoned his shirt. "I guess I'll take mine off too." He ran his fingers over his smooth white flesh. "How many chores you got to do to get those bumps?"

"A whole bunch. Till you're full growed, then plenty after that." Cole walked toward the house. "Is your ma inside?"

Noah nodded. "She fixed your breakfast, said she'd save it for you."

Cole's smirk returned. "Did she?" The thought of the kind act put more spirit into his stride. "Well, I wouldn't want to make her mad by not eating it." He turned the corner of the house and hopped onto the porch.

His bright grin faded upon sight of a young man in a black coat and trousers with a buttoned white-collared shirt sitting in a four-seat buggy. The stranger raised his open palm and nodded as Cole stopped at the door.

It appeared a suitor had come to call, a sign that took the delight of a waiting hot breakfast right out of his gut. An urge to go back and take out his new discovery on the stack of logs quickly left him. He hadn't a right to expect anything different. This wasn't his place, and neither was anything else here his.

He opened the door. Ann sat at the table with a woman dressed for church. Blond hair perched out from the woman's bonnet, and when she looked at Cole, she showed a youthful face.

Although he wore pants, there were few times in his past when he had felt so naked. "My mistake," he blurted, taking a step back and bringing the door closed.

"No, please come in," the young woman said, and Cole slowly complied. "So this must be the brother-in-law I've heard so much about."

Both women rose.

"This is my good friend, Lorna Clendenon. She teaches school," Ann said, and after her eyes dipped to the floor, she looked at Cole. "And this is my brother-in-law, Clay."

His chest tightened, pushing most of the air from his body. He had never thought simple words could do that to him.

He accepted Lorna's offered hand. "H'wdy."

The teacher's pressed lips grew to a wide grin. "My, you're tall and much bigger. You don't look like your brother Robert."

Cole's eyes flashed to Ann, who took a short breath. "He favors his pa more than Robert did."

Tim McGuire

Cole again retreated from the doorway.

"Don't let me chase you away. Ann was just telling me all about you."

"She was?" He again glanced at Ann, who once more dipped her eyes to the floor. "What might she have told you?"

"Oh, nothing special. Just what ladies tell one another."

The thought of what could have been said scared him more than waking up next to a rattler.

"Besides," Lorna continued, "I believe she's keeping something warm for you."

His mouth opened. Her meaning didn't become clear until she pointed toward a skillet atop the stove. "Oh. Yeah. I heard."

He entered the room and shut the door. The women sat once more and joined hands.

"I was asking Ann to come join me in town today."

Upon feeling the sting of the hot skillet handle against his palm, he turned to see both of them looking weepy-eyed at each other while still smiling.

"Lorna's going to be married," Ann announced, and the women hugged across the table.

"Is that right?" Cole said, inhaling away some of his tension. "Then that fella out there . . . ?" Ann's nod let him finally take a deep breath. "Well, good for you. Glad to hear it." The relief of the news brought back his appetite, and he reflexively gripped the skillet handle.

"God—" he exclaimed, releasing the handle to a crash of metal. The women quickly turned their heads to him. He didn't want to appear the fool, or show off his temper. ". . . bless both of you." He waited for them to turn away before he winced.

"I want Ann to help me pick out a dress. We only have two weeks. It's taken me almost a year to get that boy to ask me to marry him, and I don't want to give him a chance to

122

change his mind. I told Morris I wanted a ring on my finger before the summer was over.''

"I thought I might go," Ann said to Cole. "If you were taking Noah for more wood.''

Cole shrugged. "That's no trouble to me."

"Good, then," said Lorna.

Both women stood and hugged once more.

"I need to get a scarf. I'll be right back," Ann said as she went to her room.

Lorna looked at Cole with a sly smile. "Brother-in-law, huh?"

He felt her eyes scan his chest and arms probingly.

"Wasn't it fortunate for Ann that you came along?"

He nodded and forced a polite grin, then peeked at his chest.

"I mean with the barn burning and all. It appears if it hadn't been for you, I might have lost my best friend. I thank you, Mr. Hayes."

It took him a moment to realize what she had called him. "I'm used to being called Clay."

Her smile got even bigger. "Very well, Clay. Please call me Lorna. I saw the wood outside. Ann tells me you plan on building a barn by yourself. Is that true?"

"Yes, ma'am. I'm going to give it my best."

"Well, perhaps I could recruit my intended and his brother to help you."

"That'd be right nice."

Ann returned with her hair wrapped beneath a blue scarf. "I was going to take Evie with me." The women headed for the door.

"Ah," Cole said. "Where might my shirt be?"

Ann first looked at Lorna, then back at him. "It's drying on the line in back of the house."

"I'll get it," he said.

"Aren't you going to finish your breakfast first?" asked Lorna.

"No," he answered, looking at his hand. "When I get bit twice by food, I think I ought to let it simmer down."

The women went outside, and he followed.

"Noah," Ann called. "Where's Evie?

The girl rose in the back of the buckboard. "Here I am, Mama."

"Come on with me. I'm going into town with Miss Clendenon and Mr. Taylor."

"You mean Morris?" Noah cried out.

"Well, soon he'll be a married man and will deserve the respect of one, which I expect you to give him. Come on, Evie."

"I want to go where Noah's going."

"Go on, Evie," Noah snapped. "We don't want stupid girls with us."

"Evelyn Louise Hayes, you come over here right now," Ann ordered, and the young girl marched reluctantly to the buggy and sat next to her mother on the rear seat. "We'll be home before supper."

"Don't hurry on account of us. We'll make do," Cole answered. The pleasure of leaving for social reasons became etched on Ann's face. Since he'd been on the farm he hadn't seen her smile the way she did now.

Every person had to have some relief from what they *had* to do and enjoy some things they *wanted* to do. He felt a grin crack his face as he watched the buggy head toward the road into Nobility.

The heat on his skin reminded him that his shirt should be dry. He stepped off the porch, found the shirt, and slipped it on. "Let's get to work," he said as he returned to the side of the house.

Noah jumped onto the buckboard seat. "I'm ready to go."

Cole shook his head. "I don't know if we're going now."

The boy's face soured. "How come? I thought you said we were going to need a lot more wood for the barn."

"We do, but the day's near half gone. I don't want to be

up there with wolves present come dark. We still need to clean the bark off these trunks.''

Noah slumped in the seat until his face lit up, and he hopped off the wagon to charge inside the house. Within a few minutes, he returned with the musket that had once been pointed at Cole.

''Whoa,'' Cole shouted with his palms pointed out in surrender. ''What are you doing?''

''Well, you said that you'd like to have a weapon. Here's a weapon. Now, can we go?''

Cole took the rifle from the boy and inspected the hammer action and peeked down the barrel. ''This is an old cap and ball. Been near ten years since I seen one of these. It's got no cap, though. Don't even appear loaded. Does your ma have a habit of keeping her rifle unloaded?''

''She don't know how.''

He snapped his head down at Noah. ''You mean your ma held me off with an unloaded rifle?'' After the boy nodded, Cole shook his head in amazement. ''Your ma does have some grit. Does she let you handle it?''

''Sure.'' Noah's tone had a familiar confidence.

''Tell me the truth, boy. I wouldn't feel right taking this with us if I didn't know for sure she was used to you handling it.''

''Well, she saw me see her put it under her bed. That must mean something.''

''We got no powder and no ammunition.''

''Them little round balls? She keeps them and some bad-smelling stuff hid under her clothes. I know where they are.'' The boy started for the house.

''Wait,'' Cole said while he pondered taking the rifle. He didn't like the idea, but if they were going to cut more wood it might be useful. Since trading his Winchester, he wasn't comfortable without something that could shoot. He slowly nodded. ''Okay,'' he said. ''As long as you're sure it's fine with your ma.''

Noah's grin never faded. "She don't mind." He went in the house and quickly returned outside with a small leather pouch and brass flask. "Are these what you're talking about?"

Cole nodded, and he opened the pouch to find it was near full of firing caps and six mini balls. A sniff inside the flask produced the strong smell of sulfur. "Seems still good. We'll need wadding."

"Wadding?"

"Yeah, wadding, some kind of cloth you tear to stuff inside the barrel to hold the shot in place."

Noah appeared confused until his face lit up yet again and he ran to the wagon with Cole not far behind. He jumped into the bed and lifted a small rag. "Is this good enough?"

Cole nodded. "That'll do. Needs to be in strips to get down the barrel." He propped the musket on the seat and walked to the horse, leading it to the front of the wagon. Within a few minutes he had harnessed the animal. He came back to the bed and noticed an embroidered flower on one of the strips Noah had already shredded. "Where'd you get this?"

"It's Evie's."

"Evie's? You shouldn't have took what belonged to her."

"She ain't supposed to have it, no way. She holds it when she sucks her thumb, but Mama told her she had to stop sucking her thumb. She hid it out here so Mama couldn't see her, pretending she was going to come with us. I hate her anyway. Stupid girl."

Cole climbed into the driver's seat and after a short thought shook the reins to start the trip to the hills. "Hate? That's a powerful word. I don't know if I'd be using it against one of my kin."

A moment passed before Noah responded, "Well, she hates me."

"You know that for sure? Seems to me if she were wanting to come with us she couldn't be hating you too much."

Noah stepped over the seat and sat next to Cole. "Didn't you hate your sister?"

"Never had one, nor brother either. I don't have any kin now. Sometimes wish I did, maybe to visit on occasion. But it just didn't work out that way." He paused to see Noah leaning back with crossed arms. "I don't think you ought to hate your sister. She's likely the only one you'll ever have."

"She's always pestering me, following me around."

"That's 'cause you're her big brother, likely the only one she'll ever have. You might ought to think about that." He turned ahead to see the distant mountains. While still staring straight, he thought about when he was a youth. He spoke in a soft voice. "Could be a day come you look back and wished you had thought about it."

Ann breathed deeply as they approached the edge of Nobility. She was so happy for Lorna on this special occasion and felt honored that she had been asked to help with the dress, but that honor would necessitate showing her face in Jed Farlon's store.

Morris steered the buggy to the front of Farlon's Emporium and reined in. He, Lorna, Ann, and Evie all climbed onto the shaded boardwalk.

"We won't be too long. Do you have any money?" Lorna said to Morris, who shrugged and pulled out his empty pockets. She picked a coin from her purse and handed it to him. "Don't wander off too far, and don't let me find you in any saloon. We won't have any money to waste in them from now on."

He rolled his eyes as a child would to a mother, which is about what their relationship had always been. Morris began walking away, only to be interrupted by her faint whimperish objection. "Oh, Morris, dear." She showed her cheek to him. He turned around and, after looking to see who might be watching, gave her a peck. A contented smile beamed on Lorna's face. As he strode off, the two women and the girl walked into the store. Ann was last to enter, after a long, deep breath.

They walked to the counter, Ann with a firm grip of Evie's hand so the girl would not touch or, worse, spoil anything that might have to be paid for. When she got to the counter, she tried to focus on the goods on the shelving instead of the man in front of them.

"We need to see about making a dress. Do you have that catalog from Chicago?" asked Lorna.

"Yes, ma'am, it just came in yesterday with the mail on the stage," Farlon said to her, then looked to Ann with a warm smile. "Good morning Mrs. Hayes." He gave the large catalog book to Lorna, who immediately thumbed through the pages.

Ann raised her head, surprised by his good manner. "Good morning, Mr. Farlon." Encouraged by his mood, she felt now would be the time to lighten her guilty conscience. "I appreciate your kind patience with my debt. I'm hoping to be able to give something toward it soon."

He raised his palm as if to stop her confession. "Don't let it worry you, Mrs. Hayes. With what was put down against it, it balanced at near eighty dollars. I know that you still have your crop to get in. So I can wait." He smiled at her, then pointed at the book for Lorna's attention.

Ann was amazed by what she'd heard. As if by some divine grace, her most troubling concern had been taken away. She betrayed her glee with a smirk. "What was put down?"

He looked to her with a puzzled face and answered in his usual quick tone. "Nearly a hundred and twenty dollars' worth of merchandise. A man came in here a few days ago with a rifle and saddle. I gave a hundred dollars for both, even though I didn't think much of the saddle. He took some supplies, flour, peaches, and some overalls if I recall. He told me to put the rest toward your bill. But I did get more for it than I thought I would that very same day, so I felt right splitting the profit with your bill. I thought you'd know about that."

Ann looked at Lorna, whose look of astonishment gave

GET YOUR 4
FREE* BOOKS NOW—
A VALUE OF BETWEEN
$17 AND $20

Mail the Free* Books Certificate Today!

FREE* BOOKS
CERTIFICATE!

YES! I want to subscribe to the Leisure Western Book Club. Please send me my 4 FREE* BOOKS. Then, each month, I'll receive the four newest Leisure Western Selections to preview for 10 days. If I decide to keep them, I will pay the Special Member's Only discounted price of just $3.36 each, a total of $13.44 ($16.35 in Canada). This saves me between $3 and $6 off the bookstore price. There are no shipping, handling or other charges.* There is no minimum number of books I must buy and I may cancel the program at any time. In any case, the 4 FREE* BOOKS are mine to keep—at a value of between $17 and $20!

*In Canada, add $7.50 US shipping and handling per order for first shipment. For all subsequent shipments to Canada the cost of membership in the Book Club is $16.35 US plus $7.50 US shipping and handling per order. All payments must be made in US dollars.

Name _____

Address _____

City_____ State_____

Zip_____ Telephone_____

Signature_____

Biggest Savings Offer!

For those of you who would like to pay us in advance by check or credit card—we've got an even bigger savings in mind. Interested? Check here. ☐

If under 18, parent or guardian must sign. Terms, prices and conditions subject to change. Subscription subject to acceptance. Leisure Books reserves the right to reject any order or cancel any subscription.

Tear here and mail your FREE* book card today!

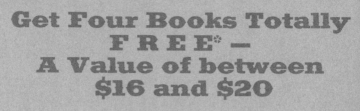

Get Four Books Totally FREE* – A Value of between $16 and $20

Tear here and mail your FREE* book card today!

PLEASE RUSH
MY FOUR FREE*
BOOKS TO ME
RIGHT AWAY!

LeisureWestern Book Club
P.O. Box 6613
Edison, NJ 08818-6613

way to a sly grin. "I guess your brother has taken more thought of staying longer."

Lorna's idea hadn't occurred to Ann, but neither had the prospect of her debt being knocked down by an unexpected source. As she contemplated the suggestion of a man to whom she wasn't related staying with her family perhaps on a permanent basis, her heartbeat quickened. Such a possibility shouldn't be considered, especially since he had said he was leaving as soon as he built a barn. However, it took Lorna's shrill scream to get that thought to leave her head.

"Ann, look at this! Isn't it pretty? So modern!"

She looked at the picture Lorna pointed to and agreed that the dress did appear beautiful. Lace lapels that wrapped around the neck stretched down the front all the way to the hem. She imagined her friend wearing it, but soon the picture of herself in the dress flashed before her. The dress's features changed to the modest white dress she had worn just over eleven years before. A cold sting shot through her. She had already known the delight of being chosen as a wife and felt ashamed for begrudging her friend such a feeling.

"Oh, Lorna. That will look lovely on you."

"We have that material right here in stock," said the storekeeper. Lorna's exuberance was heightened with Farlon's announcement. The group moved to a table where all types of cloth were bundled. Within seconds Farlon had pulled the desired fabric from the stack, and Lorna immediately unfolded it in front of her figure.

Without words and just an admiring nod from Ann, Lorna's eyes began to well.

"Why don't you step in the back. Mrs. Farlon can help you pin it to you to see what you'll need," said Farlon, and the bundle of jumping beans in the form of the schoolteacher did just that.

Ann looked to find Evie, who had wandered to the front window. She went to her daughter with thoughts of when the day would come when she would help shop for her wedding dress. As she stroked the girl's hair, a loud voice crept near the store's open door.

She stepped through the doorway to see a man in a cavalry uniform across the street talking in a high voice to a gathering near the marshal's office. He had a black beard, and his right arm was limp by his side.

Although she clearly heard him speaking, she had to get closer to decipher the words. Since Lorna would need at least a few minutes with Mrs. Farlon, Ann cautioned Evie to stay at the window, and then out of curiosity she strolled nearer the orator.

"You all need be aware," the soldier said.

"Oh, what a more beautiful day it is with your presence, Mrs. Hayes."

The distraction came from the man in front of her, who had turned to show his plaid coat and notepad. "Good morning, Mr. Kennemer."

"It's good to see your sweet face in the town again," he said, tipping his cap. "What brings you to us today?"

"Oh, Lorna Clendenon and I are here choosing a dress. She's to be married in two weeks," she said while peeking at the soldier.

"Oh, what fine news. I'll have to give it a bit of a mention in the next edition."

She stood on her toes to peer over the assembling crowd. "Who is this man? What is he talking about?"

"Oh," Kennemer answered with a disgruntled look on his face. "He's a man from the army spitting out such blarney about another outlaw in our midst. It seems we may not have got who we think we have in jail."

Ann stood confused. "Who do we have there? I thought it was the man that shot Marshal Thomas."

"Aye, and so it is, ma'am. But the major here says that there is another man who might be dead, or might be right here waiting to gun down our entire population," he sarcastically stated. "He's saying there's another 'Rainmaker' about."

Ann's breath stuck in her throat. As Kennemer returned to jotting notes on his pad, she listened to the soldier.

"The Rainmaker is a man without conscience. Over three hundred men lie dead due to his action at the Little Bighorn. And I've come from Colorado, where he single-handedly is responsible for the deaths of U.S. cavalrymen under my command, and likely for the demise of a mine owner, and the man's missing wife. Should you see this man, do not give him quarter, but flee for your life to the deputy or myself. He stands—"

"Oh, Ann," shouted Lorna, drawing Ann's attention behind her to the store. Lorna's excited waving from the sidewalk pulled Ann reluctantly from the mass. The speaker's words slurred to a chattered jumble, but Ann overcame her curiosity and retreated to the store.

As she neared the sidewalk, Lorna stepped inside, allowing Ann a glance back to attempt a last idea of who it was she should be wary.

An awful coincidence might have occurred. It wouldn't be likely that such a man as the one being spoken of would show traits of kindness. But what of the other coincidence, the one of two strange men in the area?

Another urgent request from Lorna turned Ann to the real reason for her trip to Nobility.

After Cole had loaded the remaining logs onto the buckboard, he stopped and pulled out the red bandanna to wipe his neck and brow. Keeping an eye out for any movement in the surrounding brush, he caught sight of Noah trying to balance the long musket.

"I thought you were going to teach me to shoot it," the boy cried. "Can't you teach me now? We got enough wood to build a hundred barns with."

Cole examined the load of three trunks. Though he knew he would need plenty more, it was a full load for the small

131

wagon. He walked to where Noah stood fumbling with the musket.

"Here, now. Let me have it. That's no way to be holding something that can blow your toes plum off." He took the musket from the boy and blew away the dust from the sights.

"Can that thing really shoot?"

"Sure can. I seen many of them shot when I was about your size."

"When you was soldiering?"

"Before that," he answered. He cocked the hammer and checked the sights. "It was during the war. The States War."

"I heard about that war. Were you fighting in it?" Noah asked with excitement.

"I didn't fight in that one. I drummed the lines in place, but that's sure enough where this come from."

"You did what?"

Cole aimed the rifle at a mock target. "I was a drummer. It was the only job they let me do. I would pound the drum and the men would march to the beat. See, when armies go to fighting, they get in long lines. And with all the blasting and exploding going on, they need something to keep their steps together, so they ain't scattered about. So they listen to the drumbeat."

Noah knelt to pick blades of grass. "Then what do they do?"

"Well, then they listen for the order to fire and commence shooting."

"At each other? Ain't the other army shooting back?"

"Yup, along about the same time."

Noah shook his head. "That's dumb. Why don't they hide and shoot?"

Cole paused while a painful memory passed. "Well, there's them that do that, too."

"Do you ever see them?"

"Oh, yeah." He nodded. "Yeah, I saw one right up close. Shot an officer right off his horse."

Nobility

Noah smiled. "Wow, right off his horse?"

Cole took a deep breath and again nodded. His father's death wasn't something he felt the boy should have swimming in his mind. "Let's not talk about wars. You were right saying it was dumb. Let's leave it there."

Noah rose and brushed off his hands. "So, are you going to show me?"

"You have to watch close," said Cole, placing the stock to the ground and pointing to the muzzle. "The shot goes in here." Taking the flask, he delicately poured black powder into the hole. "You need to be careful about the powder. Too much and it blows up in your face; too little and it won't fire the ball." He poked a mini ball and a wad of the cloth down the muzzle and removed a long metal rod from under the barrel. "This is the ramrod." Sticking the rod into the barrel, he shoved it farther and farther inside, just as butter is churned. "Make sure that the shot is as far down as you can get it." He removed the rod and slid it into the sheath under the barrel. Cocking the hammer, he pulled a cap out of the black pouch and inserted it on a nipple under the hammer. Then, with a click of the trigger, he gently eased the hammer forward and down.

"It's loaded. Once the trigger's pulled, the hammer pops the cap, making a spark to light the powder and fire the ball."

Noah reached for the rifle with an excited smile, only to have it yanked farther away by Cole.

"You can't handle this like some stick. You have to handle it as if it were a snake."

"I never handled no snake."

"Well, if you did, do you think you'd go grabbing at it?"

Noah shook his head

"I thought not. And you wouldn't go around pointing its head at people, trying to scare them."

"How come?"

"Because you ain't gonna, that's why. It ain't right to try to scare people thinking it's funny."

133

"Okay," Noah said. "I promise I won't shove no snakes in front of people trying to scare them. Now, can I have the rifle?"

Disgusted, Cole shook his head. "That ain't what I said."

"You said I couldn't grab at it like a snake. I said I never grabbed at no snake. You said if I did, I shouldn't be shoving snakes in people's faces. I said—"

"Whoa!" Cole shouted. He looked at the boy's confused face and reminded himself what it was like to be that age and given a chance to shoot a gun, trying to listen to a grown-up tell you something. "Let's start again."

He delicately handed the rifle to Noah. "Now, the first thing is, like I was trying to tell you, this thing don't care none what it's pointed at when it goes off. Once that trigger's pulled, it just blows a hole in whatever might be there. Understand?"

Noah nodded while accepting the rifle as cautiously as he would take an egg from a hen. His arms slowly moved as Cole placed the rifle stock onto the boy's shoulder and the barrel into his left palm. The rifle wobbled.

"You got to keep it steady, or you'll miss what you're aiming at."

Noah's control of the rifle didn't improve.

Cole grasped Noah's arms and gently guided them into position. "Get on your knee and prop your elbow on it. Then make believe you see something out there that you want to hit. Did you find something?"

Noah nodded.

"All right. Now ease the hammer back. All the way back till it locks. Once you're ready, don't pull the trigger. Squeeze it like you're wanting to inch it backwards."

Noah pulled the hammer into position, squinted one eye, and tightened his grip around the trigger. The hammer struck the cap, and the booming blast of the shot sent him onto his back. A plume of white smoke engulfed both of them.

As the smoke drifted, Cole smiled at Noah's prone figure. "Are you okay?"

Noah spit powder residue from his lips and nodded. "My fingers feel funny."

"Ah, they don't look hurt. That buzzing will go away. Did you hit what you was aiming at?"

"Yeah, a big ol' cow."

"Cow? It ain't a good idea shooting cows. They mostly belong to somebody who would take offense. Better stick with coyotes and rabbits. Besides, I didn't see no dirt fly up. That cow musta been ten feet off the ground for you to hit him."

"Well, I'll shoot better this time," Noah said as he aimed the rifle.

"You got to reload it first," Cole said, and he watched the boy's face sour.

"I wish I had one of those guns the marshal has. They don't have to be reloaded. You can shoot them a hundred times."

"Just six," Cole said. "And those take cartridges. The powder and bullet are already in them."

"I know," Noah blurted. He began to aim the rifle once more. "I wish I had one of them guns." He filled his cheeks with air and whooshed out the sound of a gunshot. "Then I could be like the Rainmaker and go around shooting people, not no coyotes and rabbits."

At first Cole was stunned, then he wanted to grab the boy and shake the words back into his mouth.

Visions of when he was a boy returned to his head. He had shared the same feelings at nearly the same age. Anger wasn't going to shame the boy from those thoughts. It hadn't changed Cole's mind when he was young.

"That's what you're wanting to do? Shoot people?"

"Yeah," Noah said with a bright smile. "Not people I know, like you or Mama. Maybe Evie. No, not even her. I'd

135

just shoot people I didn't know and didn't like, just like he does.''

"The Rainmaker?"

"Yeah, him."

Cole turned his head and bit his lip. What Noah said was likely what most people thought. "Did you see this man?"

"No. He was in the back. Mama wouldn't turn loose of me to go and look."

Cole turned back to him. "Then how did you know it was him?"

"Because the marshal said so. He said he was a real mean man."

Cole hesitated, taking the muzzle from Noah before he spoke. "Did you believe him?"

"Sure," Noah answered with his familiar confidence. "Why? Do you know him too?"

Cole shook his head and put the stock to the ground. "No, I don't know that man they have in jail. It's likely true that he done what they said he done."

He took a deep breath as Noah looked at him with a ponderous smile. "But I do know a lot of men just like him. Some bad and some not so bad. Been around some of them a long time." He looked into the boy's eyes.

"I can tell you there are men such as the Rainmaker that ain't quite as bad as people think. And they don't look forward to killing no people. Not good or bad ones. You see, killing a man is a hard thing, even when it need be done. You're asking yourself, faster than you can think straight, that you're the one that's ending this man's life and should you do it? Sometimes you tell yourself no, and other times you end up doing it before you can settle the answer."

"You ever kill anybody?" asked Noah.

Cole first thought to lie, but he hadn't lied to his young friend before and starting now wouldn't help his peace of mind.

He nodded. "Yeah. I have killed."

Noah's eyes widened, something Cole feared would spark a wildfire of questions. However, almost as a reward for his honesty, a reason came to his mind.

"When you're in the army, sometimes you have to kill."

"Oh," Noah said with less enthusiasm than Cole first imagined. "That's where you've killed people, for the army?"

"Yup," he said, nodding. He looked at the sun, which had reached the crest of the far mountains. "Better get a move on before we lose the light."

They both walked to the wagon.

Cole drove the buckboard, arriving at the house just before the sun departed for the day. He hopped down and began the task of unloading the timber. Noah came off the wagon, tired from the day's activity, and walked toward the house.

Ann stepped from inside the house to the edge of the porch. Cole turned to see what looked like a smile on her face as she rubbed her hands on an apron. "Supper will be ready soon."

As her son passed by, she rubbed his head and went to the buckboard. "Well, I see you men cut more wood today."

Cole nodded as he untied the restraining ropes. "Yeah. We'll still need more. But we're getting enough to start some of the carpentry."

Her friendly manner was a nice change, a change he didn't know exactly how to deal with. Just as her face began to glow amid the twilight, a turn of her head chased away her smile.

"Where did you get that?" she asked, her voice laced with its usual firmness. Cole peered to see her pointing at the wagon and with a swing of his head saw what drew her anger. The musket lay propped behind the seat. She looked back at him. "What have you done?"

That twist in his gut he was more used to returned. "The boy asked me to show him to load and shoot it. I made sure

137

there was no harm. I taught him how to proper use it.''

She stepped close to his face, and her eyes glistened as she shouted. ''No harm! No harm! How dare you! What do you know of harm? What do you know about teaching a boy? Damn you, Mr. Cole!''

Cole was caught without a proper answer as Noah and Evie came from inside. The boy raced over to his mother. ''Don't be mad at him, Mama. I made him teach me.''

''Hush, son. You and your sister go back in the house.''

''No, Mama, please. It ain't his fault.''

Ann turned to him. ''Noah, hush. This doesn't concern you.''

Cole squinted to see the boy in the dim light. ''Do as your ma says.''

Noah took one step back from Ann. ''No. I ain't gonna. Not until I tell you what I got to say,'' he stated in a defiant voice. Both Cole and Ann were surprised by his courage. ''It ain't Uncle Clay's fault. I told him a lie. I told him it was fine with you to teach me to shoot. If you're gonna get mad, get mad at me. You can whip my britches and I won't cry. Just don't blame him. It was my doing. Not his.''

Ann took a moment to answer his plea. ''That doesn't make a difference. You're just a little boy, and he's—''

''No, I ain't a little boy. I'm almost eleven years old—''

''Your ma's right,'' Cole interrupted, bringing all eyes to him. ''It weren't my place. I ought not to have done it till I knew she was good with it.'' When he was finished, he looked at Ann.

''Noah. Go inside now. Mr. Cole and I need to talk.''

The boy turned around, kicking the dirt as he went to the house.

When the front door shut, Ann brought her attention to Cole. ''I know you think it was all right to do what you did and then say you're sorry. But it's more than that.''

''Sorry is all I can say. If I need to leave, you tell me.''

She turned her back to him.

"But before I go, Mrs. Hayes, I think there's something you need to fess up to. That boy of yours has a lot of questions. I admit, there's times when I lose myself thinking that he's mine. But he's not. He's yours. He wants to know how some things are, and someone needs to show him. Hell, when I was his age I'd already shot rabbits and birds for supper. There's wolves out there that could come in here."

She turned her tear-dripped face to him. "That gun killed his father!"

Cole was stunned. His argument flew from his mind. He shook his head slightly. "I'm sorry. I didn't know."

She sniffled her voice clear. "That's why I never want him using it. It's what killed my husband," she said through panted breath, and stared at the ground. "It's been six years. Robert would find our stock out beyond our property. Shot dead. He took it as another sign of Owen MacGregor trying to get our land. One day he had enough and said he was going to tell the MacGregors to leave us be. He left with that gun—I tried to stop him. But he said he wouldn't use it, he just needed something to show them he was mad. The next day, Owen MacGregor came here with the news that Robert was dead. They found him on their ranch," she trembled, "with a hole in his chest. They said the gun must have gone off when he pulled it through their wire fence." She sank her face in her palms.

Cole never was comfortable with a woman's tears. He didn't know if it was proper, but he wrapped his arm around her shoulders. She folded her arms as if to keep warm or to shy away from him, he didn't know which.

"That Owen MacGregor came here, with his face showing his false pity. All he could say was that he was sorry. He even said that if I wanted him to take my children so as not to be a burden, he would see they were raised right," she said in disgust. "I should have spit in his face. Robert knew how to handle guns. I know they killed h.m, but Clement

Thomas couldn't prove nothing, so he said it was an accident.''

"Does your boy know?" asked Cole.

Ann slowly nodded. "Noah was barely four years old. He didn't understand at the time.'' She looked up at him. "It's not an easy thing telling your child that his father's dead. I tried, but Noah couldn't bring himself to believe. As he got older, every time I tried to tell him he just pretended I wasn't saying what I was saying. Like he really didn't want to know. He wanted to believe that his pa would come home someday.''

She leaned closer to him, and he hugged her tighter.

He remembered the deaths of his own parents. "It's a tough thing to learn. The learning to say good-bye. It ain't ever easy, no matter how old you are or how old you get.''

Their eyes met. His arm drooped from her shoulders. "I'm sorry about the musket. I should have knowed the boy was storying to me, but something in me wanted to teach him something I think he needed to know. I won't do nothing again without you knowing.''

She smiled and looked to the ground. "Let's leave it be. I know how my boy likes to tell stories to get what he wants.'' She returned her gaze to his eyes. "I know there are things done that we all wish we could change. Jed Farlon told me what you did against my debt. That, and what you've meant to Noah, for all you've done for us, it's me that should be saying sorry.'' She leaned even closer to him and their eyes locked on each other's, until her bumping his chest made her break off her stare. "We need to go in. I need to be getting supper on the table.'' She patted her face with the apron.

He nodded and watched her walk to the house. Scratching his head, he peered at the twinkling stars in the black sky as he made his way inside.

The children sat at the table while Ann stirred the big pot. Cole took his place next to Noah. Ann ladled a stew of meat, potatoes, and corn into the bowls before each of them. After the blessing, which he was beginning to learn, everyone ate their meal. Not a word was spoken until Ann broke the silence.

"Lorna Clendenon picked out a beautiful dress for her wedding."

"She and her mother will sew it together," Evie added. "I hope they get it ready in time."

"I'm sure they will," Ann said, then looked at Cole. "She asked if you would be there."

"Me?" he asked, surprised. "I don't know if I ever seen that. With a bride in a pretty dress and a preacher and all."

"What all have you seen?" Noah asked.

Cole looked at Ann, thinking she would chide the boy for asking questions with his mouth full, only to see an inquisitive glint in her eye as well.

"A bunch of things."

The answer didn't satisfy Noah. "Like what?"

Memories of a life of wandering flashed in his head. Although thoughts of a hard life alone came to mind first, he took a moment to recall the ones he could repeat for littler ears.

"Most of the things west of Missouri. I've seen prairies so wide you don't think they'll ever end, and grass so tall it come all the way to your chest. Sand so deep, you think you'll sink in it over your head, and rivers and lakes so still you'd swear you could walk across."

The children were wide-eyed. "What else?" asked an excited Noah.

"You need to finish your supper, son. You too, Evie." Ann's orders were complied with in a hurry so Evie could listen to more.

Cole swabbed his bowl clean of the stew with a biscuit and joined the children in clearing the table.

"Both of you need to get in your beds," Ann said. Noah and Evie protested.

"I'll tell you more if you do what your ma says."

Cole's offer lit a fire under both of them. In no time the boy and girl were in their nightclothes and tucked under bedcovers.

"What else have you seen? Have you seen any buffalos?"

Cole slid a chair over by their bunks. "I've seen a lot of them. So many hides bunched together, it looks like the ground is burnt black." He also thought of when he worked for the army shooting the animals until the ground was stained red.

"What was the prettiest?" Evie asked.

Cole looked to the floor. "There's a sack full that could take that. But there's one thing that I do remember."

Ann stopped cleaning dishes as he spoke.

"There's a place a good piece north of here up in the mountains. In the winter, everything is white. There was no green of trees or brown dirt. And the wind cuts through you to the bone, it's so cold. You get awful hungry, but there ain't no game to shoot. Everything got so quiet, I'd swear I was the only one alive. About the time I lost the feeling in my toes, and I was sure everything surrounding me was just like that for miles around, I come across a small valley with a mess of ponds of boiling water, shooting up higher than a two-story house, and the water hotter than you could fire in a kettle. Steam puffing up into the clouds, and mud bubbling like water."

Both children laid their heads on the pillows. Even though they squinted, they refused to keep their eyes shut.

Cole continued. "The stink was so bad, like hunerds of eggs had busted open and gone rotten. You could only get so close so as to get warm without scalding the skin. I had a mind to get in and take a bath in one of them ponds not quite as hot, but the thought of having to get out amongst the cold kept me from it."

Ann walked to stand behind him.

He chuckled. "The thing that struck me most was that

steaming water was the furthest thing I ever expected to see there. It tells you a little about life. Not everything is what it looks like. Just when you're sure you know everything about something, it shows you something else you didn't expect to see."

The children's eye blinks became strained. Cole rose and pushed the chair under the table. "It's time for sleep. I'll tell you more tomorrow." Slowly, he crept to the door, turning to find Ann behind him. "Thank you again for supper."

She nodded her appreciation.

"And again, I'm sorry about the rifle."

She shook her head with a polite grin. "No need."

He bedded down against the side of the house, wrapping a blanket around him and pulling a sand-filled flour sack under his head. His thoughts turned to what needed to be done the next day.

A nudge in the back awakened him. He twisted around to see the stiff breeze flap a blanket around Ann's face in the darkness. The cool air carried the smell of dust. Soon sand would be piled around the house.

She waved her hand for him to follow. He stood, taking his blanket and makeshift pillow into the house. She shut the door and put a finger to her lips. A glance told him the children were still asleep.

He nodded that he understood. She quietly crept back into her room. The wind began to howl through the cracks in the house. He crouched onto the floor and pulled the blanket around him once more, unsure whether he could get back to sleep. It wasn't the sound that kept him awake. Rather, his mind stayed alert because of one other experience he hadn't expected.

Chapter Ten

The pile of sand driven by the night's storm sloped from near the roof. Cole shook his head. Had he slept in his normal spot, it would have become his grave. He took Ann's shovel and began the task of digging out the house. Dust spilled off the spade's edge. After a few more jabs into the drift, it was clear a day's work would be needed to get things back the way they were.

The wagon, too, was buried into the side of a windswept dune. The newly cut timber was completely covered. Chickens scratched the dirt in search of their feed, which surely had been blown into the desert.

Noah came from the house, rubbing his eyes in the dawn's light. "Wow, look at that. Did that happen last night?" he said, pulling up his suspenders.

Cole nodded and pointed at the chickens. "See if you can get them some feed. And Bender's around back. He's going to need the sand brushed out of him."

Ann came outside also. "My, we're lucky it didn't take the house with it."

"That's a fact." He stopped digging to face her. "I guess I have to say I'm lucky I'm not under all this. I have you to thank for that."

She turned away from his gaze, something she often did anytime he tried to express his gratitude. Not sure if she minded seeing his chest bare, he picked his shirt off the ground and slipped it on. As he did, she went back inside.

He never knew where he stood with her, one of the ways a woman could confuse a man. Her soft shoulders could still be felt in his arm from the night before. Now he appeared to be just the drifter that happened by a week ago.

The sun was overhead by the time he had reduced the sand drift to a small mound. In a short while he had dug out the buckboard and timber. Noah led Bender from behind the house as Ann and Evie came out.

"Bender had a mountain of sand in his tail, but I got it all out of him," Noah proudly announced. "But it sure did make a mess of the chicken coop."

Barely an instant went by before Ann inhaled in a rush and exhaled a shriek. "Oh, no!"

She hurried to the back of the house, followed by both of her children. A bewildered Cole went as well. Ann knelt at the back side of the coop. As Cole walked behind her, she peered under it, then stood and brushed off her apron with a sigh of relief.

Looking down, he saw what had worried her so. A broad-leafed plant with long purple stems stretched out from beneath the shaded underside of the coop.

"Is it okay, Mama?" Evie asked eagerly.

Ann nodded with her palm to her chest.

Cole shook his head in amazement.

"That's what you make a pie out of, isn't it, Mama?" asked Noah. "What's it called again?"

"Rhubarb," Cole answered.

She grinned. "That's right."

He put his hands on his hips. "I never knew you had that out here. I haven't seen that since I was a young'un back in Kansas. I couldn't imagine it could be growed here."

"Well, I brought it with us from Missouri. It first died off, but once we put the chicken coop here, it came back up. I always have guessed the morning sun was all it could take. It's been growing ever since."

"And my mama's pie is real good," said Noah.

"One of my favorites too," Cole agreed, still looking at Ann.

"Well, Lorna said her daddy was asking if I would bring a pie to the wedding," Ann said. "My heart nearly stopped when I thought it had been blown away."

"I'm sure it will be just fine. This cool air—and what the chickens leave—is just what the rhubarb needs." Cole pointed at the coop. "Well, I'm sure it makes good use of it."

Ann smirked. "Well, let's leave it be. I'll cut the stalks the day before, and I'll need some help to make the crust."

Evie immediately raised her hand. "I'll help you."

Ann rubbed her daughter's head. "I was counting on it. Now it's time I cooked dinner." The four of them walked back to the house.

After the midday meal, Cole returned to the work of digging away the dust.

"Are you going to do that all day?" Noah asked.

A nod was Cole's answer, one Noah didn't want to accept.

"When are we going to go get the other wood we chopped?"

Cole shrugged. "I don't know. I thought I ought to finish this first."

"What if someone steals our wood?"

"I told you before, I don't think that's likely."

"How come? Don't other people need it to build something?"

Cole turned to him with a glare, but the boy didn't shy away. "There'll be time to go and get it. We don't have to do that right now. We can't leave your ma with this mess."

"You two go ahead," said Ann, standing on the porch. A bright smile came over Noah's face while a look of confusion swept over Cole's.

"That wouldn't be right," he said.

"No, it's all right. You two go on and tend to what you had planned. You can finish later what you have left."

"Are you sure?"

She nodded contentedly.

Cole jabbed the shovel into the small mound and brushed off his hands. "Okay, boy. You got what you want from your ma. Go get Bender hitched to the buckboard."

"Thanks, Mama," Noah shouted.

Cole gathered the saw and ax and placed them in the bed. He helped harness the horse to the wagon, and they both climbed onto the seat.

"There's one thing you forgot," Ann said at the door. She stepped back inside and reappeared holding the musket. "You said you might be needing this." Noah jumped down and ran to his mother. "Now, you listen to your uncle Clay. Whatever he says, you do. You hear?"

"Yes, ma'am," her son answered as he took the rifle and brought it back to the wagon.

As Noah climbed to the seat, Cole peered at the hint of a smile on Ann's face. It appeared she had taken heed of what he'd told her, and perhaps had cleared her mind of some of her worries. As he shook the reins, one more notion popped into his head. Maybe she was clearing her mind of her worries about him as well.

Like most trips made more than once, the ride to the hills seemed to take less time. Along the way, Noah bragged about his improved marksmanship. Cole encouraged him to keep a good mind about what he intended to do, but warned that along with the bragging comes the need for proving.

Not more than an hour after their arrival, Cole had loaded the remainder of the felled timber. Noah kept practicing the musket lesson from the previous day. Cole heard the boy's frustrations with the rifle. While he wiped his brow with the bandanna, he went to Noah.

"Here, now. What's the trouble?"

"This stupid thing won't do right," Noah said, pinching the rifle's hammer between his thumb and finger.

Cole took the rifle from him. "You know, I learned something a long time ago: that things without ears don't pay no mind to all the cussing you give them. They just do what they want, 'til you figure out what they want, then you do it. Then the both of you get along a bunch better." Cole wrenched his thumb around the hammer and cocked it. "Don't pull up. Pull back."

"How'd you do that?"

"Years of practicing my figuring without my cussing." He closed one eye and peeked down the barrel. "You ain't put no powder down it yet, have you?"

"No. I was learning how to hold it like you told me."

"Okay, then," he said, handing the weapon back to the boy. "Put in the shot and let's see what you've been bragging about."

Noah opened the black pouch and began loading the musket under Cole's careful instruction. Once he had cocked the hammer, he placed the cap and squinted into the sights.

"Do you know what you're aiming at? Not no cows, I hope."

"Nope. A big rattler."

"That'll do. Blow its head off."

Noah squeezed off the shot, sending fire and smoke from the barrel. The recoil moved him three steps back from where he first stood, but the fear in his face from the day before wasn't there.

"Did you hit it?" asked Cole.

"Yeah. Shot right in two."

Both of them smiled. "That's good, but remember one thing. When you're shooting at anything, especially bigger than snakes, aim for the head. If you hit it in the gut, then it can still run, or come after you. You wait before going up to it. Make sure it's down and it don't move."

He hoped that the boy's nod meant that some words had sunk in, but he knew drilling the lesson twice more was better for Noah's memory than any words could be.

"Now this time I want you to pick out a real target."

Cole kept silent, and Noah labored with the loading procedure. Only Cole's nods and head shakes guided Noah along until he inserted the cap. He braced the stock against his shoulder.

"Have you picked a target?"

The boy sighted the musket. "That cactus over there."

Cole peered at the small thorny plant some fifty feet away. "Fine. Balance the barrel until it's level with that cactus."

The musket still wobbled slightly as Noah closed one eye.

"Steady it on your knee."

Noah did as Cole told him and again aimed the musket. He put his finger around the trigger and the shot went off. The white cloud drifted away to reveal the still-pristine cactus.

"I hit it. I know I hit it."

Cole chuckled. "One thing about shooting. It leaves little doubt about the truth. That's enough for today. We only have two balls left. Let's save them for another time." They walked back to the wagon, and Cole started Bender on the way home. "You done good today. Just keep thinking about what you did, and don't go noodling another way to handle that weapon."

Noah's confused face shot up, "What's noodling?"

"You never been noodling?" Cole smirked. "Noodling is the name given to the practice of catching fish by hand. It

149

comes from after a fellow gets tired of throwing a line in the water, waiting on the fish to bite. He just jumps in, feels around for the fish, and snatches them right out of the water."

"Did you ever do that?"

"In my younger days," Cole answered with a nod and a wink. "Pretty good at it, too."

"Stop," Noah shouted. Cole reined in hard, thinking the boy had been struck by lightning. "We got to go and try that on Jasper."

"Huh?"

"Try noodling on him. Whatever you called it."

"What are you talking about?"

"Just go where I show you. It's not real far."

"I'm not going nowheres till I know what you're talking about."

Noah slumped his shoulders. "Catching fish. There's a big ol' fish nobody never caught in a creek just over that hill." Noah pointed a few feet ahead. "He's busted every line that's ever been."

"I don't know about this. You keep getting me in trouble," Cole said with folded arms.

"Please," the boy urged in the sound of a mild yodel. "You said that if you bragged about something, you had to prove it."

Peeking at the sun, Cole gauged that a good part of the day was still left. Another feeling of remorse for what he was about to do crept into his head, but the boy's eyes persuaded him that the diversion would be harmless. "How far did you say this place was?"

Noah's smile lit up his face. "Not real far." He pointed the same distance as before.

After several miles, they came upon a brook cutting through the rocky terrain. Noah jumped down and ran to a spot where the water pooled into a small pond before continuing downstream. "He's in there."

Cole went to stand next to him. "You sure he's in there?"

"Heck, yes. Morris Taylor told me that Jasper has been in there for a hundred years, maybe. He said his brother Henry and their pa tried to catch him and they nearly got pulled in."

After slipping his boots off and sliding his pant legs up, Cole slowly stepped into the icy water. He suppressed his shock over the numbing cold and uttered only a few babbling moans. "Why did I let you talk me into this?" He turned to see Noah's squinted eyes and furled brow.

"It's cold, ain't it?"

"Just a mite," he gritted. He carefully slid one foot past the other over smooth stones and stabbing gravel, then felt a slick object brush his toes. "Something moved down there."

"It's him! It's Jasper!"

Rolling up his sleeves, Cole reached beneath the surface, fumbling with all the slippery items on the bottom of the creek. Having circled most of the pond without success, he felt assured he had fulfilled the dare with his pride intact. "I don't feel nothing. I guess your fish must have left."

Noah frowned, a sight Cole wasn't going to let slow him from getting out of the cold water. With his hands gliding over the submerged edge of the pond, he touched the outline of a sizable crevice in the rocks. Fine slick tubes filled his fingers, but an instant later his thumbs were crushed by a clamping bite. Reflex made him yank his arms above the water's surface. A catfish the size and weight of a small saddle hung from his thumbs. Fins stuck out like spikes. The fish's tail arched halfway up the side of its body.

"You got him!"

"He's got me!" Cole yelled, and wagged his hands to jerk free of the jaws.

"Don't shake so hard. You'll lose him."

"That's what I'm aiming to do." Still in Jasper's biting grasp and his arms weakening from the massive fish, Cole trudged to the shore, whipping his arms to snap the animal loose. With its sandpaper teeth still digging into his skin, he slammed the fish against a boulder, breaking the animal's clamp and dropping it to the ground.

Cole rubbed his blood-soaked thumbs. "You didn't say it was no catfish," he snapped. "I thought you were talking about a trout. Look at that thing. Nearly chewed my fingers right to the bone."

"Yeah, he's a big one, for sure." Noah's smile gleamed with admiration. "And you're the one that caught him. I'm going to tell everyone I know. I can't wait till I tell Henry Taylor my uncle Clay caught ol' Jasper."

As Cole shook the feeling back into his fingers, his ire faded into a chuckle. "Boy, the trouble you get me in."

Noah jabbed the catfish with a stick, causing it to flop about, all the while pumping its mouth open and shut.

"Can we take him home? I'm sure Mama will cook him."

As the boy poked at the catfish, Cole remembered another animal that had helplessly fought for life. A lump in his throat accompanied painful memories of the Appaloosa struggling against his grip. There were plenty of reasons to kill an animal. However, he could think of more good coming from letting this one live.

"Let's let him go," said Cole. Noah stared openmouthed. "Look, I got more reason to eat that thing than you." Cole looked back at the pond. "But if he's lived in there for a hundred years, seems a shame to end it now." He returned his gaze to Noah. "Maybe someday you can bring your kids here. And you can catch him for them. As ornery as he is, I think he'll still be around."

"Do we got to?" Noah had the same pleading look on his face he had used to sway Cole to come to the stream.

"I think we ought to." Cole took the stick from Noah and slipped it into Jasper's mouth. With both hands, he lifted the fish to the pond's edge and, with a final glance at Noah's disappointed face, dropped it in stick and all.

"Well, I'm still going to tell everybody that we caught him."

"*We* did?" Cole asked in mock contempt, then looked at his hands. "I guess you better. It'll give reason for me explaining why my thumbs are crooked."

They both walked to the wagon, when a faint whistle from the east stopped Cole.

"Did you hear that?" he said, peering at the flat plain.

"Hear what?"

"That whistle. Is there a train around here?"

"No. What's a train?"

Cole frowned. "If you didn't know what a train is, how'd you know there weren't one around here?"

"I don't know. I ain't never seen one."

The truth of the boy's remark became clear. Again Cole looked into the distance, sighting only cactus, sand, and yucca. A quick glance at the sun told him there was more time left in the day. It took only three scratches of his chin to decide what to do. "How 'bout you and me go see what's over there. If we get too far out without seeing nothing, then we head back to the house."

A gleaming smile grew on Noah's face. "Okay with me. Let's go."

They climbed into the seat, and Cole steered Bender in the direction he was certain he had heard the sound. It was a short time before Noah began nodding off. Cole sat amazed at how young ones could always find sleep when traveling even over rocky terrain.

They approached a small rise. As they came nearer, it was clear the ground hadn't been mounded by wind and rain, but rather by pick and shovel. Cole stopped Bender and tied the reins to the brake. He walked to the steel rails bolted down end to end. This he'd seen many times, from when he was a boy all the way to his days as a soldier and scout. He had hammered a few spikes in railroad camps after having wagoned in butchered buffalo. It was pleasing to see something he recognized. While admiring the track, he noticed there was no rust. Neither were there scrapes or gouges in the rails, as there were in the mashed spike heads, which showed glistening steel.

"What is that?"

Cole twisted around to the red-eyed Noah.

"That there is a train track."

The boy quickly joined him, standing next to the rail.

"Looks like it might have just been laid down, too." As Noah began hopping from one wooden tie to the other, Cole squatted to examine the rails.

"What's it for?"

Still looking down, Cole replied, "It's what the train runs on." He remembered that the boy didn't know what a train was. "See, there's a big engine, burning coal and huffing steam, that hauls a mess of cars full of stuff like cattle, or crops—"

"No," Noah said in a loud voice, which pulled Cole's attention to him. The boy pointed farther down the track to a four-wheeled cart on top of the rails. "What's that for?"

Cole rose and stared at the distant waving image. "It looks to be a handcar."

"What's it for?"

"It's what they use to get up and down the rails without the engine." He walked toward it. "They must have left it behind."

"Who did?" asked Noah, following.

"The workers. The men setting the rails. They must be farther down the track, maybe already around the hills." When they came to the car, Cole inspected the flat wooden platform, steel wheels, and the teetering two-handled lever in the center.

Noah stood in awe, appearing fearful of the strange machine. "Why is it here?"

"Well, I seen them do this before. The ones driving it likely caught those on the engine, and they all went ahead. They'll be back for it, you can count on it."

"No, why is it here?"

The peculiar question stopped Cole's inspection of the car. The answer was obvious to him, but it took him a moment to realize how this appeared to Noah. "Don't you see? The railroad's coming. As a matter of fact, it's here. Or will soon be. Looks like a good thing, too. If my figuring is right, might just come close to your place, if not go right through it on the way to town."

"What's that mean?"

"Well, might mean money. The railroad brings people with money. If it stops near your place, them people might spend some of that money. I seen it happen."

Noah pointed at the car. "How many people can you get on that thing?"

"Well, they don't ride on this. There's a bigger car hauled by the engine." As Cole continued telling Noah more about trains, the boy's mind appeared snarled in the idea like a fly in a web. The example of the musket lesson crept into Cole's head. Action always did better than words.

He looked around to see the rails stretched in both directions of the barren horizon. "You want to take a ride?"

Noah's face again lit up. "Where?"

"On the rails, just a little spell."

"We're going to take it from them?"

"Ah, we ain't going to take it far. They'll find it." He pulled the boy onto the platform. "You get on that side and pull that handle up while I push this one down."

Noah slowly took hold of his end of the lever. Cole's fingers wrapped around the iron bar. Although he wouldn't admit it, he felt giddier about the plan than the ten-year-old appeared. "Are you ready?"

Noah warily nodded. Cole eased the handle down and the car slightly jolted to the side and slowly rolled south.

The boy's mouth opened and his eyes widened. "We're moving."

Cole winked. "Hang on." With another stroke of the handle, the car's speed increased. Again, he yanked up and plunged down and the squeak of steel on iron filled their ears. Cole peered over Noah's shoulder. A small grade lay ahead. He quickened his stroke so as to build speed.

Noah locked his arms atop the handle, rising with Cole's every downstroke. His mouth was still wide open but had curled into a wide smile. It was clear that all his fear had been left back beside the track. His hair plumed over the back of his head. He leaned closer and yelled above the squealing wheels. "Can we go faster?"

Cole shoved the handle up and down at a quicker pace. The car screeched around a curve as they crested the grade.

"Faster!" The boy's shout could barely be heard over the howling wind. Knowing he would never satisfy Noah's demand for his newfound delight, Cole needed to shift the boy's attention to something else. A glance to the side provided a distraction.

"Look," he yelled.

Noah turned his head. Mesas sprinkled with green trees and cactus rose from the valley floor below as the car whizzed past. Noah released the handle and faced the view. His hair splashed away from his face. He stood erect, arching his back, and raised his arms out from his side. His fingers spread apart as if to catch the wind, and he closed his eyes. "Are we flying?"

Cole laughed. It had been a long time since he had ridden on rails or enjoyed sharing a new experience. As his eyes soaked up the joy on Noah's face, he caught a glimpse down the steepening slope of an object on the tracks. He stopped his stroke, and as the car rambled faster, he focused on the fast-approaching object. Barricade. Behind it there was a ravine but no track.

"Hold on," he shouted. Noah quickly grabbed the wild handle. Cole threw the brake lever forward, prompting the piercing cry of sliding metal against metal. Sparks shot from under the slowing car. The friction released its putrid scent.

Noah's mouth was still open, only now it showed a young boy's panic.

"We'll have to jump," Cole screamed. He let loose of the handle and grasped Noah's shirt. They both leaped from the car as it smashed through the barricade and plowed into the dirt to a stop.

Cole took a deep breath while Noah stared at the drifting smoke from the car's wheels.

"Are we in trouble?" the boy asked.

Cole nodded. "That weren't a good thing to do. We best scatter before somebody comes looking for that." He pointed to a small band of pines and fir behind them. "Let's go through there." The two walked, then ran through the maze of trunks, slowing only once they were clear of the small forest.

"That was fun," Noah proclaimed through his panting.

Feeling a fool, Cole could provide only a nod as an answer. He viewed another vast plain, but its unique grass came almost to the knee. "Where are we?"

Noah shrugged. "I don't know. I never been here."

Cole walked north, hoping the twisting train track hadn't confused his sense of direction. Noah followed in his newly cut path through the grass.

While Cole felt more foolish with each step for getting lost, a glimpse to the side stopped him. A single tall oak branched over the plain. Under it, a curved slab of granite peaked above the grass. There was but one reason for that type of marker. A glance at Noah showed that he saw the stone, too.

"You know of somebody buried here?"

Noah shook his head.

They approached the site respectfully. The tree's shade had kept the grass low. A small picket fence surrounded a grave below the headstone. The engraved epitaph contained no words Cole had seen before. While trying to decipher the dates, Noah stumbled backward. His shoulders quivered and his mouth fell open with more panic than he had shown even when the handcar crashed.

"Is that somebody you know?"

Noah's eyes welled with tears as he nodded. Only after a gasp of breath could he speak. "That's—that's my pa."

Cole's gut tightened. He stared at the stone once more but still couldn't make sense of the jumble of letters. "Are you sure?"

The boy's tear-dripped face glared in horror at him. "That's what it says," he said in a crackling voice. "Robert A. Hayes. Husband and father. That's my name. That's my pa." Noah collapsed to his knees.

Cole found it hard to breathe as well. He had seen many men die and had had a hand in sending a few to their graves himself. At the time he never thought about what misery became branded on the kin of dead men. But he knew what it felt like to bury a father.

He exhaled a quivering breath and knelt, placing his hand on the boy's back.

Noah's weepy face inched up to stare at the stone. "Mama told me he was here. I never wanted to believe it. He can't be gone—not dead. He can't be!" His head fell back into his hands.

Cole pulled the boy closer. Whatever words he could think of wouldn't cut through the hurt his young friend was feeling.

The tree's shade gradually shifted to the east.

Cole whispered, "If you want, we can stay. But your ma might be worrying about us if we're gone after dark."

Noah climbed to his feet, wiping his cheeks with his sleeve. "Can we come back sometime?"

"You bet." With his arm over the boy's shoulder, Cole led them back to the path cut through the grass, angling toward the mounted ridge. He finally met the train tracks, using them as a guide back to where Bender patiently waited. He headed the horse to the southwest and back home. The sun crept behind clouds, and Cole strained to see through the twilight.

"Is your pa dead?" Noah asked, sniffling.

"Yeah." Cole drew the bandanna from his chest pocket and handed it to Noah. "That officer shot off his horse, that was my pa."

"You saw him shot?"

"I saw the whole thing."

Noah gulped a breath. "Did you cry?"

Cole shook his head. "He wouldn't have wanted me to."

"Henry Taylor said he didn't cry when his pa died, but Morris did. He said men aren't supposed to cry. I guess I ain't a man yet. How come men ain't supposed to cry?"

A life full of lessons slammed into Cole's head, but not one contained a good answer to the question. He couldn't argue the truth of the statement, but making the matter clear to a young boy who had just discovered his pa's grave wasn't simple. He didn't want to lie, so he thought the truth as he saw it was the best reply.

"That's the side of men that they'd as soon not show. They feel that others may not think as much of them as they once did." A glance at Noah showed that the fly was still snarled in that web. "It's kinda like that old musket, or even a cannon. Sometimes when it gets loaded too much, or is fired too fast, it cracks. And then it can't be trusted. Even if it's fixed, it'll never have the same faith put in it as it once had. I ain't saying it's right, but grown men are kinda like them cannons. They don't want those that place faith in them see them crack."

Noah rubbed his glistening eyes with his fist. The buckboard rumbled over the plain and arrived at the moonlit farm.

Cole stepped down and began unhitching Bender. Noah passed by him, hands in his pockets and head down. There was little Cole could do for him. It was certain that the matter troubled the boy, and Cole's message seemed to do nothing for his spirit. The sight of such a heavy load, one that had

159

brought gray-haired men to their knees, weighing down this young one gnawed at his gut. He needed to help his friend, even if it meant saying words he'd never said before.

"Noah."

The boy faced him.

"Crying, it ain't a bad thing. Don't let it trouble you. When you feel you have to, find a spot you feel safe in and let it go. That's what I do. And I know that's what the Rainmaker does, too."

Noah looked slightly cheered, which sparked Cole to grin.

"I wouldn't be telling you this for you to spread." He resumed unhitching Bender, but Noah's voice stopped him.

"Are you a noble man?"

The question amused Cole. "I ain't sure what that is."

"That's okay," came a reply from the darkened porch. "I think I do."

Chapter Eleven

The sun began chasing the stars from the sky. The brisk air was calm. As was his habit, Cole awakened long before the dawn's light. He stared at the pile of raw-cut timber. Although he hadn't planned it, and would need far more wood to satisfy his vision, it seemed like a good day to build a barn.

Any structure needed strength to remain standing. He picked the spot that would be the center. With a few swipes of a shovel, the sand vanished and the spade's sharp edge stuck into solid ground. Using his weight on the back of the spade, he soon stood in a knee-deep hole.

A short time after the rooster's crow, light shone through the house windows. It wasn't until sunlight had etched over the horizon that Noah shot out of the house and climbed the mound of extracted dirt.

"What are you doing?" he said, his stumbling spilling clods of dirt back where Cole had dug.

"I was trying to get the dirt out of this hole."

"Can I help you dig?"

"You'd be more help if you quit kicking it down here."
He let out a moan, put his hands on his aching back, and
arched erect.

Noah stopped his play on the mound and stared at Cole.
"Are we going to build the barn today?"

Cole cracked a grin. "I thought it would be a good idea."

"What can I do?"

Looking at the house, Cole answered, "How about you go
see if your ma has some coffee cooking?" The boy returned
to the house. The errand allowed Cole the solitude to drag
one of the shaved poles to the hole and sink an end. He
surrounded it with tamped dirt and water and soon had it
freestanding.

Noah came down the porch, one foot barely in front of the
other, eyes fixed on the cup of sloshing coffee. Cole took the
now half-full cup, wiping the dripping streaks from the sides
and bottom. "Thank you, boy."

"When are you going to be finished?"

"I just started! Heck, we probably have a couple weeks'
worth of work ahead of us. Maybe more."

"What can I do?"

"How 'bout you finish piling dirt around the pole while I
start on digging another hole." The boy frowned. "By the
time you're done, me and you can plant the next pole."

"Noah, come eat your breakfast," Ann called from the
porch.

"Not now, Mama. I'm working on the barn."

Cole rubbed Noah's head. "Better eat first. You'll need
the strength."

Between breakfast and dinner, seven of the posts were
standing. Soon after the midday meal, Lorna and Morris
called on the farm and admired the work. Morris was volunteered to assist in the project by his bride-to-be, so the
women could devote the afternoon to wedding plans. Having
to keep a watchful eye on a ten-year-old's safety about the

heavy timber, while constantly monitoring each motion of the clumsy Morris, gave Cole little time for concentration. Nightfall ended the day's work with only two cross-beams mounted firmly.

Lorna and Ann were busily setting the table for supper as the men entered the house. "You men got a good deal accomplished today," Lorna commented after the blessing. "I'm sure Morris would be glad to help out tomorrow."

Cole glanced at her soon-to-be-husband, who appeared as undelighted with the offer as Cole himself did. He held back his initial reaction. "That'd be right neighborly."

"Good, then. What time would you like us here? We could be here first thing in the morning."

A mouthful of fried chicken gave Cole time to consider his options. Since he was an early riser, and knew he could get more done when left to himself, he thought the polite thing to say was the wisest. "I wouldn't want you to go to the trouble. Noon or so would be just fine."

Supper ended and the women cleaned the dishes. Cole went outside to ponder on the next day's work. Soon, Lorna and Morris said their good-byes and left the farm. Ann sent the children inside to tend to their nightly chores, and once alone she came to stand beside him. "It looks as if you did get a fair piece done, in spite of your help." She smirked.

"I once heard somebody say something about a man having too many thumbs. That description suits nobody better than Morris." They both giggled.

"Well, I do want to thank you for being nice to my friends."

"I felt obliged to be friendly."

It took a moment before she faced him. "You know, there was also something said once about a man's kindness and manners. A trait respectful of his family."

Cole brushed the dirt with his boot. "I ain't got no family."

"Well," she said, folding her arms. "Somebody toted you

163

around for nine months, kept you warm, made sure you're fed.''

"That was a long time ago," he answered in a soft voice.

"It appears it stuck to you."

He looked to her. "My ma, she was one to see to it you got done what she told you. And she could do it in a way without a harsh word said, but would make you feel lower than a snake if you didn't get it done. She was a stickler for doing it proper.'' After shifting his gaze to the dirt, he again faced Ann. "It's something I've noticed around here, too."

She nodded as she spoke. "Thank you. I'm sure that puts me in good company."

"It's not an easy thing raising a boy, much less a daughter too, on your own. You should be proud of both of yours."

She smiled her reply, then rubbed her arms. "It's getting cool out here. I'm going inside." She turned for the door, then stopped. "You're welcome to sleep inside, if you like."

Surprised by such a proposition, he let his manners answer before he considered all the benefits. "I'll be fine." She nodded and went inside, leaving him to regret the hasty decision.

When dawn broke the following day, Cole had shaved two of the long trunks. Noah again was first out of the house.

"How come you started without me?"

"I figured you needed all your rest. We got plenty to do today." Horse hooves clopping dirt turned Cole's head, and he spotted Lorna and Morris. "I was hoping to get a lot more done before I got all this help," he muttered aloud.

Having finished shaving the remaining timber, Cole roped the end of a beam. He had strewn the line over the previously elevated cross-beams and tied the other end to Bender's harness. He knotted another rope in a loop around the trunk and climbed to stand atop one of the cross-beams, holding the other end of the rope. As the horse slowly pulled, Cole lifted the beam one groaning yank at a time until finally it sat astride both cross-beams.

While he rested his aching arms, he glimpsed both women

on the porch staring at him. Confused as to what interested them enough to stand in the heat to shake their heads and whisper into each other's ears, he ignored them and concentrated on the next task. The rest of the day and most of the following was spent completing the frame.

Supper was seasoned with the satisfaction of his vision taking shape. Few meals had that taste. Once he had cleaned his plate, he again went outside to gaze upon the structure. Circling it, he stopped briefly to stare at each flush joint, every visible nail head driven into the wood, and pushed against the support posts just to test their sturdiness. He picked up a four-inch plank and patted the board into his hand.

"Looks like the bones of a whale I once saw in a book." Cole twisted about to see Lorna grinning on the porch. "It's really starting to look like something. You should be proud of yourself, Clay."

Accepting admiration from a woman was an uncommon experience for Cole. "Nice of you to say. Morris, he should get some of that too."

She grinned a little more while she leaned against a pillar. "I'll be sure to pass on that you said that. It would give him pleasure to hear it." Her grin shrank a bit. "I'm sorry his brother, Henry, isn't here to help. He seems to find something to do when I ask him to come."

"Oh, that's all right. I'm kinda used to doing things on my own."

"Yes." She paused. "I've come to see that. Frankly, if I can say, this work that you've done has put a different light on you. That day when I first saw you, your face wasn't one that welcomed a kind impression. However, since I've been out here the last few days, I've changed my mind."

"Is that a fact?" he said, amused by the notion. "Why is that?"

"Because of what you just did, Clay. You smiled. It makes

165

you seem friendly. People might think differently of you if you smiled more.''

The truth of the matter made him nod. ''Yeah, well, I hadn't reason to practice it much.''

''Maybe now with you living here with your sister-in-law, you'll have more reason to practice it. I know it's changed her, too.''

He jerked his head at her smug face. ''How come you say that?''

''Because,'' she said in matter-a-fact tone, ''I see the way she looks at you.''

Morris and Ann came outside. Lorna turned to greet them with an expression that suggested she'd forgotten what she'd said, but her remark still lingered with Cole.

''Morris can come out tomorrow, but I'll be home. I still have some things to get done.'' Lorna kissed Morris's cheek, which he acted shameful of. ''I only have a week.''

''Don't go to the trouble,'' Cole said. ''I'll need to go back to the hills and cut more wood before I can do anything else.''

Morris seemed relieved.

''We'll be leaving, then,'' Lorna said to Ann, and the women hugged. The two visitors climbed into their buggy and headed off the farm to waves from Ann and the children. Cole felt obliged to raise his hand as they passed by, and Lorna winked at him. ''Remember what I said.''

Ann shooed the children back to their chores and came next to Cole, wiping her hands on her apron. ''What did she mean?''

''Nothing,'' he answered, shaking his head. He patted the plank in his hand again. ''Nothing I could make sense of.''

Morning broke the next day with Cole having already harnessed Bender to the buckboard. After breakfast, Cole and Noah, the boy shouldering the musket like a soldier, went to the wagon.

''Will you be back before supper?'' asked Ann.

"Heck yeah, Mama. We'll be back before sundown."

Wide-eyed at this cocky remark, Cole looked at Noah, only to be more surprised when the boy's mother simply shook her head in mock disgust. Cole snapped the reins. Once in sight of the tall pines, Noah rubbed his eyes from his short nap and bragged his intentions.

"I say I can cut down more trees than you."

"Is that right? How come you think that?"

"I don't know. I just feel like I can."

He reined in. "Well, let's get to the proving." Cole led him to the tallest pine among the bunch. Looking up, he gauged the tree to be nearly forty feet high. He peeked down to see Noah squinting at the high branches. "There's a lot of wood in this one. Are you game for it?"

The confidence was gone from the boy's face, but as with any male, admission of his limitations would come only as a last resort. Noah took the ax, leaned the handle against his thigh to spit in his hands, lifted the tool, and stared at the trunk. Cole expected the edge to rip into the bark, but Noah drooped the heavy head to the ground.

"Why do they call him the Rainmaker?"

"What? Why are we talking about him? I came to see you swing that ax."

Again, Noah lifted the ax only to put it back down. "Is it because he can make it rain?"

"No. It ain't because of that. Do I need to cut down the tree?"

Noah raised his hand. "No. I can do it." He took a deep breath, respit in his hands, lifted the ax, and stuck the edge deep into the trunk. "Look at that. I did it."

"That you did. Good job," Cole said happily. "About fifty more just like that will fell this tree."

"Fifty more?"

Cole nodded. Noah yanked the edge from the trunk and chopped into it again. "Well, if he can't make it rain, why do they call him that?"

"Hell, boy. Nobody can change the subject quicker than you. Like a bolt from the blue." Cole knew the answer to all the questions, but his interest lay in why the boy asked them. "How come you want to know about him?"

Noah shrugged, then continued stroke after stroke of the ax. "I just think it would be something special to be him. Go anywhere you want, anytime you want, without having to tell nobody. And you don't have to go to school. I never been anywhere except up here, and that is because of you. I want to see a lot of places and go when I want."

"It ain't all that special." Cole tucked his thumbs in his pockets, and Noah stopped his assault on the tree. "Riding around from town to town ain't a quality most men care for for long. When it rains, you get wet. When a cold wind blows, it cuts through you like a knife, and when it's hot, there ain't no shade and you can't get a drink of water because you done run out and the next water hole may be a day away. You're your own cook and liveryman, you darn your own clothes, and I guess the worst is, you're your own company. You go days where the only people around is you."

"I don't care. Why is that so bad?"

"You run out of things to talk about real quick." The more thought he gave the idea, the more solemn he felt. "After a short time, you start thinking that if anything happened to you, if you got stuck in a river, got throwed off your horse, and broke your leg or the like, nobody would ever know. You're all alone, and when you are for some time, you start feeling lonely."

He cracked a smile when Noah's head dipped. "And as far as schooling, I'll say this. There was a day I felt the same, just about when I was your size. Didn't take to no book learning. But now, there's times when I wished I'd gotten a little."

"How come that is?" Noah asked as he resumed chopping at the tree.

"Oh, there's things that are easier to know about rather than finding it out yourself firsthand. And then there's words on a page. I have found use for that. If I had something to do over, I would have liked to learn to read."

Noah stopped midswing. "You don't know how to read?"

The admission wasn't one of which Cole was proud, but it was worth the shame if passing it on would benefit his young friend. "There are some words I know what they say, but when they're strung out in a long row with some others, then I get loster than calf cut from the herd. I never thought I'd need it when I was in school, so I never paid much attention, but it's kinda like not washing your drawers. Someday the lack of it is going to let something bite you."

Noah giggled as he took aim at the fresh cut in the pine. "Heck, I know how to read. Miss Clendenon says I can read good when I want to."

"I heard the same. Nothing wrong with that." As Noah swung the ax, Cole thought one more thing needed to be said. "The next time you're thinking about the Rainmaker, instead of thinking of the things he can do, remember some of the things he can't."

The afternoon passed with Noah's confidence increasing along with his skill with the ax. Three more pines were felled and cut into halves. The sun dipping in the west was a signal for the trip home to begin. They arrived on the farm at dark and ate a fine supper.

After the meal, Cole noticed Noah shaking his finger. "Splinter?" The boy shrugged. "Let me have a look at it." Noah reluctantly allowed Cole to grip the finger. A black speck showed through the skin. Cole nodded at the boy. "Yup. We'll have to cut it out."

"Cut it!" Noah said, jerking his hand away.

"It'll just hurt worse if you don't tend to it now. It'll get a lot redder and then turn blue. Might have to take the whole thing if we don't get it out now." After a moment's thought, Noah offered his finger again for his uncle Clay to get a better look. "You got a needle?" he asked Ann.

Evie happily brought a long sewing needle from Ann's quilt basket. Cole winked at the girl and stuck the needle into the candle flame.

"Why are you doing that?"

"Haven't you never had a splinter dug out of you before?" Noah shook his head. "Well, the fire kills whatever might have been on the needle so I don't put it in you. He gripped the fingertip steady and poked at the speck. Noah winced with each poke. "This ain't hurting you, is it?" Noah defiantly shook his head. "Didn't think it would, not a man of ten years such as yourself." A thought flashed into Cole's mind.

"Let this stand as a lesson," he said, clearing through the dead skin to stab the splinter. A drop of blood oozed from the hole. Cole drew the bandanna from Noah's pocket and wrapped it around the finger. "Sometimes it's worth the pain to get something over with rather than put it off. It often hurts worse later." He looked at Ann, then Noah. "Get some shut-eye."

From sunrise to sunset, day after day, they shaved the trunks into poles and sawed the poles into thin planks, using the sturdy branches as logs for support. It would have been best to let the pine cure to avoid warpage, but Cole felt an urgency to complete the work as soon as he could.

The roof was the most work by far. Cole stood atop the beams and lifted each of the lesser-sized logs by rope and nailed them in place. Morris came by, mostly due to orders from Lorna, and finally seemed to be getting the hang of hammering nails without bending them into the wood. Cole showed him that long single strokes would drive the nail flush more efficiently than short taps.

Noah was anxious to try his improved craftsmanship with the saw. Cole watched like a queasy new papa as the angle of the blade increased with each of Noah's strokes, making for a beveled edge that was impossible to fit to a flat surface.

However, Cole found that his correction—pinching the hot saw blade—was needed less and less as Noah's pride in his work bloomed like the flower on a cactus, even though it was taking twice as long. Despite his mother's whining like a lost puppy, Noah showed caution while moving atop the structure. Cole assured her that her son had listened to every instruction and had earned the duty.

The barn door side was built on the ground. The three of them had a hand in cutting each piece of wood down to proper size to be jointed with another. When it was complete, Cole cinched a knot to it, strung the rope through a pulley at the top of the barn's apex, and tied the rope to Bender's harness. With the horse towing the load, Cole guided the end up to where it met the barn's frame and joined it flush.

The heavy work behind them, Morris spent his time tending to his own farm while Noah and Cole concentrated on the barn's interior. A crib was built for the fall harvest and two stalls were constructed, one for the horse and the other for a milk cow that Ann was planning to buy. Noah argued with Evie that Bender should get first pick of the stalls since the horse was male and would be older than the cow.

Last built was a small frame bed jointed between the support poles and lined with fine straw for Cole. The sand-filled sack did well as a pillow.

With the sun still making clear that it was summer, Ann and Evie kept in the house most of the time. Cole and Noah finished the barn's sides and enclosed the barn. Once the barn was done, both of them stepped back to admire their achievement. Although he had ideas of including a pen for future hog farming and maybe moving the coop closer, Cole let his eyes soak up the sight like a bread dipped in gravy. He felt Noah's arm wrap around his waist, and he rubbed the boy's head. They stood there together until sunset.

When they went into the house, they smelled the cornbread that steamed on the table. Ann served chicken giblet stew, which was quickly gobbled down by both the hungry workers.

The following morning, the leftover stew was breakfast as Ann nervously hurried about the stove. "Today is Lorna's wedding, and I won't have time to spend with you two," she said as Cole and Noah ate. "I still have to finish pinning Evie's dress and my own, and you need to bathe, Noah." She turned around and eyed Cole. "Both of you."

"Am I going?" Cole asked. She didn't answer.

"Is he going, Mama?" asked Noah. Cole waited, unsure which reply he was rooting for. Social gatherings weren't something he sparkled at.

She turned and nodded as she came to the table with a pan. "Lorna said she wanted all of us there." She met Cole's eyes. "And I guess he's part of us."

Noah yelled his delight, while Cole felt he'd been punched.

"Now, I don't want to have to chase you about to remind you. I've got to make a pie." She laid a cloth on the table, and she and Evie chopped the rhubarb leaves from the stems.

"Noah," Evie said as she cut. "You can't eat the leaves."

"I know that," the boy answered in a voice that showed his irritation. "They make you sick."

"Kill you dead," Cole added. "Come on. Let's leave the women the house. We got things to do ourselves." Cole winked at the boy and rose amid Ann's muttering about kneading dough, mixing the proper amount of flour, sugar, and egg.

Fighting the urge to tinker more with the barn, Cole moved the barrel tub into it and stood firm against Noah's objections to bathe. Once the boy was done, he himself relaxed in the water he'd brought from the stove. He couldn't remember the last time he'd had a hot-water bath. Having scrubbed clean, he lathered his cheeks and chin and took Ann's straight razor to the stubble.

Noah came back into the barn, his collar tight around his

neck and his hair slick and parted in the middle. "I wish I could shave."

"Don't be wishing part of your life away," Cole said as he felt for his whiskers. "You don't get the chance to get it back."

"But Henry said that when you start shaving, that tells you you're a man."

Cole whipped the soap from the razor. "That does account for part of it, but I think there's more to it than that."

"So when do you get to be a man?"

He took a deep breath, sure in the knowledge he wouldn't finish smoothing his face until he satisfied the boy's question. "It ain't something that you wake up one day and have it handed to you. Although nature will grow your body when the time comes," he said as the boy stared at him. "It takes a good while for the rest to settle in. Like being polite to folks you don't know without someone telling you, and paying for things that you bought instead of stealing them. I've met men with gray beards that hadn't learned that yet." He thought to resume shaving.

"Is that all?"

Cole let the razor sag once more and looked into Noah's eyes. "There's something called responsibility. And that is what you make of it, because it's you that's responsible for it. Folks will put your name next to how responsible you are, because they think a man should be that way. If you want your name to be well thought about, then you should do what's right. Not all of them will think the same way, but as long as you know you're doing the proper things on your own, most will think of you as a man."

"I don't understand. When's all this happen?"

"Give it time," Cole said as he scraped off more whiskers. "My bet is, you'll know it once you're there."

Confused, Noah aimed his face toward the door. "Oh, Mama said come to the house. She got's some of my pa's

173

clothes she picked out for you. She said she let some out to fit you.''

The razor stopped again. ''She did?'' Noah nodded and left the barn.

Vance stepped out of the jailhouse. While heading to Donovan's, he heard his name called from behind. When he turned he saw his father mounted on a palomino with a white star and mane and fitted with a black Mexican saddle and bridle. Brice rode alongside as the two pulled up next to the boardwalk where Vance stood.

''A new horse?'' asked Vance.

Patting his mount's neck, MacGregor nodded. ''Isn't this a magnificent animal? I had him brought from down south, a hacienda near Albuquerque. He cost me a good price, two thousand dollars. You know greasers, they'll want every dollar you have. But this one is worth it. I plan to stud him.'' He raised an eyebrow at Vance. ''Wouldn't be a bad idea for you either, son.''

Vance ignored his father's familiar harp to take a wife. ''What brought you two in town? Did you hear about Martha Parsell losing a nickel in the street?''

Owen MacGregor chuckled at the remark. ''No. But I'll look for it before I leave. I came here to talk business with the law. Let's go inside.''

''We can talk here. I was on my way to eat, and if I go sit down with you, I might starve.''

MacGregor nodded. ''Okay. It seems my plans have changed somewhat. The Atchison, Topeka, Santa Fe has been stalled building trestles. They'll be done soon, and they're going to want to make up for lost time. We need to move fast to get the land we want, and that means that Hayes woman needs to vacate before the end of the month.''

''That's a little fast, ain't it?''

''Opportunity waits for no one, son. Why haven't you been out there to serve her notice?''

Vance looked away from him. He knew the answer would spark a fire, but avoiding the issue would create a bigger one. "Well, I'm not sure it's the law taking her land or you. I'm waiting on the governor's office to send me what the law says."

"The governor? Hell, that's liable to take weeks, maybe months. You can't wait on Lew Wallace. He's too busy telling everybody about a book he wrote. Some nonsense about a man that lived a few thousand years ago." MacGregor shook his head. "Writing books. No bigger waste of a man's time has ever been found."

"Just the same, I think I should wait."

MacGregor leaned forward in his black saddle to stare into his son's eyes. "You listen to me. It's your bound duty as a lawman to see that the law is done, and your Christian duty as a father's child to do what you're told. That land was meant to have people with paying businesses on it, not a bunch of kids and corn. Now, we've already been to her place, and nobody's there."

"There's a new barn standing, too. I'd think she plans on staying there," Brice added.

Vance turned to the foreman. "Do barns standing catch your interest, Brice?"

"Now, hold on—" Brice began, until he was stopped by his boss's raised hand.

"I heard George Clendenon is finally marrying off that teacher daughter of his. I would think Ann Hayes is there."

"I ain't going to bust up a wedding."

"You do as you're told, or I'll get a federal marshal out here to do your job." Vance knew the threat of someone else doing his sworn duty was real, and it cut into him like a knife. A man wearing a federal star, talking to people he wouldn't know or care for, could lead to bloodshed. Vance nodded reluctantly.

"Do it tonight. And take Brice with you in case there's trouble. Make him a deputy."

175

"The hell I will."

"By hell, you will do it," MacGregor answered in a stern voice as he reined the palomino's head around. "Do your duty by whatever means. I want that split-tail off that land."

Chapter Twelve

The buckboard rumbled over the stony dirt road. The bumpy ride jostled Cole and Ann closer together. She seemed to try not to notice her elbow touching Cole's. Her eyes would dodge his every time he looked at her.

Cole held the reins loose, watching Bender's tail swing from side to side. Occasionally, his eyes would drift to the surrounding hills and sage and the glare of the descending sun.

Ann turned to the children. "Now, we're almost there. I want you two to show your best manners. Do you hear me, both of you? It's Lorna Clendenon's wedding day, and I don't want to be hanging my head in shame because of my children's foolishness."

"Yes, ma'am," both of them answered.

Cole waited to hear a warning aimed at him, but none came. As she turned back around, her eyes matched his for an instant and she quickly blinked them to the front. Her silence made him feel as edgy as a bobcat caught in a pen

Tim McGuire

full of hounds. He wanted to say something, but words never came easy when he was talking to her.

The road led up a sloping hill. As it steepened, Cole shook the reins to keep Bender's pace steady. When they crested the top, they saw the Clendenon farm at the bottom of a wide valley. The small flat house became broader and taller as Cole eased the buckboard down the hill. Horses and mules harnessed to the many wagons were reined to a fence near the barn. Women in their Sunday-best dresses and bonnets herded running children in front of the house.

"You remember what I said," Ann reminded her two as the buckboard passed through the gate.

Cole reined Bender to a stop at the edge of the porch. Noah jumped onto the ground, but his mother's glare kept him from joining the frolic.

Ann looped the basket over her arm. Cole quickly tied the reins to the brake and stepped off the buckboard. When he came clear of Bender's nose, a tall young man had lifted Ann from the wagon and placed her gently on the ground. His smile at her showed more delight than that of a mere polite gentleman.

"Thank you, Henry," she said. Her grimace of worry had given way to a grin that brought out the beauty of her hazel eyes. It was the look Cole had always thought was there, and it was aimed at another man. He gripped Bender's harness to walk the horse to the barn, thinking the evening may be better spent if he stayed with the other beasts.

"There stands Annie Hayes, just as pretty as ever." The booming welcome came from an older man dressed in a dark coat. A black string tie looped from his white collar. His thick black mustache was stretched level above his gaping smile. His silvering temples faded into the rest of his black hair. He stepped off the porch and hugged Ann. Henry helped Evie from the buckboard. The older man turned to Cole and offered his hand. "This must be the man Lorna was telling me about. I'm George Clendenon."

178

Cole shook his hand and nodded. "Clay . . . Hayes." He hadn't polished the delivery of his new name yet.

Clendenon eyed Cole from head to toe. "You don't look much like your brother Robert." He snapped a solemn face at Ann. "God rest his soul." His smile turned back to Cole.

"Well." Cole glanced at Ann. "I've been told I favored my pa."

Ann sighed unnoticed.

Clendenon nodded, and after a moment's pause pointed at the cloth-covered basket. "I'm hoping that's what I think it is." He lifted the cloth corner and sniffed. "Oh my, it has been a long time since I've enjoyed your rhubarb pie."

"Lorna told me you spoke kindly of the last one." Ann looked inside past the open door. "How is Lorna?"

Clendenon shook his head in mock disgust. "Like any nervous bride. She and her mother are fretting like chickens that seen an ax. Ain't nothing wrong about nothing in there, but they wouldn't be happy if they both weren't worried about something. I was happy they run me out of the house."

Ann giggled. "Let me go see if I can do anything to help."

"No need, Ann. Millie's in there helping. If they need anything else, Henry here can get it for them. Oh, I'm sorry," Clendenon said as he looked at Cole. "This is Henry Taylor. The groom's older brother."

Henry's expression had less respect than contempt as he reached out his hand to Cole.

Cole completed the handshake. "Pleased to meet you." He noticed the tension on Ann's face.

Ann darted her attention to her son. "Noah, why don't you help your uncle Clay tend to Bender. I've got a pie that needs a place to sit, and I'm still going to try and help. You never have enough womenfolk to help." She went into the house.

Noah waved at Cole. "Come on. I'll show you where the horses go."

Cole led Bender past the rigid-standing Henry on his way

to the barn. When they arrived at the corral fence, Cole reined the horse to a rail. Noah climbed up on a post. Cole didn't want to ask the question, but he needed the answer. "Who's Henry?"

"He is Morris's brother, thinks he's a growed man but he's barely nineteen. He was in school just last year." He bowed his head. "I don't like him much."

"Why is that? You sure talk about him a lot."

Noah looked up at Cole. "Because he likes Mama. Thinks he's going to marry her. Treats me like he's my brother or something, ordering me to do things. I hate when he does that."

"Yeah, he does show an eye for her." Cole gently petted Bender's neck. "Do . . ." He hesitated. "Do you know how your ma feels about him?"

"I don't know. She never talks about him."

Cole smirked. "Come on, boy. With all the women inside, let's go hear all the lies being told by the well."

Ann knocked on the bedroom door and was invited inside. She opened it to see Lorna Clendenon wearing her white wedding dress while her mother knelt sewing the hem. "Oh, Lorna, you do make a beautiful bride."

Tears streamed down Lorna's cheek. "Everything is awful. The dress is too long, I look a mess, everyone is here waiting."

Ann came and took her hand. "You hush. Everything is fine. It's just the wedding jitters you're having. I can't remember a prettier dress I have ever seen, and your mama is making it right." A smile came over Lorna's face as Ann hugged her.

Cora Clendenon gave a wink to Ann as she stood. "I'll go and see if Reverend Brown is here." She left the room to the two friends.

"Mama said Millie ought to be my maid of honor," Lorna

sniffled. "But I would rather have asked you to stand next to me."

They hugged again. "When a woman gets married, she should have her family next to her," Ann said. "Anyway, I won't be far away." Lorna's eyes continued to well. "Wipe away them tears. This should be the happiest day of your life. Why, you're going to be Mrs. Morris Taylor today. He will be a good husband to you."

Lorna's face hung down as she muttered, "Something else I had to settle for."

Ann's grin faded.

"Oh, now you know it's true. Ever since I was little I've been chasing after Henry Taylor, but he wouldn't even look at me after Robert . . ."

Ann looked away.

Lorna gripped Ann's shoulders. "Oh, Annie. I'm sorry. I didn't mean . . . it's just that . . ." Both women looked into each other's eyes. "There was only one thing that I wanted while I was growing up—to be Henry's wife. But once he thought he could have you, well, there was no use trying. I had to get his little brother to pop the question to keep from being an old maid." She paused. "You know he loves you, don't say it ain't true."

Ann took a deep breath. "Henry Taylor's a fine man. He's going to make some girl a good husband." Her head dipped. "But I gave my heart a long time ago." She looked back at Lorna. "Now I'm a widow woman raising mine and my husband's children. I ask God to give me the strength to raise them right, and if he lets me do that, then that is all I can ask for."

Both women embraced once more. As they parted, a moment passed.

"What about that other man, your brother-in-law? Wouldn't be the first time a woman married twice into the same family."

The question cut Ann's breath. "Don't think that, Lorna."

181

The secret of the façade held her tongue. She wished she could tell the truth, but gossip could cost her her home and her children's safety. Still, the idea of Lorna's suggestion had already found a place in the back of her mind, and she tried to rid it from her thoughts. "You should be thinking of your future husband, of Morris."

Lorna rolled her eyes, her lips crinkled, her chin quivered.

Ann clutched Lorna's hand.

A smile firmed the bride's lips. "Well, you're right about one thing. Morris will be a good husband. He does everything I tell him to do."

They laughed. Ann eased her grasp of Lorna's hand and walked to the door. She winked. "Morris is a lucky man today."

Cole leaned against the roofed well, bemused by the latest tale of George Clendenon's wild oat-sowing youth. The surrounding men howled their envious laughter.

Noah tugged at the back of Cole's shirt. "What was so funny?"

Cole leaned down and whispered, "I'll tell you when you're a little older." The confusion on the boy's face brought a smile to Cole's.

"Well, it's about time," Clendenon said. A small surrey approached from the gate and stopped at the porch. A tall man in a black suit and hat climbed out. "Welcome, Reverend."

"Sorry I'm late, George. I tried to prepare the soul of the Rainmaker to meet his maker, and time got away from me."

"Yeah, well, if you ask me, it's a waste of time. His kind don't have a soul to prepare."

"The Rainmaker?" Noah loudly asked, turning all heads to see him standing next to Cole. "The gunfighter? Is he hanging?"

"What's he doing out here? He should be in the house

with the rest of them kids,'' said an embarrassed Clendenon.

Reverend Brown took off his hat. ''That's right, son.''

''Son of a bitch is going to get what he deserves,'' shouted one of the men. Muttered voices of vengeance filled the air.

Noah pulled on Cole's shirt and whispered. ''Can we go see it? I never seen a hanging.''

Cole's gut felt twisted, as if he were in that noose. ''No.''

Clendenon waved his hands. ''Now, boys, this ain't the time for that. We got a wedding to get on with. And where's that boy Morris?''

''He's bent over his supper in the barn,'' Henry answered as he came around to the front of the house.

''He ain't ate yet?'' Noah asked.

''Not no more.''

The surrounding men howled again.

''Well, you go get him cleaned up and in that house. If that girl of mine comes out for all to see and finds he's not there, she'll have the place afire without benefit of flame.''

Clendenon led the group inside. He passed through the crowd on his way to the other side of the house. Lamps hanging from the ceiling lit the large den. Reverend Brown stood in front of the large stone hearth.

As Cole and the boy entered the house, Ann held out her arm for her son. Noah joined his mother and sister next to the preacher. Cole took shelter by the back wall.

The towering Henry Taylor came in, leading his brother Morris, who appeared more like a condemned man approaching the gallows, between the patting hands of the admiring guests. Once the slight-statured groom took his place by the Reverend, a throat-clearing grunt from Brown signaled the commencement of the event.

The crowd on the other side of the room parted, clearing the way for the waiting Reverend and Morris. A girl holding pretty yellow flowers came through to stand in front of Ann and the children. A long moment passed, then George Clen-

183

Tim McGuire

denon, with his veiled eldest daughter on his arm, walked the bride one step at a time to her intended.

The guests encircled the bride and groom. Clendenon kissed Lorna's cheek and gave her arm to Morris. The couple held hands and turned to face Reverend Brown, who cracked open his Bible before his voice boomed into the silence. "Dearly beloved."

Morris repeated Brown's instructed vows, careful not to mistake a word. He took a ring from his brother's hand and slipped it on Lorna's finger.

Cole smirked when Lorna swore to obey her new husband. As she peered down to Morris, it seemed that shoe was being nailed on the wrong horse.

He glanced at Ann and saw a streaking tear dangle from her quivering mouth. Her glistening eyes seemed ready to launch another. Despite her furrowed cheeks, it was the happiest he had seen her.

On the pronouncement of being man and wife, Morris lifted Lorna's veil and kissed his new bride. Women bellowed sweet words of endearment. The proud father and mother were first among the tearing faces to congratulate the newly bonded couple. Henry nearly shook his stunned-faced brother's hand off, then carefully place a smack on his new sister's cheek.

Clendenon raised his hand. "Everybody, please make room for their first dance as Mr. and Mrs. Morris Taylor." The circle widened. Reverend Brown gave the spot in front of the hearth to two men. One of them knelt to prop a guitar on his knee while the other tucked a fiddle under his jaw. The fiddler drew the bow across the strings, playing long high notes.

Morris held Lorna's hand. They both stared into each other's eyes. She placed her other hand on his shoulder and they both swayed to the tune's slow rhythm. The gentle strumming of the guitar whispered its harmony. Women with bright smiles leaned against the chests of their men. The enjoyment of watching the two dance around the circle showed in everyone's smile.

George Clendenon led his misses into the circle, and soon, like leaves coming off a tree, partners both young and old joined the celebration and danced to the melody.

Cole felt a tug at his shirt. Noah waved him to bend down.

"I want you to dance with Mama."

Cole glanced at Ann, who stood next to the girl with yellow flowers. "I ought not to do that."

"But if you don't, then Henry Taylor is going to ask her."

The boy's gut feeling was the truth. Henry Taylor stepped in between the dancers toward Ann.

Cole looked into Noah's eyes and saw concern. "I ain't no good at this."

"You said that you owed me. Please. My mama is a widow woman, I know that now. But I don't want her dancing with him."

Cole rose and peered over the heads of the dancers to see Ann. He had known more comfort preparing to slap leather with another gunman in the middle of a street, but he had a promise to honor. He dodged through the dancers, heading in a straight line for Ann. As he approached, Henry had already arrived. Ann seemed startled by the two men standing in front of her.

"Would you do me the honor?" Henry asked.

"Oh, Henry. I would love to," the girl with yellow flowers excitedly accepted.

Shock came over Henry's face. "Millie?" The girl took his arm and pulled him away, all the while his face locked on Ann.

Cole inhaled and offered his open palm. "Would you like to dance?" The proposal was more like an apology. It wasn't until he saw a slice of Ann's smile that he exhaled. She placed her hand in his, and he took a step back to guide her into the swarm of moving people. A bump into Clendenon awakened him from his dreamy confidence. He was in the middle of a river not knowing how to swim.

Her hand came to rest on his shoulder. He found the soft touch of her side. It seemed she knew she would have to lead, and he followed her steps to the slow country waltz. The worry of knocking someone to the floor faded as he stared at her face.

She stepped back, took his left hand into hers, turned beneath his stretched arm, and took his right hand above her shoulder. Her hair had the scent of the autumn night's breeze. The pace slightly quickened, and he matched her prance to the fluid meter of the fiddle's sweet cry. A glimpse to the side caught Noah's happy smile.

The music slowed, and Ann turned beneath his arm once more to face him. With one last long cry of the strings, her sway stopped close to his chest. Her hazel eyes were lit up by her smile, and this time it was aimed at him.

Applause signaled the end of the dance. He never thought he'd be sorry to hear it. Ann dipped her head.

"I need to see to Lorna." She gave him one last glance and went to her friend.

He turned to see Noah standing behind the table ladened with pies, cakes, and all types of food brought by the guests. Noah stared at him as he approached the table. "Are we square?"

"Yup, all square. Did you like dancing with Mama?"

He shrugged. "It didn't hurt much." Noah's curled brow made Cole chuckle. "I'm only fooling, boy."

Mrs. Clendenon came next to Noah and cut out a piece of the rhubarb pie. Glancing up at both of them, she offered each a slice, which they accepted.

The tart taste took Cole to his youth. The difference between the pies past and present was a mature appreciation for good home cooking. Also, he reflected on the years gone by, and what he'd been through since. Had he known then what the rest of his life would bring, he would have shown more favor for a home-cooked meal, along with just having a home as well.

Crumbs and smeared filling painted the corners of Noah's mouth. His fondness for the dessert was no mystery to anyone. With his plate soon bare, he began cutting another slice, until Ann's voice stopped him.

"Noah, clean your mouth. Why don't you get Mr. Clendenon a piece?"

"Yes'm." The frown on Noah's face didn't slow him from doing what he'd been told. Few privates showed the same respect for their sergeant as Noah did when his mother spoke. He cut out a slice and weaved through the crowd.

Ann came to the table but was quickly shadowed by Henry. "Can I get some pie for you, Ann? Or maybe some cider?"

She presented a polite grin to him. "Why, thank you, Henry. That would be nice."

Cole tried to ignore her conversation with Henry, and how she volunteered a smile so easily at the young man fetching her drink. As she stood alone, Cole felt a need to speak. "This is mighty good pie. Best I've tasted for many a year."

Her answer came almost as a whisper. "I'm glad you like it."

His appetite disappeared. He wasn't sure what he'd done, but the woman he had danced with didn't seem the same one now accepting a cup from the returning Henry.

He took a deep breath, and thought of stepping outside, when Noah hurried through the crowd to tug on his mother's arm.

"Mama, Mr. Clendenon said to come quick. Deputy MacGregor is outside, and he wants to talk to you. And there's another fellow with him."

Her eyes widened as she glanced at Cole. She went toward the door, followed closely by Henry. Noah followed, too, until stopped by Cole. He looked down at the boy and spoke in a calm voice. "You better stay here." He winked. "It could be trouble. I'm good at that."

He shouldered his way through the gawking guests and went outside. He sidestepped George Clendenon in the doorway. The deputy stood flanked by a shorter man who appeared to be a ranch hand and was nursing a healthy wad of chaw. Ann was farther from the door, with Henry just behind her.

"I'm sorry to take you from the party, Mrs. Hayes. It sounds like a fine time," Vance said. "I'm here not by my own choosing. But I've got to serve notice to you, Mrs. Hayes . . ." He paused as if something had caught in his throat. "To serve notice to you that without your husband, as I know you are, you've got to leave your place."

Gasps and mumbled confusion as to what was said lit through the crowd like a fire.

"What are you talking about, MacGregor?" yelled Henry.

"This doesn't concern you, Henry. It's not your business," the deputy replied.

Henry stepped in front of the bewildered Ann before she could speak. "I'm making it my business. You got no call to come out here on my brother's wedding day and raise a bunch of hell."

"You ought not to talk to the deputy that way, son," said the ranch hand as he walked closer to Henry.

"Brice," Vance warned, but the man didn't stop until he came face-to-face with the defiant Henry.

"If I were you, I'd be quiet and let the deputy do his job."

"Why are you here, Canton? Did daddy send his favorite dog to guard his boy?"

Brice punched Henry, sending the young man on his back.

"You shouldn't have done that." Cole's voice hushed the shrieking guests. He strode to stand over Henry and offered a hand up. "Is it a part of that badge to punch a kid?"

Henry refused Cole's and Ann's help and got to his knees on his own.

"You want part of this too, mister?" Brice muttered. "I don't want to shame you too much in front of all these folks."

Cole stared at Brice. "You're a long way from there, friend."

Brice smirked. "I admire a man who has backbone." He twisted around slowly and spat out tobacco juice, then recoiled around a backhanded slap.

Cole caught the blow with his right hand, snapped Brice's arm rigid, and wrenched it forward, locking the shoulder. He kicked Brice in the gut, exploding the wad of chaw out like a bullet. Brice dropped to one knee. Reaching his left hand to his right hip, Brice drew his pistol. Cole ripped the gun from Brice's grasp, kicked him to the ground, and spun the revolver's aim back at its owner.

"Do you want part of this?" Cole growled at the panicked ranch hand.

"Drop the gun, Hayes," Vance shouted, pointing his pistol at Cole, who then flung the gun away.

Henry climbed to his feet, glanced at Ann, and marched to the deputy, spouting insults on his way. He punched Vance to the ground. "Do you want to fight? Fight me."

"Henry, don't!" Ann cried.

Vance rubbed his jaw and slowly rose. "No. I don't want to fight you, Henry." He turned to face Ann. "I'm sorry to bust up the wedding. Things got carried away more than I wanted them to. I think we all need a few days to settle things. I'll be out to your house on Saturday, Mrs. Hayes. We'll talk about this then. Brice, get your gun and get on your horse."

"You come to her place and I'll be waiting on you," Henry said.

Vance didn't challenge the threat as he holstered his pistol. He and Brice mounted without further words and rode off.

The guests ebbed back inside, and George Clendenon tried to shift the mood back to the celebration. Henry walked over to Ann, who inspected him for wounds like a doting mother. As they both walked past on their way inside, Henry glared at Cole.

"Where'd you learn to fight like that?"

Cole peered behind him to see Noah smiling. He rubbed the boy's head and prodded him for them both to join the others. Sure he had made a mistake in showing his temper, he went inside. The guests looked as if a grizzly bear had just entered the house. All the manners he had tried hard to show wouldn't be remembered.

Ann wore her shawl and was hugging Lorna and Morris. The bride's tears weren't from joy. Cole was sure he had shamed Ann into leaving the party. She gathered Noah and Evie and led them outside. He trailed behind the family of three to the buckboard, feeling once again the outsider. Once the children were in the wagon, he shook the reins. If he had had his own horse, he would have started for Mexico that night.

Owen MacGregor heard angry voices grow louder as he rose from his chair. The study door swung open, and Vance charged in.

"Keep this son of a bitch out of my way from now on," he yelled, pointing at Brice as they entered the room.

"Mr. MacGregor, I was just doing what you told me," said Brice.

"Like hell you did," Vance snapped.

"Shut up, both of you," MacGregor ordered. "Now, what the hell are you talking about? Did you serve the Hayes woman that notice?"

Vance sighed. "Oh, we went out there. And when I told her, young Henry Taylor took up for her. When I told him to stay out of it, Brice hit him."

MacGregor turned to his foreman. "Is that so?"

"Mr. MacGregor, it ain't exactly like that. That Taylor kid

started sassing your son, and I thought I'd teach him a little respect for the law.''

"Well, what's wrong with that?"

"I didn't need his help," Vance said. "He almost got himself killed. That brother you weren't worried about stepped right into it. When Brice tried to slap him down too, Hayes kicked him on his ass faster than lightning hits the ground. When Brice pulled his gun, Hayes took it from him like he was a kid. If I hadn't stopped Hayes, he'd have put a bullet in that thick head.''

"You let some farmer beat you down and hold your gun on you?" MacGregor asked disgustedly.

A moment passed before Brice answered, first looking at the wall. "I'm sorry, Mr. MacGregor," he said to his boss, "but that man ain't no sodbuster. The way he handled a pistol, he ain't been plowing dirt all his life.''

MacGregor pondered a few seconds, then faced his son. "Well, what are you going to do about it?"

Vance sat in a chair. "The way things turned out, I postponed giving official notice until Saturday. I'm hoping everybody's tempers will have cooled by then."

"I know that Taylor kid's won't be," Brice interrupted. "He got plum hot, and said he was going to call you out if'n you came to the Hayes farm.''

Vance curled his lip as if to dismiss the threat. "Henry Taylor is sweet on Ann Hayes, everybody in the county knows that. He was just trying to look good in front of her. He'll change his mind or forget about it.''

"What if he doesn't?" MacGregor's question didn't get a reply from Vance. "Since tempers are already high," he glared at Brice, "I'll go out there with you."

"You think you being there will calm things down?" Vance scoffed.

"I don't want you out there on your own. What if this man Hayes is with him? You said he knows how to handle guns. I'll let you do your duty, but I'll be along just in case.''

Tim McGuire

"I don't need you there," Vance said, staring at the elder MacGregor.

"Son," he said in his familiar fatherly tone. "You may not want me there. But I'm going to be there."

Noah and Evie were rocked to sleep in the wagon's bed. Cole twisted around to glimpse Ann in the light of the full moon. He was driving home with the same gnawing in his gut he had come with. It just wasn't right. He had only done what he thought best at the time, a reflex that came naturally. Although he didn't think it was wrong, it wasn't a matter he felt comfortable to judge himself.

"I'm sorry if what I did put you in a bad mind with your friends."

"It's not your fault." Her calm whisper didn't settle his gut.

"Well, anyways, I felt it needed to be said."

She put her hand on his arm and looked him in the eye. "It's me that should be apologizing."

He exhaled deeply. His gut felt instantly better, but he was now confused.

"Marshal Thomas told me this day would come. He told me that Owen MacGregor had told him that it was against the law for me to be on my land. He said that since Robert's death made me a squatter, that we couldn't stay on the land, that I couldn't own it. He rambled on about some law that says it's so, but he didn't want me and the children without a home. So he said he would look away for a while, until he could think of something. But he never did."

"What kind of law is that?"

She didn't answer right away. "Because a woman can't own land that she wasn't born with. She can't get land from her husband's family."

He snapped the reins to keep Bender's gait steady. "Why does MacGregor want your land so bad? It seems he's got plenty."

192

A slight smirk grew on her face. "Greed. Stubborn pride. That's what men like him only think about. You can bet if Owen MacGregor wants something, it normally is worth his while." She paused. "Of course, there's the pride part, too. Some men can't stand for a woman to have something that they want."

"You know, now that I think about it, I saw rails just a few miles east of here. The railroad is coming, and it's coming close to your place. It might be the reason that Mac-Gregor is wanting your land so bad."

"I heard. Noah told me. That could be it, but I would have no use for trains."

"No, but MacGregor would. Trains bring people, and people bring money."

After a few silent moments, Ann spoke again. "Noah told me that you and he saw Robert's grave." Cole didn't know how to answer except to nod. "I guess it's best that he finally saw it. I never did know how to bring him there. I thank you for that."

"I know now why you stay. One thing I'd ask, but if it's not for me to know it's okay. Why do you have your husband so far from your home?"

It was a few seconds before she answered. "That was to be our home someday. Robert was always fond of trees, and when he found that spot and took me there, he said he would like to build a new house near that tree. But, with it being fall, he wanted to wait for spring. It was in between when he died."

Like many times before, Cole found himself wishing he had kept his questions to himself.

The roof of the house reflected the moonlight. Within a few minutes, Cole had reined in Bender to stop at the porch. He cradled Evie in his arms while Ann led the way inside. She opened the door, lit the candle, and pulled back the girl's bed blanket. When Cole put Evie on the sheets, Ann tucked her daughter in. Noah, once in the lower bunk, took a little

193

more time to get back to sleep. He mumbled something about working on the barn, but fell back asleep with Cole's assurance that that was tomorrow's work.

As Ann tucked in her son, Cole left the house and went into the barn. Still a bit restless from the night's events, he lit the lantern. A smoke would have been nice, had he had one; it always settled his nerves. But he'd sold his tobacco and papers with his saddlebags.

Creaking from behind stopped his ruminations. Ann entered the barn. She closed the door and walked to him, her arms folded as she glanced at the barn's interior. "Looks a bit different when lit from the dark. It appears bigger." Her eyes met his, showing a sincere mood. "I need to thank you for what you did for Henry. He sometimes feels a need for acting older than he is, and it brings him trouble. It was good of you, doing what you did."

"He only does it for you to think fond of him."

"I know that."

"Maybe . . ." he started, unsure whether to finish. "You should set him straight on how you really feel about him."

"And how do you think I really feel about him?"

Her response surprised him. He'd almost expected to be slapped, but since she seemed in a mood to know the truth, he felt obliged to answer. "If you don't mind me saying, I believe you're wanting to find someone, but Henry ain't what you're looking for."

"Is that so?" Her voice was laced with a dare. "And what would you believe it is I'm looking for?"

He smirked. "I can't say. A lesson I learned early on was not trying to figure on what a woman is thinking. You'd have better luck guessing on a turn of a card or where a single raindrop would fall."

"That seems a good policy to keep." Her eyes darted to his chest. "You have a button missing on your shirt." She stepped closer and touched where the button belonged. Her fingers drifted around his chest. She slowly raised her head and looked deeply into his eyes, whispering, "I'll have to find time to mend it for you."

He knew he may yet get slapped, but with her so near, the urge to kiss her overcame him. His lips touched hers, and he noticed they were warm and sweet. Her arms wrapped around him. He felt the contour of her shoulders, but as soon as he moved to hold her tighter, she pulled away.

"I need to get back inside in case Evie wakes up." She stepped to and out the barn door, all the while looking at him.

Chapter Thirteen

Cole blinked in the morning's light between the boards. He hadn't slept past sunup—without benefit of liquor—since the day after he left the army. Sitting on the straw bed, he recalled the happenings of the previous night. He smiled. Sleeping in daylight wasn't the only experience he'd missed in a while.

He slipped on his shirt and went outside. All was quiet. No Noah, Evie, or Ann. Perhaps it wasn't as late as he thought. He went to the house and stepped inside. Ann stood over the table serving the children breakfast. She glanced at him only an instant, then returned her attention to the stove. Cole took a breath. He hoped the woman he had kissed in the barn was the one here in the house.

He took the chair next to Noah and waited, as both children did, for their mother to join them. The morning blessing was brief, and breakfast was soon enjoyed by all.

"You never did say where you learned to fight like that," Noah said.

196

"Not another word said about that. Do you hear me?"
Ann scolded.

"Yes, ma'am." The boy finished his plate and put the
dishes in the bucket. Evie did the same shortly after, and the
pair went outside. Ann seemed to want to keep busy and
avoid looking at Cole. She cleaned knives, forks, spoons, and
plates in a large wooden tub, remaining careful to keep her
back to him.

The barn's uncompleted labor beckoned him. When he
faced the door he felt her eyes on his back, but he knew that,
like a shadow, she couldn't be caught in the suspected pose.
Once on the porch, he shut the door behind him.

After a moment's thought, he squinted to the east in the
direction of the sound of rumbling wheels. A single horse
buggy came at the house at a quick gait, leaving dust trailing
in the morning's breeze. Alone in the driver's seat, Lorna
reined to a stop and was quickly met by the eager Evie. A
gracious smile was given to the child, then the schoolteacher
stepped from the coach and onto the porch.

"Good morning, Clay," she greeted in a formal tone, but
her face showed concern. "Is Ann inside?"

Still confused by the quiet breakfast, he casually nodded
and moved aside to allow Lorna into the house. Once the
door closed, plans to resin the barn's roof filled his thoughts.

Ann twisted around to see Lorna standing at her door.
"What are you doing here? How come you're not with Morris? Is anything wrong?"

After a vain attempt by Lorna to hold a brave demeanor,
her chin quivered and the two friends came to each other for
a mutual hug in the center of the room. Ann helped her to a
chair. "Oh, Ann. It's Henry. I don't know what to do."

"What do you mean? What's he done?" she answered as
she, too, felt a need to sit.

"Last night, after you left, Henry went into a rage over
being shamed in front of you. Papa tried to calm him down,
but he would hear none of it. He swore to be here when

197

Tim McGuire

Vance MacGregor comes tomorrow and threatened to shoot him if need be." Tears ran down her cheeks. "Everybody started leaving then. On my wedding day, when I was supposed to be happier than any girl has a right to be, and my new husband went home with his big brother, whistled for like a loyal dog. I spent the whole night crying in my room. But the worst of it is that when I went to the Taylor place to fetch Morris, he and Henry were practicing with that old gun of their father's."

Ann comforted her with an arm around her shoulder. "Oh, Lorna. Didn't you talk any sense into him?"

"I tried. But both of them now have a head full of hate." Lorna pulled a handkerchief from her bag and sniffled her nose clear. "Ann, you've got to talk to him. You're the only one he'll listen to."

"Me? What can I say to change his mind?"

"Now is not the time to be coy. You know you're the reason he's acting this way."

Ann rose and stared at the wall. Even though it was the truth, she didn't want to admit it.

Lorna continued. "You know men. Once their pride has been hurt, they're bullheaded against common sense. Henry may just be my brother-in-law now, but I love him as much as I do Morris, maybe more. There, I said it. But he won't do it for me. You've got to talk him out of this. Everybody knows Vance MacGregor is the best man with a gun in the territory. He'll kill Henry."

Ann could go speak to the young man who held so much fondness for her. However, to convince Henry to give up his fool notion, she was sure she would have to proclaim heartfelt thoughts that she didn't harbor.

"You're right, Lorna," she said, still staring at the wall. "Men are bullheaded when it comes to their pride. And even more so if a woman tries to change their minds for their own good."

Chair legs scooting against the floor made Ann turn, and

198

she spotted Lorna walking to the window to peer outside. An unpleasant silence draped the room. "What about him? Your brother-in-law?"

The question surprised Ann. "What are you saying?"

"You saw him last night. He looked comfortable with a gun in his hands. Might he go and talk to Henry or maybe Vance and call this thing off?"

Ann went to the window beside her friend. Cole and Noah were working atop the barn. "Henry wouldn't listen to him."

"He might. You said it yourself. He might not want to have a woman tell him, but men have a way of talking sense to each other. We have to try something. Please, Ann. Go and tell him to talk to Henry."

Although torn in two different directions over her affections for two different men, Ann couldn't find fault with the idea. "Okay, I'll ask him. I'll ask him alone." She walked slowly outside and toward the barn, unsure of what words to use. When she reached the side wall, where Evie drew circles in the sand, she squinted and put her hand to her brow. "Son, you come down from there and go inside and pay your respects to Miss Lorna. Evie, you go with him. I need to speak to Uncle Clay."

Despite minor complaints, Noah climbed down from the roof and both children went inside. Soon Cole was on the ground, standing in front of her. He wiped the grime from his hands with a rag, his eyes darting from her.

"That's the first time you ever called me that with only the kids present. Maybe you're getting used to it."

She ignored his remark. "I have something I need to ask you. Lorna has just come from the Taylor place. She's sick with worry because Henry is out practicing with a gun. He's still planning on being here if Vance MacGregor comes."

"Then he's a damn fool. What's that got to do with me?"

She hesitated, then forced the words from her mouth. "I'm asking you to talk to him. Try to change his mind."

He stared her in the eye. "You want me to tell him he's

a damn fool? You think that will change his mind?''

"No, but you can show him that. Henry doesn't know anything about handling guns," she paused, "but you do. I know you do.''

"So you want me to go and help that kid who's sweet on you. So you can keep leading him on like a calf?'' he said with anger.

"I haven't led him on.''

"Haven't you? Then tell him how you feel. Tell him you don't have feelings for him, and he'll give up getting shot for you. Or do you have feelings for him? Do you love him?''

"I don't love him,'' she replied. With the hidden truth stirred, she felt compelled to reveal part of her soul. "Before a month ago, I only knew one man that made me feel like a woman.''

The spite faded from his face.

"It's true, Clay. Please don't ask me to say more. If I were to tell Henry what I told you, he'd be a broken man, and after would come here looking for another man to fight. I can't have that. That's why I need you to tell him that he need not fight Vance for me. Tell him that I would obey the law and leave before I would see him hurt. Please, will you go and do me this one favor?''

Cole's mouth opened, but he said nothing. After a nod, he spoke. "I'll do what you ask.'' He stepped around Ann and headed for where Bender stood.

Noah bounded from the house and off the porch. "Are we going to get back on the roof?''

"No, we'll let the resin sit a spell,'' Cole answered as he began hitching Bender to the buckboard. "We'll start back on it once I finish doing an errand for your ma.'' He quickly had the horse harnessed to the wagon. When he shook the reins, he gave Ann a last glance.

The sun was high overhead when Cole arrived on the Taylor spread. He could see Henry standing about ten paces from the wooden fence, a tin can on the top rail. With Morris behind him, Henry appeared to aim a Navy Colt revolver at the can. He fired. The can still sat atop the rail. Two more carefully aimed shots were fired with the same result by the time Cole had reined Bender to a stop behind the brothers.

"What are you doing here, Hayes?" Henry snarled.

"Word is you're planning on gunplay with the deputy tomorrow. Is that so?"

"What if it is?"

"Well," Cole said, fighting off a chuckle. "Seeing your skill with that Navy six, providing the cylinder don't get out of line or just fall to the ground, I'd say Morris here is going to have this place to himself along with his new misses."

The remark made the Taylor boys twist around at him. "I suppose you can do better?" asked Henry.

Hopping off the buckboard, Cole nodded. "I can. But I didn't come out here to tell you that." He looked first to Morris. "I was sent here by your wife. She came to the house fretting over what the two of you got planned."

"Morris ain't got nothing to do with this. I told her that this morning." Henry turned his sights on the can again.

"I don't believe that's what got her worried."

"What do you mean?" Morris asked with a blank face.

"I mean, I think it's plain she has reason to want both of you out of this fight."

Henry uncocked his pistol and turned again to Cole. "She's my brother's wife."

"All the same, I think she'd just as soon not have a husband bent on revenge against his brother's killer."

Henry glanced at Morris, who seemed confused as he shook his head. "I wouldn't want to, but I'd do it if you'd want me to, Henry."

"See there?" said Cole with a smirk.

"I told you to stay out of this. I don't want you doing nothing," Henry barked at his brother, then resumed aiming at the can. "If all you can do is spread fear, Hayes, then kindly leave my land. Tell Ann I'll be at her place at sunrise."

Cole stood behind Henry as another shot rang off, this time splintering the rail's edge. "You ever been in a gunfight? I mean, pointed a gun at a man?"

"Don't seem so hard." Henry spoke while looking straight.

Shaking his head in disgust, Cole stepped to Henry's side. "If you were to stand in front of Vance, what would you be looking at?"

Henry appeared stumped for an answer. "I would stare him straight in the eye."

"Then you'd be dead. A man don't draw iron with his eyes. You watch his gun hand. If it so much as twitches, then you fill your hand and shoot quick—straight in the heart if you can."

"What do you know about guns? I don't see you carrying one."

Cole took a step to come nose-to-nose with Henry. "A lot more than you do!" He pulled the six-gun from the young man's hand and cocked the hammer while pointing the barrel at the can. With the target aligned at the muzzle's end, he squeezed the trigger, sending the tin spinning into the air to crash onto the dirt. He flipped the pistol butt end up in his palm and offered it to Henry, who slowly took it back.

Having again let his temper get the best of him, he took a breath and stepped away. "You're going to die, Henry. The deputy carries a Colt with a five-inch barrel. Ain't but one reason for that—so as to clear leather faster than you or any other man standing in front of him. He's pointed a gun on a man, and I'd bet put a slug in some. A forty-five makes a hole the size of a nickel going in and comes out like a cannonball."

A hard swallow showed from Henry's throat. "I'll take my chances. At least I'll be a man about it."

"You don't know what the word means. You'll be a dead

man," said Cole. "If you're still of a mind on filling a pine box, then I'll ask you to keep away from the house. Be two miles up the road and I'll meet you there. If you'll do that, I'd be obliged and will help you with what I'm able."

Henry didn't answer, but aimed again at the grounded can. He cocked the gun and pulled the trigger. The hammer clicked on a spent cap. Cole exhaled, shaking his head, and climbed to the buckboard seat. He shook the reins while Henry reloaded the revolver and Morris retrieved the can.

Cole arrived at the farm as the sun began to set. Lorna's horse and buggy still remained in front of the house. He unhitched and led Bender inside the barn. He brushed the horse, knowing he would soon have to tell the women what his trip had accomplished. Before he could feel right about telling them, the barn door opened and Ann and Lorna came inside.

"Did you talk to Henry?" Ann asked. Lorna's eyes glistened in the lantern's light.

He sighed heavily. "Yeah, I talked to him. But I didn't change his mind none."

Both women showed disappointed faces, first to him and then to each other. "So is he going to be out here in the morning?" asked Ann.

"I asked him to be up the road a couple of miles. No sense having any bullets flying around here. I also said that I'd be there with him."

Lorna nodded with a gracious smile. "I thank you for that." She looked at Ann, and the two friends consoled in another embrace. They left the barn, and Cole followed. Lorna stepped up into her buggy.

"I'd be glad to drive you home," he said.

"That's all right," Lorna said as she took the reins. "But I thank you for your offer. I've been on these roads all my life." With a shake of the reins, she had the horse pull away from the house.

Ann looked at Cole. "I want to thank you too. I know you

203

tried your best." As she started inside, her low tone had him uneasy.

"Would you rather I meet Vance tomorrow?"

"No." She twisted around. "Why would you ask that?"

"I don't know." He shrugged. "You have a way of making a fellow wonder why he does things."

She faced the door and took another step.

"I'll be up early. It's best you and them kids stay here. Keep Noah close to you. Make sure he don't stray off. He don't need to be out there."

Still facing the door, she nodded and went inside.

Chapter Fourteen

Cole rose from the straw bed. A peek between the boards showed no light from the east. Unable to sleep, he slipped on his shirt and sat on the edge of the bed to put on his boots.

Wary of the action that was soon to take place, he tried to think what he could do to prevent it, but could think of nothing. He himself had been told many times to steer away from differences settled with firearms. He also had felt the fire burning inside boys wanting to prove they were men. Like some fires, it was often best to let them burn themselves out.

Not wanting to have squeaking wheels awaken the curious Noah, he led Bender from the stall, grabbed the mane, and mounted. The slow trot down the road gave him further time to think.

A brisk wind came from the north. Autumn was soon to have its chance on the land. A glance at the corn told him it was harvest time. This day could be better served for that purpose. Cool winds would soon bring cold ones, even in the desert. He'd often been told Mexico had the warmest winters. He had never traveled there, and the thought crossed his mind to find out himself.

What would be left behind? Ann and the kids would make a fine family for some man. The idea was appealing and he had seemed to be a good fit. His pretending he was a lost relative had become almost real.

Pounding horse hooves came from out of the darkness. Three riders slowed their mounts. Henry was in front, flanked by Morris and George Clendenon, who greeted Cole with a nod. "Any sign of Vance?" he asked.

"Not yet. I just got here myself."

Dawn broke with the four men mounted in still silence, unwilling to offer any words about the situation. Cole occasionally glanced at Henry, who still seemed unaware of the deadly seriousness of the matter. The Navy six was tucked in his pants' waistband.

"Eight o'clock," Clendenon announced. He snapped his watch shut and tucked it into his vest.

"Maybe he ain't coming," Morris said.

Cole snapped at him. "Don't be spouting that. If you're looking for a reason to go, then now is the time." He turned to Henry. "Same for you. If your head gets all twisted and confused hoping he don't come, then it's best to leave now. You can't be thinking about one thing and hoping for another at the same time."

"You trying to scare me, Hayes?"

"I'm trying to save your life." Cole and Henry stared eye to eye for an instant until Clendenon offered his opinion.

"Maybe he's right, Henry. You should listen to him."

Henry glared at the older man. "You're going to start this too? I thought you were on my side. If any one of you wants to leave, then do so. I came here for a fight."

Horses approached on the road. "Too late for that," said Cole, and the party all looked at the two riders approaching.

Vance MacGregor and a mature man in a fine coat and hat on a palomino rode side by side and pulled up within feet of the four men. "I was wishing I wouldn't see you today, Henry," said Vance.

"Owen, you got to stop this." Clendenon addressed the mature man.

"Nothing I can do, George. This is the law at work. I'm just here as a father looking out for his son. I would have thought you'd do the same, with the Taylor boys being part of your family now."

Clendenon cowered from the suggestion. "I've tried."

"The hell with this, let's get to it," Henry shouted angrily.

Vance raised the palm of his empty gun hand. "Hold on, Henry. I didn't come here to fight you. Now, I have work to do today and you're getting in the way. If all of you don't clear the road, I'll have to put the lot of you in jail."

"Jail?" Henry scoffed. "Well, the same might be said about you, Mr. Deputy. Only it won't be jail where you're going."

"Are you threatening the law, son?" Owen MacGregor asked, then looked to Cole. "Are you Ann Hayes's brother-in-law?"

Cole nodded. "I am."

"So I hope you know this hasn't got anything to do with you or her personally. This property was granted to Robert Hayes and no one else. Once he passed, it should have been auctioned. This should have been seen to a long time ago." He nudged the palomino.

"It ain't got anything to do with the train tracks I saw about five miles from here, does it?" Cole's question stopped MacGregor and had both father and son glance at each other in worried fashion.

"No, it does not," came MacGregor's answer after a moment of thinking. "Does that settle this matter?"

"Not yet," Cole replied. "What about me taking over my brother's place? Seems to me what is owned by a brother can be passed to his kin. There must be a lawyer of some kind in Nobility that could settle all this to the law's satisfaction better than you.''

''There's one in Santa Fe,'' said Vance. His father twisted around at him as if betrayed.

Cole continued. ''Let's give him a crack at it. Maybe something can come from it. It has been a long time, Mr. MacGregor. A little longer can't make much difference, can it?''

Vance nodded. ''It sounds good with me.'' He reined his horse around. ''I'm going back to town.''

Henry snarled at Cole. ''You done it again!'' His hand gripped the butt of the Navy six. ''I came here for a fight, do you hear?''

''Henry, don't!'' Cole's order was quickly shouted down by Owen MacGregor's loud call.

''Vance, he's drawing his gun!''

The deputy's head twisted back, and within a blink of an eye he had his Colt drawn on Henry. The double-action fired instantly, sending Henry off his horse. Writhing in pain, Henry held his wounded shoulder while all the riders viewed the incident with shocked faces.

Groaning his agony, Henry pawed the dirt for his six-gun.

Before a word could be uttered, another shot cracked the air. Henry's head snapped back and his body slumped onto the ground.

The cool wind whipped through Cole. Everyone stared at the motionless body sprawled in the sand.

Vance flashed his eyes first at Clendenon, then at Morris, and finally at Cole. ''I didn't want this! I didn't want this!''

Morris shivered. His jaw dropped, his eyes wide in awe.

Clendenon shut his eyes and shook his head.

Cole swung his leg over Bender's head to dismount and ran to the body. A bloody hole the size of a dollar bloomed from the back of the scalp.

"You all saw it," exclaimed MacGregor. "It was plain to see. He drew his gun. It was self-defense. Vance had no choice."

A now stoic Vance holstered his Colt.

Carefully reaching for the Navy six, Cole gripped the barrel. Cocking the hammer, he saw the misaligned cap. He aimed in the air and pulled the trigger. The click of the hammer sounded louder than the absent shot could.

Vance let out a deep breath.

"You murdered him," Morris cried. "His gun wouldn't have fired."

"You can't know that. It was damaged when he fell," MacGregor tried to explain.

Cole glared at Vance. "You still have business out here, Deputy?"

"No. Not today." Vance looked to Morris. "I'm sorry for what happened. But if any man draws his gun, I got to draw mine." He spurred his horse to a trot toward Nobility. Finding himself abandoned, Owen MacGregor first looked to Clendenon as if for some forgiveness. With nothing said, he rode at a gallop after his son.

The three men who had come to shepherd Henry stared blankly in their tracks at his dead body. As the wind blew in Cole's face, he was brought out from his trance, and he slowly recovered the riderless mount. Clendenon helped load the corpse across the saddle. The older man climbed onto his gelding as Cole did Bender.

Clendenon murmured his intent of guiding Morris back to the Taylor place. The two men led the third horse and headed back for where they'd come from. Cole watched them leave and then nudged Bender home.

The sight of bullets spilling blood had returned to his life. Feuds over land, money, or women often brought the spraying of lead. Once a fellow was killed, more deaths would normally follow. People who had nothing to do with it often got in the way of a careless shooter. Especially those without a way of defending themselves.

He approached the farmhouse, wanting to pull up and ride away rather then tell of the encounter. Noah was his usual spry self, hopping from the porch and spouting questions, one on the heels of another. Cole didn't answer, for he couldn't think of a reply other than the truth, and telling the boy the truth wasn't proper.

Stepping inside, he ordered Evie out of the house. Ann swept the floor, an act her face and the dustless planks showed was necessary to keep her mind busy. Once she stopped, he felt her eyes search his soul. Although it seemed she knew, he closed the door and told Ann what had happened. At first, she bravely returned to her sweeping, but soon the broom fell away as her face sank into her palms.

He put his arm around her shoulders, and this time he felt comfortable doing so. She had lost a longtime friend and onetime suitor. He had failed to prevent Henry's death as she had asked him to do.

It wasn't long before Noah cracked the door open to stick his nose inside. Upon seeing his mother's tears, he and his sister rushed into the house.

"What's wrong? Why are you crying, Mama?" Evie asked.

"Henry's dead," Cole announced solemnly. "He drew his pistol on the deputy, but Vance was first to fire."

Disbelief filled Noah's face. "Henry's dead? No. It ain't true!"

Cole nodded. "I seen it myself."

"But Vance said he didn't want to fight him."

"Henry forced his hand."

Noah's disbelief gave way to a creased brow of anger, a reaction that surprised Cole. "Deputy MacGregor killed Henry? I can't believe it. The Rainmaker should kill *him*. I wish the Rainmaker would kill Vance MacGregor."

"Don't you ever say that," Cole yelled, pointing his finger

at Noah. "Don't ever say that or wish that!" Realizing his raised voice had frightened everyone in the house, he paused to soften his tone. "Once you say that, people will never let you take it back. You stop thinking about the Rainmaker, or guns, or who ought to kill who. Do you hear me? I don't want you thinking about that man or about who ought to die. Don't ever start."

A scared nod was the boy's answer.

Cole faced Ann, who looked at him not with the eyes of a protective mother, as he had expected, but rather with the respect a woman would show the leader of the family. She wiped away her tears. "I should go and see if Lorna is all right. I know she's going to need help with Morris to get this behind them."

"I'll get Bender hitched," Cole said, and went to the door.

"No," Noah interrupted, showing responsible pride. "I'll do it." Cole grinned his surprise as the two of them went outside together.

During the task of harnessing the gelding to the buckboard, Noah remained quiet. Sure the boy's silence was the result of having shouted at him, Cole felt poorly. "I'm sorry I yelled at you."

"That's all right. I know you didn't mean it at me." The boy's contented beam returned, which gave Cole the confidence to bring up another subject.

"I need a favor from you. I want you to take Evie and your ma over to the Taylor place. You need to help both of them, especially your ma, through this." With Noah's full attention now on him, Cole said gently, "I know you can do it. Be ready for what you might see. Folks circling the dead won't act as they should. Take no offense to what you hear."

"Why ain't you coming?"

With a heavy sigh, Cole looked away from the young inquiring eyes. "I don't think I'd give people the piece of mind they're looking for."

Ann and Evie came from the house, dressed as they would

211

be for a sermon. When they came to the buckboard, Cole helped Ann to the seat, where she was joined by her son. Her astonishment clear, Cole said nothing as he stepped back. Noah snapped the reins.

With the wagon heading for the road, he concentrated on the purpose for staying behind. High clouds masked the sun, but half the day's light remained. A good part of it would be needed to get where he had to go. He followed the fresh ruts in the dirt.

The overcast skies brought on dusk sooner than expected. The glow of Nobility could hardly be made out before he reached the edge of town. The journey on foot had cost him a good deal of his wind. As he rested, he saw a scaffold mounted on four posts. With thirteen steps to the top, it was a structure built for only one purpose.

He pushed his aching legs to Farlon's store, but when he arrived, no lantern illuminated the drawn shades. The doorknob wouldn't twist. A peek through the shades further dimmed his hopes of regaining his reliable Winchester. When he shook the knob, the rattle of the door glass brought him more attention than he wanted. Now he thought of kicking the door down, but that would bring him more notice.

Scanning the townsfolk for the storekeeper, he saw the light coming from the telegraph office. Perhaps his long walk had not been wasted. He threaded through the passersby and went inside the office.

"I'm about to close up. If you want to send a wire, write it down and it will be sent in the morning."

Cole quickly closed the door and stepped to the partition. "No. I'm here for an answer to a wire sent a week or more back."

"The name?"

"Hay—Cole. A wire under the name Cole."

The operator rose and sifted through papers sitting in pigeonholes on the wall. "Here it is. Came in a few days ago."

He handed an envelope to Cole, who turned about to face the wall.

He recognized the letters of his name and tore open the envelope. Four lines of words butted end to end frustrated him more than Farlon's locked door had. It was possible the relief from his worries stared at him from the page. What he needed next was someone to tell him what it said.

"I'm leaving now" was the crusty remark just before the room's light vanished. The operator's silhouette moved against the outer twilight, but was halted when the door opened. In came a figure nearly as tall as Cole, wearing a short-brimmed hat. The outline of a uniform patch rested on the shoulder.

"Would you check on a telegram for me?"

The formal voice froze Cole. It could belong to only one man.

"I'm Major Miles Perry."

The unlit room was barren of places to hide. A man Cole thought was dead now stood feet away.

"You, too?" asked the irritated operator. He retreated behind the counter. The shuffling of paper could be heard. "Everybody wants to come in at five o'clock" was muttered. "Let me find a match."

The light would make Cole confront a past that had trailed him for over three years. Perry went toward the counter. Cole crept for the door. The closer he came, the quicker his step. He bumped Perry's shoulder. Light flared behind him when he stepped through the threshold, and he slammed the door without looking back. He strode faster down the boardwalk, listening for any presence following him. Curiosity made him stop in the alley next to the Manor House Hotel.

What had brought Miles Perry to this town?

Thinking his luck had changed with the telegram, in truth it had become the worst fate had to offer. Unarmed, all he could do was try to keep a bead on what was chasing him. He edged an eye past the corner of the building. In a few

Tim McGuire

minutes, the light disappeared from the window and out stepped Perry and the old operator, who locked the door and proceeded the other way down the boardwalk.

Standing alone, Perry shook his head at the paper in his hand, then wadded it into a ball and tossed it to the ground. The major walked into the street, stopped, picked up the wadded paper, and soon faded from view into the merging citizenry.

Once he was sure he wouldn't be seen, Cole made his way down the boardwalk. While he was pondering how he would leave town without being noticed, a shout boomed from across the street.

"Vance, wait!"

The caller was hidden in the shadows. The deputy could spot Cole and might divulge his name. Cole darted into the first building he came upon.

The barroom he'd entered buzzed with activity. Smoke hovered just above the card tables, where loud tangled conversation and laughter salted the air. Without a stake to risk, he searched for an empty chair where he could hide from wandering eyes. Making his way to the rear of the room, he saw a lone gambler with five hands dealt faceup into four columns. Three vacant chairs surrounded his table.

"H'wdy," Cole said as he approached. The greeting put the gambler's stud-banded black hat at an angle that revealed a pale face garnished with thick coal-black eyebrows and a mustache.

"This game's closed." His muttering had a lace of southern drawl.

"I ain't looking to play."

The reply made the man look Cole over once more. He casually opened his coat to expose a hip holster with a chrome revolver. "Then what do you want?"

"A seat."

Again the gambler looked at him, only to chuckle and then emit a grunting cough. "Well, then, by all means. Join me."

214

Cole sat, keeping his back to the batwing doors. It wasn't long before he saw that most of the patrons' attention was on that table.

"Since you didn't come here to seek the fortune of cards," the gambler said while resuming his one-man game, "did you come for the companionship offered upstairs?"

"No. I just needed to rest my bones a spell."

A young woman came to the table and placed a bottle of whiskey and a shot glass next to the gambler. "Thank you, dear. I believe my guest is without a glass."

She looked at Cole.

"I don't drink whiskey. How much is coffee?"

"Six bits."

"Damn! I don't guess water is much cheaper?"

"Not much," she answered.

"How much is the dirt on the floor?"

Cole's remark sent the gambler back into laughter, followed by a brief heaving hack. Managing to speak, he looked first to the woman, then at Cole. "Please bring my friend the finest brew your establishment has to offer and place it on my bill. What is your name, sir?"

The response took time to consider. "Clay Hayes."

"Well, Mr. Hayes, it's my pleasure to meet you. What an unusual delight it is to meet a man of your conviction toward spirits frequenting a saloon."

"Oh, I take a snort of hooch on occasion. I just can't stand the smell of corn whiskey." He cracked a sly grin. "Too much of it has come back through my nose."

"Well," the gambler said while twisting the cork from the bottle. "My doctor tells me that alcohol is the great sanitizer." He filled the glass. "The prescription is to imbibe liberal amounts of the remedy." After swigging the shot, he quickly poured himself another.

"What doctor tells you to drink whiskey as medicine?"

After gulping down the liquor, the gambler failed to suppress a loud belch. "Me." He offered his hand. "My name is John Holliday. Doctor John Holliday.'' They shook hands, and Holliday refilled his glass. ''I have an unpleasant malady.''

''I know. My ma had that same cough.''

''And what is your mother's condition?'' He raised the glass.

''She passed on in 'sixty-one.''

Cole's statement stopped Holliday's arm. ''My condolences. God rest the sweet woman's soul.'' He swigged his drink and continued dealing the cards.

''You don't have the signs of a man who takes to betting against himself,'' said Cole.

''I'm not. I was hoping for a house faro game to play.''

''I don't play cards, but I heard faro is a brace game.''

Holliday grinned. ''You're correct. That's why I was wanting to play for the house. Nevertheless, all they play here is that uncivilized poker.''

The woman returned with a cup of coffee and walked from the table without a word said.

''I'd say you made her mad,'' said Holliday. ''Ah, the fairer gender. Nothing in nature rivals their capacity for beauty, nor their deceiving treachery.'' He pointed above the bar where a picture hung of a naked woman lying on a bed in an empty room. ''You see how the artist took great care to draw every meticulous detail of her body, the color of the ample bosom, the roundness of the hips,'' he raised his eyebrow, ''every red hair in place.'' He gulped down another shot. ''But the face stares at the ceiling and is indifferent, as if uncaring of being depicted in such a way.'' He looked at Cole. ''They know our desire. And they use it to achieve theirs.''

Normally deaf to fancy talk, he took the meaning to heart. He thought of Ann, and the times that she had him uncertain of his own actions.

''Pleased to see you again, Mr. Holliday.'' An old-timer came to the table with his hand outstretched. Holliday reluctantly accepted the handshake. "Cyril Walker. Do you remember me?"

"Yes, of course. You're the gentlemen that shared my bottle this afternoon."

"Yessir, that's right." Cyril pulled out a chair and sat before Holliday could offer. "It sure is a sight, having you here."

"So you told me earlier. You left just as I was about to order another bottle, on your way to assist the local law."

Cyril rubbed his lips as a dog licks its mouth waiting for a bone. "Yeah, I had to go guard that boy that done shot Marshal Thomas."

"Yes, you were saying. What is his name, again?"

"Billy some such. But everybody recognized him as the Rainmaker."

Cole's eyes widened, but he kept motionless.

"Rainmaker?" Holliday said, confused. "Seems to me I've heard that name."

"Oh yeah. He's a bad one. He done killed a woman and her husband in Colorado. Murdering women and children in about every state, robbing banks and stages. I heard he's kin to Frank and Jesse James."

"It ain't true," Cole blurted, then sipped his coffee to settle his temper.

"You say that like you know this man," said Holliday.

After swallowing, Cole replied. "I know the name."

After a moment, Holliday smirked. "Then the Rainmaker you know must be a man of discretion and not one to involve himself in acts of crime?"

"He ain't no angel. But he didn't kill that woman in Colorado, and he ain't the one that done in her husband, neither."

Holliday's smirk grew larger. "Perhaps you know the Rainmaker as well as he knows himself, Mr. Hayes?"

Cole took another slurp of coffee. "I guess you could say that."

While Cyril's concentration was firm on the whiskey bottle, Holliday appeared like a gambler confident of another man's hand. "What a pity I've never enjoyed the pleasure of meeting him. I would love to have talked with him and offered some advice."

Though reluctant to reveal any more than he had, Cole couldn't help but ask, "What might that be?"

"A man of his character and reputation should consider his options. Especially if he were to find himself in a place where he's not welcome." Holliday moved the ace of diamonds to another column. "On my way here, I met an English gentleman who was looking for men skilled with firearms. His name is Lord Apperson, and he was traveling through land where hostile Indians may take exception. He said he would be quite reasonable to the fee and was unconcerned with the past of whoever may apply."

Cole looked to the floor. "And where is this fellow?"

"Well, that's part of the reason I am here and not there. I met him in Denver on his way to El Paso."

"Oh no, Texas?" Cole asked with anguish.

"My sentiments exactly." Holliday filled his glass. "When God thought up hell, he had Texas in mind." He swigged his drink. "However, if one was willing to overlook such hardships, Lord Apperson said he would be traveling south toward the Rio Grande." He pulled a small card from his vest pocket and gave it to Cole. On it was some fancy writing and what appeared to be a man wearing a suit made of silver carrying a sword and a red shield with a cross on it. "I was given that and told to join him as soon as possible. I plan to travel to Arizona."

The meaning was clear. Cole tucked the card into his pocket and gave Holliday an appreciative nod. "I'll pass it on to him."

Holliday resumed his attention to his game. Cole glanced about the room and spotted a Chinese girl carrying clothes. A dark-green shirt made Cole stare. The girl stopped at the bar, and after a brief word with the bartender, she went upstairs.

Cole rose from his chair.

"Give my regards to the Rainmaker, Mr. Hayes," Holliday said. Cole again nodded to the gambler, then stepped to the bar.

"Where's that girl going with them clothes?" he asked the bartender.

"What's it to you?"

"I might know who they belong to."

"Well, hell," the bartender scoffed. "I know who they belong to."

"No," said Cole in firm voice. "I know who they really belong to."

While wiping out glasses, the bartender held up a finger. "Wait here." He called over a redheaded gal and whispered in her ear. Figuring the barkeep was trying to sell time with the woman, Cole began to walk away, but he was stopped by her grip on his hand.

"Curly says you know about the clothes." When Cole nodded, she pointed toward the stairs. "My name's Betsy. Follow me. The owner is going to want to talk to you." She led him to the last door on the second floor. "You stay right here," she said, knocking twice on the door and then entering, leaving Cole in the hall. After a minute, she opened the door to a room decorated with red velvet chairs, a couch, and drapes. Behind a desk sat a woman with brown hair and wrinkled cheeks. She was dressed unlike her workers, in a gold-colored skirt and jacket with a frilly white blouse puffed out between the lapels.

"Please come in," the seated woman said. Cole cautiously entered, and Betsy closed the door behind him. "I'm Joanne O'Malley. I own this business. Betsy says you have an interest in the clothes worn by that son of a bitch in jail."

"That's right."

"Are you a friend of his?"

"He ain't no friend of mine. He tried to kill me. Took my clothes and gun and shot me not more than a month ago."

"And your name is?"

He hesitated before answering. "Let's just say my name is Clay."

"Well, Clay, it appears I have something you want. Let me show you what I want." She walked to a rear door to the office and opened it. On a bed behind hanging beads lay a girl younger than those he'd seen in the saloon. Next to the bed, a similar-age fellow with spectacles sat weeping.

"Her name was Lucy," O'Malley calmly said. "She was working here to get enough money to make it to San Francisco to be with her beloved Patrick. That's him crying. He hasn't left this room since he got here a little over a week ago. Now he has to go back to California without her." She shut the door. "Doc Fuller said she was in what he called a coma ever since she was beaten by that man. She stopped breathing this morning. Now, you want your clothes? I want you to kill the man that killed her."

"I heard they were fixing to hang him," said Cole, surprised.

"After a trial." O'Malley walked back to her desk. "That's if they find him guilty. Guilty of shooting the marshal. But he wouldn't hang for killing a whore, not for what he did to Lucy. I don't want him to die for killing Clement Thomas. I want him dead because of what he did to that little girl in there."

Though Betsy was as red-eyed as her hair, Joanne O'Malley stood in front of him without a hint of tears.

"I ain't no murderer."

"If you won't do it for that dead girl, you can do it for yourself. Don't you want to get even with him?" She opened a drawer and pulled out a wrapped bundle of greenbacks. "I'd make it worth your while. There's five hundred dollars in that stack."

The money would solve his need for a road stake. Ideas

of staying on the farm with Ann and the kids slammed into his head. However, even killing jailed killers was a crime. If he couldn't stay, the money could be used for the hard ride to Mexico. He never took to gunning down unarmed men. Revenge and five hundred dollars piqued his interest in the notion.

"Where's my gun?"

"The one he used to shoot Clement was taken by the deputy. I suppose it's in the jailhouse."

Cole walked to the door.

"So, Clay. Do we have a deal?"

He twisted the knob. "I'll let you know."

A knock at the door brought Vance out of his chair. He opened it enough to peek outside, his hand on his holstered Colt. Libby stood on the boardwalk carrying a supper tray. "Oh, it's you."

"Who were you looking for?" she said, and entered.

"I got to be careful with him in here." Vance lifted the cloth cover and sniffed the meat and potatos. "Smells good. You got him eating better than me."

"He's got to eat too."

"Yeah, I guess so." His grin faded slightly. "Look, Libby. I want to thank you for coming over here. It's been awful nice not to have to fret over getting him fed along with everything else. And thank Big Jim for me, too."

"That's all right. There's a rumor that you shot Henry Taylor."

Vance's face turned solemn. "I didn't figure it would take this long to get around. Yes, it's true. Henry was fired up for a fight and drew his gun with my back turned. My father yelled out to me. I just reacted. I fired twice. The next thing I knew, Henry was dead."

Libby placed the tray on the desk. "What a terrible thing. Were you hurt?"

"No." He looked away. "Not on the outside. But when

you kill a man, even when you have to, it stays with you.''

She put her hand on his arm. "I'm sorry. Is there anything I can do?"

He shook his head, not returning her gesture. She dipped her eyes to the floor. She had barely known Henry Taylor, so her sympathetic pose was an act. Her heavy sigh was meant more in self-pity. Her mind now firmly set on doing what she had come for, she picked up the tray.

"Oh, Vance. I almost forgot. That soldier is looking for you. He said he had something to tell you."

"Why didn't he come here? Did he say what he wanted?"

"No. Just that he needed to talk to you now. I think he might be over at the Manor House."

Vance frowned. "What's he wanting now? I haven't got time to chase his stories." He looked at Libby with the tray. "Are you going to be all right here by yourself?"

"I'll be fine," she answered with a confident nod. "Having done this so long, it's almost a habit."

"Don't get too close to him. I shouldn't be long," he said, walking out of the jailhouse.

When the door hit the jamb, Libby put the tray back on the desk and got the key ring off the wall. Unlocking the hallway door, she was quickly at the front cell. A sleeping Mansfield awoke to the rattle of keys. He quickly smiled.

"Oh, darling. I knew you'd come for me."

She poked a key into the lock, but it wouldn't turn. Frantically, she thumbed for another one to try.

"Where's the marshal?"

"He's out walking around town. But he'll be back soon," she said, searching for the right key.

"Well then, hurry, darling."

She inserted another key and it began to turn the latch. Before she twisted the lock completely, she gazed into his eyes. "Are you truly going to take me with you? Back to Alabama?"

"Of course," he said, widening his smile. "Now open this door quick, before the marshal comes back."

"We're going to live on your place? Plantation, you called it."

His smile became a grimace. "Yes, girl. Now, open the door."

"And we'll get married, and you'll show me off to your friends, and one day we'll have children like you said?"

Grabbing her hand, which held the key, he twisted her wrist. The latch clacked and the cell door swung open. Libby stepped back, rubbing her pained wrist. When he pushed her aside and went to the office, suddenly her dreams of living as a respectful lady vanished from behind the bars as well. "You hurt my arm."

"I'll hurt more than that if you don't help me. Did you bring a gun?"

Puzzled by the question, she shook her head.

"I'm going to need something." He rummaged through the desk and pulled a gun from the bottom drawer. His angry face turned to her. "Did you at least bring me a horse?"

Again she shook her head, her heart pounding each beat she stood alone with him. She wanted out of the jailhouse.

"Do you expect me to run out of town?" he yelled, charging at her. He spoke through gritted teeth. "Miss Libby, how do you expect us to start our life together if you don't think about such things?"

She could barely contain her stuttering breath, but she held back tears for fear of making him even madder. A glance at the back-hall door provided her with a way to escape him. She ran to the door, slid back the iron bar, and flung it open.

She stopped upon sighting a tall man standing in the doorway. His look of surprise quickly turned to a scowl. She stepped back when he came through the door. He stared at Mansfield.

"Remember me?" he said in a cold, vengeful tone.

"You," Mansfield said as if seeing a ghost. "You're that drifter. You're still alive?"

The man came closer, forcing Libby back toward Mansfield, who then aimed the gun at the intruder. He cocked the hammer and pulled the trigger, producing a harmless click. Staring at the pistol, he repeated the attempt to fire, without success. Palming the barrel, Mansfield raised the gun butt like a knife and reached for Libby.

She felt a hand clutch her arm, and she was thrown inside the open cell by the huge man. He slammed the cell door, sealing her inside.

"You'll not beat any more girls. I just came from seeing the last one."

"What do you want?" Mansfield stammered.

"I'm standing in for that little whore."

The freed killer stumbled in retreat through the office and threw open the front door. "The prisoner's escaping. The Rainmaker's getting away" was shouted from the street. "Vance, he's got a gun!"

Gunshots erupted. Mansfield fell back into the jailhouse.

"Someone's in there with him! Someone broke him out!"

Chapter Fifteen

The Colt slid on the wooden floor into the hall. Blood quickly
soaked Mansfield's shirt as he lay sprawled in the office. Cole
picked up the revolver, spun the cylinder, and saw six empty
chambers. Loud voices and the sound of boots on boards
came from the front. He fled out the rear door. Shouts from
behind made him sprint down the alley.

"He went out back!"

Cole ducked through a rail fence and jumped over another
one, not looking back for fear of slowing down. Two horses
reined to a post in back of a building gave him thoughts of
riding out of town, but once he had stopped, he saw that the
gate on the surrounding corral led only to the street, where
more cries of alarm could be heard.

Flashes from swinging lanterns came down the alley. Further running would put him in the clear and make him an
easier shot. He stepped between the horses and heard muttering voices.

"Do you see anything? I think he went down here."

As they got closer, Cole prepared for a fight. Unarmed, he found the rifle scabbards bare, but white rope shined in the moonlight. He glanced above and spotted a beam protruding from the awning. It had been a long time since he'd thrown a lariat, but with the lanterns becoming brighter, it was his only choice.

He snugged the Colt in his pants waistband and flung the loop into the air, snaring the beam. He pulled the rope taut and climbed hand over hand toward the roof.

"Hey, what's that? Do you hear something?"

He pulled hard and quick. The coarse twine burned his palms. The edge of the beam was in his grip when the roof became lit from below.

"Something's up there!"

A shotgun blast ripped shingles from the edge. He stuck his heel atop the beam and rolled onto the roof.

"Vance! Vance! He's on the roof!"

Ned Beckley's call made the deputy charge out from the jailhouse. After having gunned down his second man in a day, it took a moment for him to focus on the fleeing accomplice. "Who is it? Can you tell?"

"No. It's too dark up there. But me and Jimmy seen him climb a rope like a squirrel up to the roof."

"Deputy MacGregor." Vance twisted around to see Major Perry running at him through the crowded street. "What's the trouble?"

"Mansfield busted out of jail. He was running out the front door when I saw him with his gun. I fired, and he's dead on the floor inside. Ned and Jimmy said they saw someone slip out the back. I guess whoever it is helped bust him out. They put Libby in the cell."

"Where's the gun?" Perry asked. "Cole's gun."

Vance shook his head. "It wasn't in there."

"Then it's him. He came back for it just as I said."

Vance faced the crowd. "All of you get back."

"Did you kill the Rainmaker, Deputy?" asked a woman from the mass.

"Yes."

Perry looked at him. "You didn't kill the Rainmaker. The Rainmaker is the one on the roof."

It took an instant for Perry's statement to sink into Vance's head. Maybe it was true. Cyril came out of the Shipwreck. The old man put on his tethered hat, but before he could speak, Vance barked an order at him. "Go to the livery. Don't let anyone get past you."

Cole crouched out of view from the people beneath him. Shrieks from terrorized women was the only talking he could understand. Pistol in hand, he crept along the apex of the crowned roof. If he could get to the livery, he might get to a horse and ride it to his escape.

A loose shingle slipped under his heel. His back crashed onto the roof, sending him sliding down the slope. He hooked the pistol's butt around a stovepipe to halt his slide, but his boots poked over the awning.

As the alert to his presence was screamed, he pulled himself to his knees, then his feet. The incline challenged his balance, but he pawed his way back to the apex. Trapped at the top, he ran toward an open second-floor window of the saloon. He peeked to the street and saw a man with a long-barreled weapon running parallel to him. The wide gap between the buildings and the pursuing gun toter wouldn't leave him time to grab the sill and climb inside.

When the shooter dropped to one knee, Cole leaped from the side of the roof. While in flight, he crossed his arms in front of his face. He smashed through the glass to fall inside. A second later, a blast from a shotgun peppered the wall.

While he shook himself free of the glass shards, the whore in the room yanked the bedsheet over her bare top while her customer scrambled for his britches. Cole moved away from the window and yelled at both of them. "Get down!"

*   *   *

Vance ran to the front of the Shipwreck. "I didn't say to shoot. Where did he go?"

Ned pointed to the upper floor. "He dove through a window up there! I might have nicked him!"

Major Perry ran to stand beside Vance just ahead of a number of the town's men, armed with their rifles. "Up there! Open fire!"

Vance twisted around to face Perry. "No! There's people up there!"

"So is he," Perry shouted. Rapid gunfire from repeating Winchesters sent sparks and smoke into the air. Wood splintered from the building's shutters. Windows shattered and collapsed.

Vance barely heard himself yell, "You bastard," over the fevered barrage of bullets. He slammed his fist into Perry's jaw, dropping the meddling soldier to the ground.

Cole ducked his head from the lead piercing the walls. The whore and her customer shielded their bodies with their arms as they crawled from the bed. Wood planks cracked apart and dropped to the floor. Slugs hailed the room with the fury of a wild storm. He knew he would feel the sting of being shot any instant, or witness pain inflicted on the other two.

He sprinted out the door and down the hall. As he crossed the catwalk above the drunken gamblers below, the shooter with the shotgun burst through the batwings. Cole fell to his knees. A thunderous boom vibrated through him. A coal-oil lamp crashed onto the catwalk, igniting the wooden platform. With the choice of two ways to die, he ran at the wall of flame in front of him. He crossed his elbows over his face and plunged through the fire, feeling the slash of glass.

Vance heard another window shatter. His Colt drawn, he ran to the other end of the saloon and saw a man ablaze fly out of the window and land atop the adjacent smokehouse.

228

Ned ran out from the Shipwreck. "He jumped out the other window!"

Confident the man was dead, Vance was startled when he saw the same glowing figure reemerge and scat across the smokehouse roof. Instinct made Vance point his revolver and fire twice at the figure, which disappeared over the far edge of the roof.

"You got him, Vance!"

Ned's happy shout didn't give the deputy any pleasure. "Go around the back and see what you can," he said, running toward the spot he believed the figure had landed. As he came around the pitch-black alley, he pointed his gun at the first thing that moved. Cyril's tethered hat was all he could make out. "Damn you, old man. I nearly shot you." Smoldering embers next caught Vance's eyes. He crept, gun firmly aimed at the only illumination. "Bring some lanterns or a torch so I can see," he whispered as he approached in the darkness.

Within moments, a brighter light came from the other end of the alley and Ned's face shone in the glow. Vance heard the town's men assembled behind him. The lantern's light on the alley's opposite end revealed that no one stood between Ned and Vance. However, the next object the light exposed was the livery's outhouse.

Vance motioned for Ned to creep closer to the only place anyone could hide. "I know you're in there. Come out with your hands high." The outhouse door didn't move. "I don't want to have to shoot you, but I will!" The door remained closed.

Having killed two men this day, Vance wasn't anxious to make it three, but he steadied the Colt's muzzle at the crescent hole. He pointed for Ned to open the door. Holding the lantern outstretched, Ned reached for the door handle with the caution usually given a rattlesnake, then stepped back as he yanked open the door. Only the bench was inside.

Vance stared at the site, frozen in disbelief.

"Nothing got past me. It must have been the goddamn devil himself," said Ned with awe. "Just vanished into the air."

Vance heard a low groan and his name shouted from the street. Jimmy rounded the corner of the smokehouse, out of breath. The groaning seemed closer to Vance, and he took the lantern from the approaching Ned.

Holding the light over the source of the noise, Vance saw Cyril collapsed on the ground, rubbing his head just when Jimmy spoke.

"Deputy, someone just stole my horse and rode out of town."

Cole spanked the horse's rump to send it off his trail. Every step brought lancing pain to his side, and although his forearm had ceased dripping blood, he could still feel the wound's warmth against his tacky palm. His bare shoulders felt as if the fire still licked away his flesh.

Knowing he would likely be tracked at daybreak, he dragged a tumbleweed to cover his prints as he limped backward. Once assured he had smoothed the footpath beyond recognition to those who would follow, he abandoned the bush and walked upright toward the farm. The long trip would sap even more of his energy, but badgered by the knowledge that he'd lit a fuse to a keg of black powder in the form of a posse, he willed his aching body to continue without rest.

Only when the barn's silhouette cut into the stars did he allow himself to shorten his stride. Pleased with himself that he had made it there before dawn, he slipped in the door and collapsed on the straw bed.

His breath was hindered by the stiff presence of the revolver stuck in his waistband. He pulled it out, and although he was fond of the weapon, he stared at it as a symbol of the return to past troubles. Troubles that would likely swirl like a twister around the family that had befriended him in his desperate condition a month before.

With his discovery that Major Miles Perry was close by, he knew the life of a brother to a dead man he'd never seen—as well as the bond that had grown with Ann and her children—would soon end, and his life on the run as the Rainmaker was about to return.

Chapter Sixteen

Noah opened the door and the barn's interior became bright with the morning's light. Ann came in behind him. "Where'd you go, Uncle Clay? How come you weren't here last night?"

Cole was in no mood to reply to youthful questions.

Ann stepped in front of the boy. "Oh my Lord, what happened to you?"

"I ran into some trouble." Cole sat on the bed's edge, wincing with each movement.

"Son, go get the liniment on the shelf next to the stove." When Noah ran from the barn, Ann inspected the unhealed wounds and whispered, "What kind of trouble?"

Cole paused before he answered. "You don't want to know." She glanced up at him, her eyes shifting to his, then at the wounds.

"You need to get to Doc Fuller."

"No. I can't go into town. Not anymore."

"You could get gangrene, as bad as your arm is." He

looked away from her. "What are you scared of? Were you there last night?"

After a deep breath, he convinced himself to answer her, but Noah's quick return silenced his confession. Evie came in right behind her brother. Ann took the bottle and rubbed the ointment on his back. Cole jerked away. Her feather touch on his skin felt like bear claws.

"I'm sorry," she said. "But it's all I can do."

"It ain't you." He stiffened against the pain. Noah's face showed his anguish over seeing Cole's back. Evie moved closer to watch her mother's treatment of the wounds.

"What happened to you?" the girl asked.

"Stupid, can't you see he's hurt?" Noah said.

"Hush that mouth, son. I won't have you talking that way."

"I was in a place I shouldn't have been," Cole answered to both children. "Let's leave it at that."

Ann wiped her hands on her apron. "Go get all the cloth from my quilting basket."

"I'll get it, Mama," Evie said as she started for the door.

"No, I'll get it," Noah sniped at her. "You don't know what she wants."

"I do too."

"Be quiet before I take a switch to the two of you," Ann ordered. "Your uncle Clay is going to need plenty of rest, and you two quarreling isn't going to help."

Cole looked at Ann once the children left. "I can't rest. I got things I got to do."

"No. You let whatever it is be. You're going to have to let yourself heal or I won't be able to stop the infection."

He knew she was right. The ache in his skin subsided enough for him to gather his thoughts. With every minute that went by, the chances of a posse finding him grew larger. "Ann, I got something I got to tell you."

Her eyes didn't dodge his. As she waited for him to speak,

it seemed she knew what he needed to say was important but wasn't anxious to hear it. Her face was calm and peaceful, almost a smile. He couldn't bring himself to tell her of the trouble to come. She took the burden off his mind. "Whatever it is, it can wait."

Miles Perry paced in the barred cell. The front door of the jailhouse opened and Vance soon stood in front of him. "Deputy, you can't keep me here like some trapped animal."

"That's exactly what you are, Major. You're damn lucky nobody got hurt last night with all that shooting. If Dottie hadn't been quick with a water pitcher, the place would have burned to the ground. Jo O'Malley's ready to still make use of that gallows by putting your neck and mine in a noose because of what you done to her place. You got everybody riled up with talk of another Rainmaker running loose while I still have to wire the circuit judge that the one I had is dead from breaking jail. In fact, I wish you were some varmint so I could just shoot you, but all I can do is see you're run out of town."

"Out of town? I'm an army officer. You have no right."

"I've got all the right I need," Vance said as he unlocked the cell door. "With this badge, the ticket I just bought you, and the Colt poked in your back while I march you over to the depot." He opened the door. "Now, let's go. The stage leaves in a few minutes, and you're going to be on it."

Perry walked from the cell and out of the jailhouse. "Where is it I'm traveling?"

"As far away as I could get you."

They walked through the street. People stopped long enough to gawk or snicker. Nothing in his past compared to this indignity, but an attempt to halt his expulsion could prove even more embarrassing. When they reached the depot, the driver tethered baggage to the top of the stage.

"Here's your other passenger, Sam," Vance said. Perry

climbed into the stage and sat across from Patrick Franklin. Vance shut the door.

"Don't ever come back here, Major."

"I assure you, Deputy MacGregor, with this insult, you've not heard the last from me. I'm not a man who forgets things easily."

Vance nodded. "We'll see about that." He stepped out of Perry's view. The driver hopped onto the ground and began a final inspection of the coach. Upon his return to the seat, he was interrupted by the cry of a young woman.

"Please wait." She handed the driver a ticket. He opened the door and helped her inside. She sat next to Franklin. Her clothes were quite plain, and she didn't appear to carry any baggage. Within a few minutes, the driver climbed atop the stage and the last view of the town quickly passed by the window.

"I never want to come back here," the young woman muttered. Perry concurred, but kept his thoughts silent. Franklin did not.

"I feel the same way." The voice instantly reminded Perry of their previous conversation.

"Did you find that girl you were looking for, Mr. Franklin?" A solemn nod was the answer. "Pardon me for saying, but I assume she didn't want to join you."

"She's dead," Franklin answered. "She was beaten and killed by that Rainmaker person."

The young woman turned to him with her eyes wide. "You're the one? I heard she had someone come for her. Oh, that's awful. I'm so sorry."

"Thank you," Franklin said, then offered his hand. "I appreciate your feeling. My name is Patrick Franklin."

"Libby," she answered quietly, appearing ashamed to admit her name. "Libby Tidwell."

"My condolence as well, Mr. Franklin," Perry added. "If it's any consolation, that man in the jail was not the Rainmaker. He was an impostor."

235

"Little difference that makes to me, sir. An outlaw is an outlaw. The woman I loved is dead. I don't need to know the killer's name."

"Billy Mansfield," Libby blurted, then peered to the floor. "He was from Alabama."

"Good riddance to him," said Franklin. "With due respect, Miss Tidwell, I suspect you're looking at his present location right now." The remark brought a twitch to her cheek and a glimmer of a smile to both of them.

Perry scanned the rocky landscape from the jostling coach. "On the subject of location. Do either of you know of our destination?"

"I'm boarding a train in Las Vegas on my way to San Francisco," Franklin said. "Then I believe this stage continues on to Cerrillos."

"You're going to San Francisco?" asked Libby, her appearance sharply brightened.

"Yes, that's right. Where are you going, if I may ask?"

"I just wanted out of Nobility. It took all the money I had just to ride this stage. I don't even know where it was I bought a ticket for." The two sat looking at each other.

"Perhaps we'll journey together a bit farther."

Perry was unsure if Franklin's suggestion was meant as a prediction or an invitation; however, it was obvious that Libby took it as the latter. While the two other passengers engaged in conversation over their mutual interests, the major scratched his bushy beard and reflected on his experiences since its last trimming. He drew the wadded telegram from his pocket and unpeeled the paper. Once more he read the reply to his request for reinforcements for what he was once sure would be a glorious triumph.

To: Maj. M. A. Perry
From: Lt. Col. C. J. Hardesty; 7th Cav.
Have received news of Rainmaker.

Nobility

Stand down, repeat Stand down.
Report at once, Fort Bliss

The message pained him, as it had the first time he read it. Not only was no dispatch coming to his aid, he was sure he had been ordered not just to report but to surrender. He wasn't needed for duty, but rather to stand trial in a court-martial. Once a respected officer in the Seventh Cavalry, he now found himself a drifting outcast. His peers' ridicule would be too much to bare. Convinced only the truth would prove him just in pursuing an army traitor, he would have to provide it on his own.

The coach was nearing mountains. Green trees could be seen out from the increasing overcast. If he traveled beyond these hills, they would be difficult to traverse, especially in the oncoming night. The time had come for him to decide whether to comply with his superior's orders or continue his personal quest for the one man whose capture would salvage his career.

"Driver, stop the coach!"

The barn door creaked open and Ann came inside, rubbing her arms from the night's chill. "How are you feeling?"

Cole smiled and nodded. "A heap better since this morning. You were right about the rest. The sting is almost gone."

His reply didn't change the look of worry on her face. "I'm glad to hear it." She glanced back at the door, then at him. "There's someone here that wants to talk to you."

Cole's eyes shot to the sack pillow. His pistol lay beneath it, but it was unloaded. The shovel wasn't much of a weapon, and the hammer was outside. Without another door to the barn, he was trapped. He readied himself for a fight.

"May I let him in?"

He made no motion, but Ann opened the door. In came a short man with a dull plaid coat and cap. His hands were filled only with a folded green shirt and dust-colored pants with a black hat on top. "Good evening to you, sir," the man said, tipping his cap as he entered. "Kennemer's my name. I run the town's paper. I ask only for a wee bit of your time."

"Irish?"

"Sure that would be true, I must confess. County Fermanagh, it's—"

"I heard of it," Cole interrupted. "My ma was from there."

"Well, then, it's a delight to know you, sir." He came farther inside, and Ann closed the door.

"I wouldn't have picked you for a newsman."

"Nor I," Kennemer giggled. "Came to this country six years ago, first to mine coal, but when I saw it would serve me better to dig for something more substantial, I came here looking for silver. When I got in town, a Mr. Bernard J. Fogelman was leaving. It was him that took hold of my coat and sold me his paper for the six dollars I had in me pocket. It didn't take me long to find there was a truth that needed telling, so I took it as me destiny. It's always been a tradition of the Irish to be the thorn poking the side of tyrants. But I don't blame you for your beliefs, Mr. Hayes. You thought I would own a pub." He offered the clothes to Cole. "But there's one owned by another bright lass from our isle, Joanne O'Malley. She asked me to deliver these. She said they belong to you."

Cole took the clothes. Although he was pleased to have them back, they also brought unpleasant memories. "Why do you think that?"

"There was shooting in Nobility last night. It appears the prisoner they had in jail, the man they're calling the Rainmaker, tried breaking loose, but the deputy shot and killed him."

Ann's eyes widened as Kennemer continued.

"After it was over, I asked questions, which is me nature, and I heard that another man, a bigger man, had tried helping the Rainmaker get out of jail, but that man escaped. After a while, I happened on a man named John Holliday, and we spoke in confidence. He said he met a fellow named Hayes in the Shipwreck, and a bit more snooping and I found out about such a fellow and these clothes. And there is also an army major by the name of Perry, who's telling a tale about a man named Cole, and how that man is truly the Rainmaker.''

Cole looked at Ann, who turned her shocked face to him. ''Who are you?'' she slowly asked.

''I think it's him,'' Kennemer replied, looking at Cole. ''Are you the Rainmaker, Mr. Hayes?''

Cole took a deep breath and exhaled slowly. Punching the Irishman wouldn't keep the truth from getting out, nor would Ann think better of him for it. It was time for her to know, but he couldn't face her just yet. He kept his eyes on Kennemer. ''What do you want?''

''Only a few words with you, and I promise I'll keep your whereabouts to meself. But I'll admit, if you be the Rainmaker, the whole town's looking for you.''

Cole faced away from both of them. ''What do you want to know?''

''According to Major Perry, you were at the last stand of Colonel Custer. He said you were responsible for the slaughter by warning the Sioux.''

''That's the story he always tells. It ain't true.''

''Then what is the truth?''

Cole turned to find Ann in stunned silence, her eyes appearing to ask the same question. ''Three days before Custer was set to join up with General Terry and move against the renegades, I got a message. I had it read to me by a trooper named Potter. He said the man sending the message wanted me to find Sitting Bull and get him to come to his senses and lead his people back to the Black Hills reservation.''

Kennemer took a pad from his coat pocket and scribbled on it, while Ann let her weight fall against the center pole.

"So that night I left, set to do what I'd been ordered. I told Potter to keep to himself, and I guess he did just that, because he was in C Company, and none of them are alive today. Anyway, I made it to the river. It was night and there was no moon, so I couldn't see good, and a scout party jumped me. They took me to the camp, and would have killed me if it hadn't been for a white man named Jon that was with them. I tried telling him why I was there, but he wouldn't hear a word I said, and they tied me to a tree with a rock stuck in my mouth. There wasn't much I could do then. The next morning, I heard a bunch of commotion about white soldiers coming, and a little time later I saw Custer leading troopers down the valley. He was two days early. They got swarmed on, like a mess of bees all over a hive. The troopers kept falling back, farther and farther, trying to fire Springfields, but the Lakota had repeaters and could return fire a lot quicker. They chased Custer back up the hill, and then a little time after I couldn't see no more, the shooting stopped, except for those bucks riding back to the camp firing in the air, wearing trooper's shirts, coats, and pants. That's when I knew it was over."

"The major says you told him that it was President Grant that was the one that sent you the message."

Cole nodded. "That's true."

"He says it's a lie. It never happened."

"He was the one that give it to me. In a sealed envelope. Potter said it was signed by a name of Sam, and that's what I always knew the General as. Grant was my pa's commander at Shiloh. When my pa got killed in the war, it was the general that seen I got into the army so I'd have a place to go. He always knew where I was from then on."

"And why do you not tell them this story, that Grant ordered you to do it?"

"No," Cole said, shaking his head. "A president ain't supposed to be talking behind his own army's back. I owe that man too much. It ain't the thing to do."

Nobility

Kennemer grinned. "What a noble thing to do."

Cole glanced at Ann, who appeared shocked. After telling his story, what pained him most was that look on her face.

"So you've been an outlaw since?" asked Kennemer.

"After I was cut loose, I was told to go tell the white soldiers that more would die if they didn't let the Lakota be. I rode out and saw what they done to Custer and his troopers." A lump grew in his throat. He swallowed hard. "Most of them had been cut up, heads and arms lopped off. So I did as I was told, but when I got to Terry's camp, that's when I found out I was wanted. I've been trying to run from it ever since."

The newspaperman continued scrawling on his pad. "Just one more thing, and I don't mean to offend you. With stories such as that being told about the Rainmaker, are you the bastard that everybody thinks you are, Mr. Cole?"

Dipping his eyes to the floor, he replied, "I guess that ain't for me to say."

"No," Ann said softly. When both men looked to her, she stared at Cole with glistening eyes. "He's not." She faced Kennemer. "Can't you leave him alone, to lead a happy life?"

"Men such as he aren't meant to be happy. It's not their fate." Kennemer put his pad in his pocket and tipped his cap to Ann. "I'll be going now, but there is one thing. Miss O'Malley left me this to give to you." He drew a stack of greenbacks from his pocket. "She said this as well belonged to you." He handed the money to Cole, who took it reluctantly. "There's also a gun belt outside and some leather leggings. I'll leave them by the door. Good evening to you both," Kennemer said as he left the barn.

Cole tossed the money on the bed. "Ann, I was trying to tell you, but I couldn't get the guts." He sat on the bed. "I'll head out in the morning."

She came to sit next to him. "I don't want you to leave."

"I'll ruin your life." He looked at the floor. "The Irish-

241

man's right. Sooner or later, they'll come looking here. At first bounty hunters, or maybe someone looking to take me down to be able to brag on it. I can't bring you that kind of trouble.''

"But they don't know who you are. Mr. Kennemer said he wouldn't tell them. Everybody knows you as Clay Hayes.''

He met her eyes. "I'd like that. Nothing would give me more pleasure than to stay with you and the boy and girl. My mind's been twisting back and forth like a tree in a storm, trying to decide what to do. I knew my past would get out soon enough, and I didn't know what you'd think of me. But it's better this way. If I was to stay, then someday you'd wake up and I'd be gone.''

She placed her hand on his. "I've been thinking about something too. That one day I'd wake up and you'd be there.'' She leaned closer to him. He peered into her eyes, shutting his own upon feeling her warm breath, and gently kissed her lips. She didn't seem to mind. Her moist lips made him kiss her again while sliding his hands along her sides. Her arms wrapped around his shoulders.

His heart hadn't beat this fast in a long time. It had been years since he'd held a woman. Unsure whether he was dreaming it all, he was careful for any sign she wanted out. She showed no sign. He didn't want to be clumsy, but he sensed her patience with him, perhaps because she was thinking the same. He released her mouth and enjoyed the scent of her neck, but she stopped him when his caress nudged against her blouse collar.

She rose and took the lantern off the wall, as if to use it to guide her back to the house alone. She adjusted the wick down. All light vanished. Fabric was ruffled and buttons were popped free. The heat of her body again joined him on the bed, but when he felt her contours, he touched flesh where cloth had been.

Her lips found his while her fingers probed his chest. He

quickly had the shirt off his shoulders, and soon after that, had slipped off all his clothes. They sank to lie embraced, her neck resting on his arm while her arm wrapped around him. With tender kisses, a trust was formed without words. She pulled him closer. Her breasts pressed against his chest, and her parted thighs clearly showed her desire. When he was sure she was ready, he eased inside her. They became one in a mutual rhythm where minutes passed like seconds, culminating in the shared bliss of a man and a woman.

Wind howling under the door awoke Noah. He blinked about the dark room. No light from his mother's door meant she was asleep. Unable to return to his dreams, he quietly rose from his bunk to peek outside. Dust danced by the porch and through the corral, but his eyes locked on the open gate. Bender was gone.

He opened the door and held it tight before it could slam against the inside wall. The horse could not be seen in the thinly clouded moonlight. The fool animal must be on its way to Texas, just as Uncle Clay had said. Noah went inside and forced the door shut. Squinting into the dark room, he found the musket in the corner.

"What are you doing?" Evie whispered.

"Nothing. Go back to sleep."

"Do you have Mama's gun?"

"I said go back to sleep." Noah put the strap that held the pouch and flask over his shoulder.

"You tell me where you're going, or I'll tell Mama."

He went closer to her bunk so only she would hear his anger. "You hush your mouth." He paused, considering whether to tell her what he had planned. Maybe she'd keep quiet if she knew.

"Bender's got out, and I think he's running with the wind to Texas. I'm going to go get him."

"I want to go," she said, throwing off her covers.

"No. You stay here and don't wake up Mama. I can do it myself."

"Why can't I go? You go every time."

"Because you're just a stupid six-year-old girl. You don't know nothing about being out there like I do."

"I'll be seven before you'll be eleven."

"But today you're six. Now, you stay here, and if you tell Mama, I'll pull your hair right out of your head." He went to the door and turned to her again. "Maybe I'll bring you back something."

"Like what?"

The question had him stumped, until he thought of what she liked. "There's some pretty flowers. I'll bring you those," he said as he left the house.

Cole awoke feeling as if his body had melted into the straw. Recalling the night's events, the warmth it brought to his soul, made him want to revisit the passion he had enjoyed. His curled arm, which earlier had wrapped around Ann, was now by his side. Although the straw was still depressed where she had lain, she wasn't in the barn. The door was shut. She must have crept from his bed, perhaps to ready breakfast for him. He hoped so, not just so he could eat but so that what they had shared would still show on her face. An inner peace enveloped him, just as she had hours before.

The peace was shattered when Ann shrieked. "Clay, Clay! Come quick!"

He rolled off the bed and jumped into his pants to race out the door. Ann paced on the porch, staring blankly at the dirt. "What's wrong?"

"The children! They're not here."

He charged into the house, and his search under her bed and into the crowded corners confirmed what she had discovered. A glance at the front wall showed that something else was missing. He returned outside and put his arm around the distraught mother. Filling her with fright wouldn't help her mind. His first thought was to ride after them, but an instant later he saw the open gate. "They've gone after Bender. He must have got loose during the night."

"Oh, my Lord," she cried again and again. He took her by both arms and forced her to look him in the eye.

"You stay here. Likely they'll be right back as scared as pups. They'll need to find you here." He took a step off the porch, but she grabbed his arm and aimed her tear-dripped face at him.

"They're all I have."

He wrapped his palm around her hand. "I'll find them. I promise."

Chapter Seventeen

Clouds blanketed the sun. Uncle Clay had said something about moss growing on one side of a tree, but the rest sounded confusing. Pine and oak covered the hillside, along with high mounds and jagged gullies. His shouts for Bender only echoed back, and there was no other sound to guide him to find the horse or his way home. Noah sank to his knees, unsure of what to do next.

He wanted only to show everyone that he could do something on his own. Mama's face would glow with pride when he came strutting back with that horse. He was sure of it. Now the night had passed and morning was almost over. He found himself in the middle of the mountains, but nothing looked as it did when he came to cut wood with Uncle Clay.

He had brought the musket for the chance to shoot at a rabbit or deer or maybe a wolf. As he pinched the hammer and pulled it back, his mind wandered in the glory of such a prospect. Henry Taylor had never shot a wolf, or at least had never bragged about it. But Henry was dead; all his bragging on things he did had led only to his getting shot. A gust whipped Noah's face as he thought of that prospect.

Still the gun had the hammer back, ready to fire. Noah raised the barrel and spotted a sapling that wobbled in the breeze. Closing his left eye, Noah sighted the barrel so as to catch the tip of the baby spruce when it was pushed to the side.

A low rolling growl made every muscle in his body seize. He opened his eye and eased his face to the left. A black shadowy presence approached at a cautious pace through the trees. As it neared, its ears went flat to its head and a recoiled snout flashed red gums and white teeth, four of them shaped like knives. Its yellow eyes locked onto his own. The same sound came from behind him, but he stared straight ahead.

With every step closer, the animal's fierce snarl became braver and louder. Noah's gut stuck to his backbone, unable to suck in any air. They were going to kill him and eat him. He was sure his flesh would be ripped from his bones the next time he blinked, so he forced his eyes wide open. Instinct made him cower, angling his view onto his lap. His hands no longer felt part of his body, but they were still entwined around the rifle. The more he thought to lift it, the more he trembled.

The black one charged with a snapping bark, then stopped. Noah flinched, then was punched in his chest, and his ears crackled with the boom. The smell of burnt powder and cloth wafted into his nose when the white cloud drifted over him.

When it thinned, the wolves weren't in sight. Once he realized the gun had fired, he rose and ran down the hill. A whining cry was right behind him. He moved his legs as fast as he could, careful to keep them under him and not stumble. Once he was past a row of pines, the hill sloped to a gully where an oak with a low branch stood. The tree protruded out of the gully where one bank rose half as tall as the trunk. As the slope leveled, he gripped the rifle with both hands and hurled it up into the tree's limbs in hopes it would snag there. The butt snapped off the brittle twigs to fall over the highest edge of the bank. He suddenly realized that he couldn't get a foothold in the bank's loose dirt, so he jumped to hug the low branch. Kicking his legs, he swung atop it. A glimpse at the ground showed jaws agape and snapping in midair.

The black wolf landed on all fours and again leapt up the trunk, but the height of the branch kept Noah as safe as a treed squirrel. He heaved a deep breath, felt a sharp pinch of his thumb, and stared at his bloody palms. The tree bark had cut his skin. He couldn't help but pant faster than his heart beat. He felt dizzy and dug his fingernails into the branch to keep from falling. His stomach churned and a surge bubbled up into his throat, but he swallowed it back down, mostly for fear of splashing the gathering pack below. It would only make them madder.

A few more deep breaths settled his stomach and cleared his head. Now four wolves yelped at him. However, as he surveyed where he was, a warm wave ran through him. Although they scratched up the bark, the wolves had already proved they couldn't climb up to him. Nothing else was in the tree. And there was a lot of daylight left.

Even though he was safe, he wanted to cry, but that would make him sure he was no man. He had hoped to find Bender and bring the family horse home, but he'd gotten himself nearly eaten by wolves, stuck in a tree, and could only wait for someone to come looking for him like he was a lost baby.

Some of the pack began baying, as if complaining that he wasn't playing fair by staying in the tree. Two of them took turns leaping up the trunk. Another tried to run up the bank, but the bank's crescent curve forced it back to where it had started. As Noah watched, he saw the musket lying atop the edge of the bank. If he were to jump to where it was, the wolves would still be separated from him by the high rim. Maybe he could run fast enough to get home before they figured out how to climb it.

He glanced down again and counted three wolves. The black one with the yellow eyes was missing. His idea now scared him more than the prospect of staying in the tree. The view through the forest was blocked by the oak's branches. His breath quickened once more. A whirring howl shot through the forest, and soon the three animals on the ground joined in the cry. Their attention slipped from him, and they all tried again to climb the bank. For a moment Noah thought they'd found another interest that would take them away from the tree. Soon he would be safe, and he could run home and tell Mama how he'd scared off a pack of wolves.

With frenzied howling, the three wolves ran from the tree and were lost from his sight in the dense forest. A distant blurry black image could be seen through the thicket. Now he realized that the one with yellow eyes had found a way around the gully; it ran as if it was after something. Noah watched and followed the lone wolf's path, peering in the direction it was headed. An open expanse of land now shone through the tangled branches, and he sighted the wolf's prey.

His gut jumped into his chest and his heart pounded when he recognized the figure that stood alone in the field. He tried to suck in air to yell, but there was no room left in his body. Finally, he screamed with all the breath he could muster.

"EVIE! RUN!"

The black wolf had cleared the forest and was on a dead sprint at his little sister. Noah search for a way to head the animal off, but it ran too fast. Then he glanced at the musket below him. He was on the ground before he even thought to jump. Two strides and he had the weapon in his hands. Evie screamed, and he watched her run, but the wolf was halfway to her.

The muzzle was blurry, so he wiped his eyes clear of tears. After pouring powder into the hole, he pulled a single ball from the pouch and stuffed it and a wad down. Evie's screams sounded distant, but if he dared look again, he would be too late. The ramrod was in his hands and down the barrel.

He shoved it twice and yanked it out, slammed the butt to his shoulder, and thumbed the hammer back. When the wolf leaped, he took a wobbling aim and pulled the trigger. The hammer fell but there was no shot.

His hands frozen, he saw the wolf take Evie facedown. Its mouth was full of her hair, shaking her back and forth like a rag doll.

Unsure what he'd done wrong, he pulled the hammer back to look at the spent cap. He pinched it out and felt around for a fresh one. His sister's screams became muffled, then ceased. She had to be dead. Noah grunted anger, gripped the cap, and placed it on the nipple. His aim still wobbled, so he dropped to one knee and steadied the barrel on the other. His left eye closed, he put the barrel's end in line with the biggest part of his target. He squeezed the trigger.

The explosion sent him onto his back, but he quickly rose and ran clear of the white smoke. The wolf was down, and it didn't move. He ran through the tall grass, thinking only once about the rest of the pack. Although his ears were still ringing from the shot, he could hear their cries.

Upon arriving where Evie lay, he saw the black wolf. Fur and flesh were scattered in the red-splashed grass. The pack's howl turned his attention to Evie. Blood streamed from her neck where two gashes had ripped the skin. He knelt slowly and rolled her onto her back. He had gotten her killed. The sweat on his brow felt frozen by the wind. Unable to steady his raging pant, he dipped his head and touched her stomach. He didn't know any prayers to say, except that he was sorry for hating her all her life.

He felt pressure against his palm. An instant later, he felt another. She was breathing. She was alive. He put an ear to her chest as Uncle Clay had with his mother, but he didn't know what to listen for.

The once-distant howls echoed nearer. He dropped the rifle to lift her in his arms. He'd always bragged he could carry her; now he had to prove it. He took a step, only to stop and glance at the musket. It was his father's gun, but his arms were filled with his sister. He would have to come back for it.

The wolves' howls drew his attention to the trees. The pack came at him. He ran, Evie's head bouncing from side to side, blood spilling from her neck. He focused on a boulder stuck out of a small but sharp rise. Once there, he placed Evie on the angled slab face, climbed atop it himself, and pulled her to the top.

The pack had found the black one, and all at once they pointed their noses straight up and starting yelping. They continued the chase and were quickly at the boulder, but when they leaped, their nails couldn't help keep them from sliding off the rock. The rise, like the high bank, was too steep for them. They kept jumping, snarling, and snapping inches away from Evie's feet. When he was sure he couldn't stay on the rock, he lifted her again and ran through the woods. The wolves' piercing calls followed him. The beasts would find a way up and be right behind him any second. His legs ached and his arms cried out for rest, but he forced himself to go on.

"Oh God, please! Oh God, please!"

He darted through the trees, and the view in front of him opened to a dry chasm with an old split oak lying across it. He glanced back and heard the wolf cries echo, then moved Evie for a better hold. Carefully he stepped onto the log and put one foot in front of the other. The high pitch of the wolf cries no longer echoed. He concentrated on the other side of the chasm, centering his weight while balancing Evie.

When he had set foot on solid ground, he placed her on the dirt, twisted around, and saw the three wolves stopped at the other edge. When one cautiously attempted to try to cross, Noah furiously grabbed the log. Rapid jerks and tugs budged it off his side. The wolf quickly backed away as the old oak crashed down the chasm.

He lifted his arms and wanted to cheer himself for outsmarting them, but his sister was hurt and he had to act quickly. He picked her up. Ahead lay high cliffs. Tired and confused, he wanted only to rest, and he thought they would be safe there.

The last grains of powder kept the small fire glowing just as Uncle Clay had said it would. The cloudy skies were turning dark. As Evie lay next to the flames, her neck wrapped by his shirt, Noah stared at his sleeping sister.

The fact that she hadn't uttered a sound since she was bitten by that black wolf scared him. Maybe she was already dead and he didn't know it. He forced the thought away. If he tried to shake her awake it might hurt her worse.

He recalled times when he had enjoyed pulling her from her top bunk by yanking the blanket she was wrapped in. Her screams of terror had given him great delight. Another time he had dangled her long hair over the table candle, just to see if it would burn. Mama whipped his britches hard for that.

He'd always hated the idea of having a little sister. There was nothing she could do that was any fun. There were times when she helped him sweep the house, but he didn't want to give her any of the glory. She had never told Mama what happened to three missing eggs, even though she had seen him throw them at Bender to see if the horse would get mad.

Uncle Clay said that hate was a strong word and that it shouldn't be said about your own kin. He thought of when he'd said that word, and he felt sick staring at her now, knowing he'd almost lost her forever. She would've been just a lump in the ground, like his pa.

"Evie, you can't die. It's okay if you want to sleep, but you just can't die." He wanted to give a reason for her to live. "You don't want to miss Christmas, do you? Now that I know where them trees are, I can bring one home, just like the one Miss Lorna would set up in school." His throat tightened, and warm tears dripped on his cheeks.

"I'm sorry for all the times I said I hated you. I really don't. And if you wake up, I promise I won't call you stupid no more. Even when you do a stupid thing, like always telling Mama something I was going to tell her first."

He sniffled his nose clear. "Don't you worry about us. I know it's getting to be nighttime, and I know you want to be in your bed. But I'm going to get us home. Mama's going to come, you just watch. She's probably out looking for us now, wondering why we're not getting ready for supper." He looked up at the low cloud that reflected the light. "Mama's going to see this fire and she's going to find us. And when you wake up, I'll let you tell her all about it." He swallowed the lump in his throat. "But you got to wake up, Evie. Go ahead and sleep. Just don't die." He looked up again at the yellow glow against the dark clouds.

The reflection of the fire was seen by another pair of eyes, which then peered at the musket that undoubtedly was responsible for the gaping hole in the dead wolf lying near it. A soldier's weapon from years gone by. A weapon whose use was familiar to him. Another glance at the distant fire glow led to thoughts of who had lit it and a scratch of a scruffy beard that hadn't been shaved in weeks.

Chapter Eighteen

Awakened by a shout, Ann raised her head from the kitchen table. She rushed out into the noon sun and saw two figures approaching from the east. One was tall and appeared to carry a bundle, and the smaller one was coming at her more quickly.

"Noah?" she cried. She ran toward them, and once she was past the barn she recognized her son holding the musket. She held her arms out, and he was soon in her motherly embrace, pressed against her bosom. During the night, she had thought she would never hold her son again.

She wiped her tears and his with her fingers. "Where were you? Where's Evie?" she said, her voice crackling. He pointed to the other figure, which now took shape as an army soldier. Noah began talking, but she didn't hear a word. Noticing the man's beard, she knew it to be the one she'd seen in town while shopping for Lorna's dress. She quickly concentrated on the coat-wrapped bundle in his arms.

"*Evie!*"

She raced up to the soldier and opened the coat. "Oh, Lord. No."

"She's alive, Mrs. Hayes. Barely, but she's alive," said the soldier. Ann looked at him, too shocked to speak. "I found her and your son in the mountains. It seems they had ran into some wolves. I fear they would've killed the girl if it hadn't been for the boy."

Ann glanced at Noah, who didn't show any pride about the remark. She feared the wounds to Evie's neck had become infected. "Please, take her inside." She led the man to the house and had him lay Evie on the lower bunk. She wet a rag and cleaned the wounds.

"I'm sorry I couldn't do more for her, Mrs. Hayes. She was unconscious when I found them, and barely breathing."

"I thank you for your help," she replied as she tended to Evie. "Mr. . . . ?"

"Major, ma'am. Major Miles Perry."

"Major Perry, I thank you again for bringing my children home to me." She looked to Noah for an instant. "What happened?"

Noah told the story of pursuing Bender and the encounter with the wolves. When he described how he'd shot the wolf that attacked Evie, Ann felt a shiver down her spine.

"Your son is a hero, Mrs. Hayes. It was quick and sound thinking to do what he did. Especially how a boy of his age knew to handle such a weapon that hasn't been common for years."

"Yeah, Mama. I was telling Mr. Perry—"

"It's Major Perry, son," the officer interjected.

The correction didn't ruffle Noah's enthusiasm for telling his story. "I was telling Major Perry how I was taught by Uncle Clay, when we were cutting wood for the barn. He said he might know Uncle Clay. Where is he?"

Ann paused from nursing the wounds when she remembered the conversation in the barn with Kennemer. She resumed her attention to her injured daughter. "He's not here. He went looking for you."

Noah's reply was laced with frustration. "I knew that would happen. And he's going to be mad, too. I know he would have liked to talk with someone he knows."

"Mrs. Hayes," Perry said in solemn voice. "I'm looking for a traitor to the Army of the United States. A man known as the Rainmaker."

"Noah, go fetch me more water. I need to clean this rag," said Ann, and her son was quickly outside.

Perry continued. "A few days ago, an impostor thought to be him was killed escaping from the Nobility jail, and another man believed to have assisted in the jailbreak escaped capture. I'm anxious to talk to the boy's uncle. Because the Rainmaker's true name is also Clay. Clay Cole."

This man was here to take away what little happiness she and her children had known in five years. "Major Perry," she said, keeping her eyes away from him for fear they would reveal her deceit. "My brother-in-law is Clay Hayes. He's from Missouri." She turned to him. "I appreciate all your help, sir. I'm sorry I can't tell you more, but my daughter needs urgent care and my attention is needed with her."

Noah reentered, toting the filled bucket.

"Very well, then. I won't bother you further." Perry stepped to the door. "If you should see the Rainmaker, he's a tall man. The last I saw him he wore a green shirt and had leggings up to the knee, and he wears a black broad-brimmed hat."

Ann nodded and grinned politely. "I'll watch for him."

"Mama," Noah said with a look of amazement. "Uncle—"

"Son, I'll need you to help me with the bandaging," said Ann.

"I'll go into town to summon a doctor for the girl." Perry left the house and closed the door. Ann told Noah to tear strips of cloth, then she went to the window to see the soldier walking toward Nobility.

*   *   *

Cole nudged Bender to keep from slowing down. He figured the gelding would wander for fresh grass, but he didn't know what would attract two kids. More than a day of searching and he hadn't found Noah or Evie. Trying to think of what to tell Ann, he glanced up and saw the barn's peak over the horizon.

One of the few things he had promised to do, not finding her lost children would be harder to explain than a lost battle to a commander. When he rode past the barn, he took a deep breath for the short, empty story he had to tell.

He tugged slightly on the horse's mane, and swung his leg over its head and dropped to the ground. He took another deep breath and looked to house. Noah burst out the door.

"Mama, Uncle Clay's come back!"

Cole blinked twice, sure it was a mirage. The boy ran to him, and Cole dropped to a knee. He grabbed Noah's arms and stared long enough to see the hair drooped over the eyes, dirty nose, freckles. It was really him. Cole pulled the boy to his chest and squeezed tight, unsure why such a feeling should come over him. "Where'd you go?"

Noah told his tale with a bright smile, but when he explained how Evie was attacked by a black wolf, Cole's blood boiled.

"That was a damn fool thing to do! Didn't you know there were wolves up there? Didn't I tell you? Now your little sister's hurt." His chiding eroded Noah's smile. He took a breath to temper his words. "There's some things even a man doesn't chance. When you knew Bender was gone, you should've come for me. I know you like to think you're growed, but you're not. You're ten years old. I'm happy you did what you done, but there's times when you have to stop and think things through before you do them." When there was no other lesson he felt he could pound into Noah's ears, he asked about Evie. Noah pointed to the house.

Cole rushed inside and saw Ann kneeling by her daughter. "She's starting to take fever."

He felt the girl's brow. The heat made him place his cheek on the girl's. "She's burning up." He looked around the room for a cure to the fever. Water would do, but it wouldn't suck out the infection that poisoned the girl's blood. As he searched, Noah entered the house.

Cole felt bad about what he had said to the boy, but it had needed to be said. He couldn't fret over hurt feelings with the girl still struggling for life. The idea of struggling for life brought a memory and a possible answer.

"Do you remember where we caught that catfish, ol' Jasper?" he asked Noah. An unspirited nod was the reply. "Take every bucket we got and fill them with river mud and water to the brim." Noah had a look of confusion. "It's a man thing I'm asking you to do. It'll help cut into the fever. But I'm needing you to get it and be back like a shot. Hitch Bender to the wagon and be back here as fast as you can. Can you do it?"

Noah's nod became faster with every word. He ran from the house and began the task he had been given. Cole turned to Ann.

"Don't worry. He can do it." He took the rag and wiped Evie's brow. Ann touched his hand and looked deeply into his eyes.

"I'm not worried about Noah. I know he can do anything you ask him to." She faced away from him. "There was a man, a soldier, that brought Evie to the house. His said his name was Perry."

Cole paused, then looked to the girl and continued wiping.

"He said he was looking for the Rainmaker."

Cole dipped the rag in the water bucket and wrung the cloth. As Ann explained about Perry's warning, Cole thought about the dreams he had allowed to dance in his mind, about what he had accomplished with the barn, with the boy, with Ann, with himself, and about what he had let himself hope for. When he unfurled the rag, it was nearly bone dry.

258

"Where'd he go?"

"He left here on foot more than two hours ago. He was headed in the direction of Nobility. I know now why you said that about leaving. A short time ago, I would have done anything to stop it. Now I know if I keep you here, then I'll only risk getting you hurt."

"Don't ever think that. There ain't nothing else in my life that ever mattered more than you and these kids. I couldn't feel different if they were my own."

"Still," Ann said, shaking her head. "If you stay here, then somebody will come for you, someday." She dipped her head. "And something could happen." He raised her chin with his fingers. "I can't have that. I lost one man when he fought to stay here. I won't see that happen again."

He grinned. "That ain't going to happen to me. Trust me." Her eyes glistened and her jaw quivered. He gently kissed her lips.

"Please go," she said.

Noah snapped Bender's reins enough to get the gelding at near a full trot. The old horse didn't like galloping, but it couldn't be helped. He had to get home and warn Uncle Clay.

The vision was still clear in his head. That Mr. Perry that liked to hear himself called major, standing to talk with that mean fellow that punched Henry. Brice was what Deputy MacGregor called him. The two of them didn't appear to know each other when they started talking. After having sneaked close enough, hiding behind the sagebrush, Noah heard most of what was said.

He shook the reins harder. He almost steered Bender over some small dunes that would have turned the wagon over. Dusk made them hard to see. Water lapped over both bucket rims as the buckboard rumbled over the stony path. The light from the house emerged once he crested the hill.

Brice had told the major that whatever went on in this

valley was the business of Owen MacGregor. He said he'd help where he was needed once he heard that Major Perry wanted to tell Vance MacGregor about Uncle Clay trading something with somebody named Custer and some Indians. The look on both their faces is what scared Noah the most. When they talked about coming to the farm, they didn't smile at all, meaning that they weren't there to visit. The last person showing that face was Vance MacGregor, and the next day Henry Taylor was killed. "Faster, Bender. Faster."

He reined in and stomped on the brake. The smell of burning wood surrounded the buckboard as he jumped off and ran into the house. "Mama, Mama, where's Uncle Clay? Where is he? I got to tell him something."

His mother showed that confused and angry face whenever he shouted at her. But she pointed toward the barn, and Noah ran outside before she could speak. His mother yelled what sounded to him like an order not to go just when he opened the barn door, but he was sure she couldn't have meant that.

"Uncle Clay, where are you," Noah called as he stepped through the doorway. The straw bed was empty. The only light came from the lantern that hung from the far end stall. "I need to tell you something!" He went farther inside. "Are you in here? I got something I need to tell you. The army man—"

Noah tripped over the shovel and went face first to floor. Unhurt, he now could see behind the stall. The tan boots that stepped toward him were covered with dark leather. He continued to peer up, sighting the top of the leather, which stopped at the knees of dust-colored pants. A long narrow holster stuck with a shiny gun hung from a brown belt with loops filled with bullets. He saw a dark-green shirt with seven buttons, and a black hat held by two hands. In an instant, Noah remembered Major Perry talking about the Rainmaker having been last seen wearing clothes like these. The dim glow lit up Uncle Clay's face.

His heart pounded and he wanted to laugh his delight,

because he knew he was smiling ear to ear. "Wow! You're really him. You're the Rainmaker. I knew it. I knew it could happen. I was hoping for it so hard."

Uncle Clay didn't show the same face. "I didn't know what you'd think of me. I didn't want to scare you."

"Heck, you didn't scare me," Noah said while getting to his feet. He walked slowly and held out his hand, just to press his finger against the gun. "So you're really him. Does Mama know?"

"Yeah, she knows."

Noah gazed upon him. "Wow. I wish Henry Taylor was here. I mean, I wish he weren't dead at all, but if he could be around just for one time, this would be it."

"What were you yelling when you came in here?"

"There's a fellow that says he knows you. His name is Perry."

"Miles Perry? Did you talk to him?"

"Yeah," Noah answered, nodding. "He said he knew you."

Cole dipped his head. "What else did he tell you?"

"Nothing. Except, I saw him and Brice from the Mac-Gregor ranch talking. And they said your name, and that they were going to get Vance MacGregor to come here."

Cole's head shot up. "When did they say that?"

"Just when I was coming back with the water. I saw them, but I don't think they saw me." Noah looked at Cole from head to foot. "Why are you dressed in them clothes? You ain't leaving, are you?"

The time had come, but he didn't have the guts to tell the boy. "What makes you say that?"

The boy smiled. "Nothing. I thought you might. But I guess I was just crazy for thinking that."

Cole picked up the checkered shirt and pulled the telegram from the pocket. Before he was to put it in his shirt pocket, a thought hit him. "Did you say you read good?"

Noah nodded. "Pretty good," he admitted with some re-
luctance.

Cole gave the telegram to Noah. "Good enough to tell me
what that says?"

Noah unfolded the paper and stared at the message, then
at Cole, squinted again at the paper, and stammered the
words.

> *Clay Cole; Have news from Claire. Well done.*
> *Account with fee and bonus*
> *in your name with Wells, Fargo.*
> *Deepest Thanks and Regards—J. Thorsberg.*

He looked again at Cole. "What's that mean. Who's he?"

With a deep breath, Cole answered. "Oh, it's a long story.
He's a fellow back east. He promised to pay me if I helped
out his daughter when she was in Colorado. She went there
to find her husband and got in a big mess. I kept her from
trouble."

"How much money?" Noah asked, eyes wide.

"Never you mind." He took the telegram from the boy.
"You brought the mud, did you? We best get in the house.
I need to show your ma an old injun trick."

Vance hung the key ring back on the hook. The floor was as
swept clean as it could get, but he still didn't feel like sleeping, so he slumped into the desk chair. He took a deep breath
and reflected on the day's events.

The man who had taught him respect for the law now
rested in peace just the other side of a fence from his killer
under a nameless marker. If Clement knew that, it was doubt-
ful how much rest he would take. Still, the old marshal would
likely be proud of his deputy. Although, with two men, not
much older than boys in their graves, the peace of Nobility
was as he'd left it.

Clopping hooves stopped outside the jailhouse door—a

party of three he'd just as soon not see burst inside from the dark. "What the hell is he doing here? I told him never to come back," Vance asked his father.

Owen MacGregor glanced at Major Perry, who entered ahead of Brice Canton. "Now, hold on, son. There's something you need to hear."

"Stories about the Rainmaker running loose? I ain't interested. Now, the three of you can leave."

"I know where he is, Deputy," said Perry in a cold tone. "He's living on a farm not more than ten miles from here."

"The Hayes place," added Brice.

The news had Vance stumped for a reply, which must have showed on his face. His father smirked at him.

"I told you you'd want to hear this."

Vance shook his head. "I've heard the same bull before. How do you know it's him?"

"Last night I found a boy and girl up in the mountains alone. The girl had been attacked by wolves, so the boy led me back to his farm as I carried her. While we walked, he told me about a man he called Uncle Clay. The boy's description of the man couldn't have been any clearer if he'd drawn a picture. Very tall with broad shoulders, scars on the face, blue eyes—"

"That's the same man Ann Hayes has said was her long-lost brother-in-law," MacGregor blurted. "Clay Hayes."

"His name is Clay Cole," Perry continued. "The boy said that his uncle had claimed to have been robbed of his gun and clothes and was left for dead by a bank robber.

"Mansfield," muttered Vance.

"Exactly," said Perry. "So, you see, Deputy, when Mansfield came into town wearing Cole's clothes, he was mistook for the real Rainmaker. And Cole has been living and walking among you all the time."

A momentary silence was broken by MacGregor. "We need to go out there tonight and get him and turn him over to the major."

Tim McGuire

"It's the middle of the night. I'm not riding out there to wake up a man who's done nothing to break the law and haul him off to jail, just because the major thinks this is the man that he says he's been looking for. As far as the law is concerned, Clay Hayes has done nothing wrong and deserves to be left be."

Perry shouted, "He's a traitor to the army, damn you!"

"I don't care if he's Robert E. Lee himself. I don't have reason to put him in jail."

"Both of you stop your barking," MacGregor yelled. He pointed to Brice and Perry. "You two, wait outside for now." When they closed the door behind them, Vance felt his father's eyes piercing him like hot pokers.

"I ain't doing it, Dad."

"Son, listen to me before you close your mind to reason." He put his hand on Vance's shoulder. "You have a great opportunity staring you right in the face." Vance's puzzled expression made him chuckle. "Don't you see? There's a man out there that can make you famous. Hell, I couldn't care less what the major says about this man Cole. But I do think that he may be right about who Cole really is. Even if he's not, no one will ever know that for sure, but what they will know is how Vance MacGregor brought the Rainmaker, the true one, to justice." He peered into Vance's eyes. "Hell, son, governors are elected in such ways."

"You expect me to throw a man in jail over that?"

"It would be better if you killed him. No chance of him getting away. Everybody would just as soon an outlaw met his maker as fast as possible."

Vance was stunned. "I can't believe what you're saying."

"Believe it. It's all true, and it can happen. You never took to thinking how a businessman must think to survive. Do you want to wear that badge the rest of your life? I don't think you do, and if I'm right, this one chance is sitting right on your doorstep, begging to be taken."

Vance turned to the wall, trying to ignore his father's rea-

264

soning. However, the more he heard, the more he found himself thinking the same way.

"Vance, you could be known as the greatest lawman in the Southwest. New Mexico will soon be a state, mark my words. And with statehood comes the need for leaders. First to head a group of rangers, just as those in Texas. Next, well, there are other ways to serve one's state. Governor, senator, maybe the president. It all starts with something to spark the legend. This may be that spark. Son, don't let it pass by. Don't let the Rainmaker get away."

Ann sighed as she folded her arms and leaned against the back of her chair. Cole watched her rub her neck and lean forward again to stare at her daughter. Mudcakes were packed around the girl's neck and forehead to suck the heat from her body.

"How long has it been?" he asked.

"Nearly four hours," she answered in a concerned whisper.

Cole glanced at the window. "The sun will be up soon." His eyes caught the sleeping Noah. The innocence of the child curled up in the chair hardly reflected the events the young one had been through in the last two weeks. Events that would challenge a grown man's courage, and this young boy came through it while still showing his bright smile. Cole's praise for the deeds came in harsh words. A punch in the face would gladly be accepted if they all could be taken back.

A groan from Evie turned his attention. Ann continued to hold her daughter's hand while repeatedly pressing a palm to the girl's forehead. "She's still so hot."

"That's a good sign. Fever's got to come to a boil before it breaks. But we need to freshen the mud." Cole dipped his hands in the cool water and packed more mud around Evie's neck, head, and chest. The wounds showed signs of healing.

The compress not only chilled the fever but also worked as a salve.

As the night passed, light from the window slowly took over the room. "Why are you still here?" asked Ann, staring at Evie.

At first he thought she spoke to the girl as a question to the Almighty. When he held his reply, she faced him. He felt his heart beat a hundred times. He hoped she would know the answer. In a flash, all the times he'd spent with Ann and the children ran through him. "Do you want me to go?"

Her eyes darted to the Colt on his hip. "I want you to live."

His memories were flushed away with her words. He didn't appear to be the man who had become part of her family.

Ann went to stir the broth simmering on the stove. While Cole sat torn between which future to take, a pattern on Evie's cheeks made him come to her side. Beads of sweat spotted her skin. He rubbed his fingers with it for a taste to be sure. It was then that salt was sweeter than fruit.

"Come quick."

Ann rushed beside him, and she gushed a breath of relief upon the sight. She touched Evie's head, face, and chest, her smile widening with each move of her hand. "She's cooling down."

He nodded. "It's broken."

Ann hugged her child in a thankful embrace, then snugged the blanket under the girl's chin. She rose to stare into his eyes and wrapped her arms around his back, sinking her face against his chest. Her muffled whimpers were a joyous sound.

She wiped her tears away and peered into his eyes once more, but soon was distracted by the window. The worried look on her face returned. "You've got to go."

Cole looked to Evie. "There's still time yet. I'd like to see she makes it through."

"No," she said, shaking her head. "You've given me

more than I've ever had a right to ask for. It's because of you that my children are still with me. Please go. You've done all you can do. Now do something for yourself, and for me."

He glanced over at the slumbering Noah, but Ann had him look at her and shook her head. He held her close one last time, pressing her soft body to his chest so as not to forget it. Reluctantly, he took the black hat from the table and stepped to the door.

"Take Bender," said Ann.

He shook his head. "I'll not take your horse. You have a crop to get in and one to plant next year." With a last gaze at Noah, and the begging eyes of his mother, Cole opened the door and walked out onto the porch.

"Noah, wake up, son." A tug of his shoulder and the sound of galloping horses approaching outside quickly brought him alert. He rubbed the last bit of sleep out of his eyes to see his mother holding the musket. "You stay inside with your sister."

"What's wrong, Mama? Where's Uncle Clay?"

She stopped only long enough to look at him, then quickly went outside. Noah ran to the window. Dust rose in the air from four horses that came to a stop in front of the house. Noah went to the door and cracked it open to peek and hear.

"Get off my property," Mama said, aiming the musket at Vance MacGregor. His pa was next to him, along with Mr. Perry and Brice.

"That's another matter we will see to later," said Mr. MacGregor.

"Now, Mrs. Hayes, stop this foolishness and put down that rifle, before someone gets hurt," the deputy ordered. "We know that your brother-in-law is in fact the Rainmaker. Where is he?"

Mama pulled back the hammer of the empty musket. "He's gone. He left last night. Now, leave!"

267

Upon hearing the news, Noah felt his stomach sink.

Mr. Perry turned his head to Bender, reined to the corral post. "He couldn't get very far on foot."

"He took another horse." Noah knew his mama had to be lying.

"Is that true?" Mr. MacGregor asked. "Where'd he get one?"

Noah knew the feeling that his mother must have felt. He had had the same feeling many times. He charged out of the house. "I got him one. Mr. Grover let me borrow the brown mare."

Noah saw his mama turn a worried face to him just when Mr. MacGregor yelled at him. "Go back inside, boy."

Noah spoke the first thought that came to mind, one he had heard from Henry Taylor many times. "Go to hell."

Mama's eyes widened, but he knew she would have to wait till later before she washed his mouth with soap.

"Sounds like you need to teach your son some manners, Mrs. Hayes," said Brice. "By the end of a strap." He pointed at Noah.

Mama pointed the musket at him. "I'll blow your head off if you move toward my boy."

Brice chuckled and pointed at Noah. "Looks like he's took up stealing, too. Where'd you get that rag, son?"

Noah looked at the red bandanna that stuck out from his pocket. He looked to his mother, who then looked back at Brice.

"Is that yours?" she said with a grimace. "It was here the night my barn burned to the ground."

"Simmer down, Mrs. Hayes," called Vance. He shook his head at both his father and Brice. "We're not here for you."

The clopping of hooves shifted everyone's attention to the cornfield. Around it rode the small man who talked funny and wrote newspapers.

"What the hell?" blurted Mr. MacGregor. "What are you doing here?"

The man tipped his cap at Mama. "Good day to you, ma'am. I see this is where the party is. Someone neglected to invite me."

Brice nodded. "You're damn right."

"Pity. It's a good thing I was awakened by the sound of you riding out before dawn and decided to follow you. Otherwise, I would have missed the great battle of four men attacking a single woman and her two children."

"Kennemer, this ain't got nothing to do with you."

"Oh, but you're wrong, Deputy. You see, in this country of yours, it was one of the first things written down that the law's business is everyone's to know." He smiled, which seemed to anger the other four men.

Vance turned back to Ann Hayes. "Where's your brother-in-law, Mrs. Hayes? He's a criminal and he must be brought to justice."

"He ain't done nothing," Noah said defiantly.

"He's a traitor," Perry shouted.

She pointed the muzzle at the soldier. "You leave him alone."

Vance's hand moved toward his pistol. "Put down the gun, Mrs. Hayes."

She swung it and aimed at him. Vance drew his gun, but before he could bring it out of his holster a gunshot pierced the air. Everyone froze in place, then glanced around in a confused fashion.

"Where'd that come from?" commanded Mr. MacGregor.

"It came from up over that hill," the major said while pointing to the east. He looked at Ann. "I didn't think he could get very far." He kicked his horse and rode in that direction. The other men followed, with Kennemer tipping his cap as he rode by.

Ann first looked to Noah. Her face was filled with fright. "Son, you stay here with your sister." She dropped the musket and ran after the men.

Noah wanted to follow, but first he went inside to where

269

Evie was still sleeping. There was no sense in staying to watch her. He saw his mother run past the window while holding up her hem. Noah left the house, being sure to shut the door, and ran east.

Chapter Nineteen

Cole lowered the Colt from its skyward aim when he sighted five riders approaching over the hill from the farm. His lack of will hadn't let him walk away for the last hour. Now he would have to test his courage.

When the riders came within range, he steadied the Colt on his left arm. "That's far enough!"

They all reined in. The ranch foreman pulled a rifle from its scabbard. Cole fired. The foreman's sorrel collapsed, pinning him under it.

"The next one's in your head."

"Drop your gun, Hayes, or whatever your name is," Vance yelled. "Give up. You can't get away."

"I only see one of you strapped with a hogleg, Deputy. And that's you." Vance made a motion for his pistol. "You pull that iron and I'll make you the same offer as I did your foreman."

"Surrender now, Clay!"

"You know me, Miles. I never knew the right thing to

do.'' Cole peeked to see Kennemer pulling alongside Vance. ''Are you part of this too, Irish?''

''Good morn to you too, sir,'' Kennemer answered with a smile. ''And no, I'm not part of them, but I wouldn't miss seeing this for a cask of fine Irish whiskey.''

The remark made Cole smile. ''I see you brought your old man, Deputy. Did he come for a chance at me, or to help you haul off the widow and kids?''

Vance looked at his father, then back at Cole. ''Neither. I'm the law here, and I came because I heard that an outlaw calling himself the Rainmaker was in my territory.''

''You didn't come out here just for that.'' A thought entered Cole's head. ''I bet you'd like to take me in across a saddle. It would make that badge a lot shinier to you and folks in town.''

Vance nodded. ''It would prove Nobility to be a town of law and order.''

''Well,'' said Cole as he dropped the aim of the Colt. ''I'm going to give you your chance. Whichever of us comes away from here will get to say they bested the other. But, for my part, I want your word as the law that you'll leave the Hayes woman be.''

Vance looked to his father, who then shouted at Cole. ''He can't make that promise. She's got no title to that land.''

Cole re-aimed the Colt ''Then I'll empty both of your saddles right now.''

''Wait!'' Vance shouted. ''I'm the law. If it's a gunfight you want, it'll be me that will take the law's side.''

''Don't be a fool,'' warned Perry. ''He won't shoot you in cold blood. I know him.''

''You're telling people I killed more than two hundred men at the Little Big Horn, Miles. What's two more?''

Perry faced Owen MacGregor. ''This is a mistake.''

MacGregor whispered, ''Don't worry, Major. My son is the fastest man with a side arm I've ever seen.''

"That's the trouble, Mr. MacGregor. You've never seen the Rainmaker."

Cole dropped his aim once more as Vance came off his horse, and he caught sight of Brice reaching for his fallen rifle. Cole fired, splintering the weapon's stock, then put the aim back on a startled Vance. Brice put his hands up as if being robbed. "You don't listen good, do you? Any more from you and your boss gets shot."

"Brice," MacGregor ordered. "Leave this to Vance."

Cole kept his aim at the deputy, then peeked at Kennemer. "You write all this down. I expect you to put it in your paper."

The Irishman nodded, showing a mixture of awe and fear in both his face and voice. "Aye, that I will."

Vance walked with his palms up, well within range of any pistol. "How are we going to do this?"

"We'll just do what comes natural." Cole glimpsed the tin star on the deputy's chest. "This is between you and me. Take off that badge."

Vance slowly removed the star.

Cole lowered his aim and holstered the Colt. He clasped his left hand over his right in front of his gun belt and locked his eyes on Vance's gun hand. "Okay, son. This is your chance. Make your play."

Before him was a man not much more than a boy. There was a time when he thought slapping leather with another man was a part of living each day. Age and experience had taught him that only one of them got to keep breathing. He was facing a quick youth with a five-inch barrel. At seven inches, the army Colt was a poor weapon to draw, but his skill had always proved the better. A twitch could make the difference between hearing a shot and not. Time had healed the wounds to his head and others to his leg and shoulder, but he knew a shot in the gut was seldom survived. Fate had shown him the misery of death by lead: soldiers in war and a father squeezed with pain for days. Some he sent to the

grave, rowdy cowhands crazed by the bottle or women, or
thieves seeking others' fortunes. And those seeking reputation. In younger days the risk never came to mind, but today
it was there. If he should not hear the shot, he could only
hope the bartered reward would come to pass.

A flinch of the elbow had Vance's gun clear of leather.
The short barrel could be seen, and it arced up. A shot
cracked the silence, and then another, Vance's shot, boomed
through the air, with the bullet pelting the dirt.

Cole watched the deputy fall to the side. Then he looked
down and felt for the first time his drawn Colt, smoke wisp-
ing from the muzzle. A breath later, he saw the deputy holding his bloodied hip.

"VANCE!" The scream of the elder MacGregor echoed.
MacGregor swung his leg over his horse, but Cole's pointed
pistol stopped the dismount. "Oh my God, son. Please don't
kill him!"

Cole strode to stand over the helpless lawman. The short-
barrel revolver had fallen beyond the deputy's reach. Cole
picked up the weapon and tucked it into his belt, then aimed
for Vance's head, a shot that would leave the same mark
Vance had left Henry Taylor. He pulled back the hammer.
Vance's eyes were as wide as silver dollars.

Cole felt a presence surround him. He peeked to the hill's
crown and saw Ann and Noah standing watch. People would
believe the Rainmaker a cold-blooded killer, but Robert
Hayes's brother wasn't and neither was Noah's uncle Clay.
Although he thought the deputy deserving of the shot, he
pulled the trigger with his thumb firmly around the hammer
and eased it to rest. He rammed his boot heel into Vance's
gun hand. The further agony he caused wasn't fatal and
would keep that quick gun off his back.

He went over to the older MacGregor. "You still have
your son." He cocked the Colt's hammer. "And I'll have
your horse."

At first, MacGregor appeared bewildered and unwilling to

concede the palomino. He pointed to Perry's mount as if to suggest that Cole take it, but Cole shook his head. MacGregor dismounted and ran to his wounded son.

Pistol still in hand, Cole climbed onto the palomino and looked to the unarmed Perry. He glanced again at the two still standing atop the hill, then again at the man who had brought so much trouble to his life. "You're lucky today, Miles."

Face drawn, the major stared back at him. "Someday I'll be even luckier."

Cole nudged the horse to a trot and pulled up next to Kennemer. He removed the folded telegram from his pocket and handed it to the newspaperman. "See she gets this."

After Kennemer scanned the message, his head popped up at Cole. "And how do you suppose I should do that?"

Cole smirked. "You're a smart fellow. You'll come by it somehow."

With a kick to the palomino's flanks, Cole had the horse charge up the hill. He hadn't long before he would feel the shadows of men on his trail once again. Blue sky was to the south, which meant a fair night for the ride that was to come. When cresting the hill, he heard the call from behind.

"Uncle Clay!"

He didn't pull up. He hadn't time. Mexico waited for him. "Uncle Clay, stop!"

The echo bounced around in his head. Parting was better left wordless, but the misery etched in the ten-year-old's voice pounded his ears. A glance behind showed the pursuer's determined young face. If he didn't stop, he would likely be followed to the border. It was more than a conscious mind could ignore, so his hand reined the palomino in. At first, the tiny figure of the boy at full sprint urged him to resume his flight, but he recalled his lessons on the right thing to do, the ones he'd hope would take seed in the young one's mind, and the horse stood firm.

Noah stopped running, his breath coming in pants, his eyes wide and mouth agape. "You can't leave."

"I don't have no choice," Cole said, swinging his leg over the horse's head to dismount.

Noah gulped breath and rapidly blinked his eyes. "But you said you'd stay here. With Mama, Evie, and me."

"Things is different now."

Noah gritted his teeth. "Then you're a liar! You said you would stay. You're a liar. I thought we were friends."

The words opened Cole's gut worse than a sharp knife could, but he knew why they were said. He dipped his head to the dirt and knelt on one knee, thinking of what to say so his young friend would understand. "I'm sorry you feel a need to say that. I know it seems true. I want to stay. I like to think I'll be back. But there are reasons I've got to do what I got to do now."

"You don't have to run," Noah strained to say. "I saw. Vance tried to shoot you."

Cole shook his head. "Folks don't consider that making it right, even if they heard the truth. But I ain't leaving because of that." He paused. Noah's frown always made it difficult to think. "You see, there's times when a man has got to think of what's best for them he cares for, instead of himself. There'll be days like today, when men I don't even know will come looking for me. It wouldn't trouble me for my own sake, but I couldn't live in peace, knowing that I'd draw them here where you and your ma and Evie live."

Noah appeared confused, as he often did whenever Cole tried to make sense. "Do you remember why it was best letting Jasper go?"

Noah nodded, his words choked. "You said, even if I didn't want to, that I ought to."

Cole peered into the boy's red eyes. "It was the right thing to do."

"But we can go with you."

"No."

Noah swung his head from side to side. "You can't leave. No, no, no, no."

"Don't make this harder than it has to be, boy." Cole sensed his tone getting loud, and that wasn't what he wanted Noah's last remembrance of him to be. "Your ma needs to stay here. This is where she was intended to be. This is your family's place."

"Then I'll go with you."

"You can't go where I'm going." Cole pushed his black hat back and grinned. "Besides, you can't leave your ma alone. She's going to need you more then ever now. You'll be the man to protect her and your sister."

Noah gulped a breath and looked behind him, where his mother slowly walked toward both of them. He faced Cole. "What about you? *You'll* be alone."

Cole pressed his lips together. He saw the red bandanna in the boy's pocket and drew it. "I may be by myself," he said, wiping a tear that dripped down the boy's cheek, then clutched the cloth. "I'll never be alone."

Noah wrapped his arms around Cole's neck. "Don't tell nobody I cried." Surprised by the boy's hug, Cole slowly put his arm around his young friend and squeezed tight, unable to keep his own tears back.

"Not if you don't tell on me." He held Noah's shoulders and looked him in the eye. "Noah Hayes, it's been my pride to know you. I'll be bragging on it to everyone I come across. You sure enough got what it takes to be a man, and you're going to make a fine one."

Cole rose and took the palomino's reins. He climbed into the saddle and turned the horse south.

Noah felt his mother's hand on his shoulder as he watched his uncle Clay ride to the top of the hill. A shadow passed by his eyes. He looked up to see a large black bird gliding in the wind. It reminded him of one of the stories he had been told while he and Uncle Clay cut down trees. Birds could go anywhere they wanted, Uncle Clay would say, but wherever it was they went, they couldn't stay there for long.

The black bird swooped down to soar to the south, just as the black hat disappeared below the hill's crown.

NOBILITY TOWN CRIER

PRICE ONE PENNY
SATURDAY, NOVEMBER 1, 1879

P. KENNEMER, EDITOR

VANCE MacGREGOR ELECTED TOWN MARSHAL

RAILROAD BOON TO COME TO TOWN AND BRING PROSPERITY

"RAINMAKER" LIVING AMONG US
MAJ PERRY'S ACCOUNT OF 7TH MASSACRE

Tuesday's special election to fill the official post of City Marshal since the murder of Marshal Clement Thomas was won by Deputy Vance MacGregor, who ran a campaign to restore law and order to our town in anticipation of the coming of the Atchison, Topeka, Santa Fe Railroad next year. His first official act after Wednesday's swearing in was to arrest MacGregor ranch foreman Brice Canton for numerous fires set that destroyed several barns, homes, and livestock in the area. The new marshal jailed Canton toting a shotgun while still recovering from injuries sustained to his right leg and hand from recent gunplay with a stranger said to be an army traitor.

Maj. Miles Perry of the 7th Cavalry said the stranger was responsible for the massacre of troops led by Lt. Col. George A. Custer at the Little Big Horn river in Montana on June 25, 1876. Maj. Perry stated that he personally has pursued the suspected traitor since that time and vowed to continue until the fugitive is brought to justice by a military court. The stranger's whereabouts are not known nor is his true name except to be referred to by notorious reputation as "The Rainmaker."

LAND AUCTION HELD

An auction was held to settle the claim to land deeded originally to Mr. Robert Hayes, who died six years ago from an accidental bullet wound from his own weapon. The land, which lies northeast of Nobility, parallels federal land grants held by the ATSF and is considered prime for industry investment, had been in dispute since Hayes' death for reasons of right of inheritance. Gov. Wallace decreed that the law states that the wife of the deceased is not a legal heir to the property, though is due any acquest from the marriage. The territory's taxes from such transaction are expected to consume any said revenue.

Those present at the action included cattleman Owen MacGregor, Jim Donovan (still mourning the disappearance of his adopted daughter, Libby Tidwell), noted businesswoman Joanne O'Malley, and a host of other eager investors. The top bidder for the 160 acres, which sold for a record $4,500.00, was Hayes' widow, Ann. When asked of her plans for the land that she has farmed for the last seven years, she replied, "To build a new house near a tall oak tree, raise my children and be left in peace."

EDITOR'S NOTE

From one of Erin's sons to another, "May the road rise to meet you," Mr. Cole.

DIABLO
DAVID ROBBINS

The wide-open boomtown of Diablo is a tinderbox in the blistering Arizona sun, just waiting for a spark to set it off. It looks like every prospector, gunman and hard-luck case west of the Mississippi has hit town, desperate to get what he can, and to hell with everyone else. The homesteaders hate the prospectors and the miners, and both sides hate the cowboys and the ranchers.

Lee Scurlock is the spark Diablo is dreading. He is riding to escape his past in the dirty Lincoln County War, and trying hard to mind his own business at the stage relay station when three cowboys take it into their heads to make trouble. When the shooting stops, one of the cowboys is dead, and Scurlock finds himself in some serious trouble—trouble that will follow him when he rides with the stage into the blazing man-made hell of...Diablo.

——4254-1 $4.50 US/$5.50 CAN

Old Marsden

FRANK RODERUS

When he was born his parents named him Alvin, but that was a good long time ago. These days pretty much everybody just calls him Cap. Maybe he isn't quite as spry as he was back in his trapping days, but he can still sit a horse and his aim is almost as fine as ever. Most of the time, though, he is perfectly content to regale his granddaughter with tales of his exploits. But when someone kidnaps that lovely little girl, Cap isn't about to leave her rescue up to somebody else. He won't rest until she is home safe and sound—and until whoever took her learns just how much grit Cap still has in him.

___4506-0 $4.50 US/$5.50 CAN

Dorchester Publishing Co., Inc.
P.O. Box 6640
Wayne, PA 19087-8640

HIGHPOCKETS

DOUGLAS SAVAGE

In the autumn of his days, Highpockets stumbles upon a half-frozen immigrant boy, nearly dead and terrified after being separated from his family's wagon train. For one long, brutal winter Highpockets tries to teach the boy all he needs to know to survive in a land as dangerous as it is beautiful. But will it be enough to see both man and boy through the deadly trial that is still to come?

___4400-5 $3.99 US/$4.99 CAN

LES SAVAGE, JR.
MEDICINE WHEEL

Bob Hogarth arrives in Wyoming's Big Horn Basin with nothing but a small herd of cattle, the result of stubborn scraping and saving back in Texas. He is determined to do better, to own his own ranch, to become a man of substance. But there are lots of folks who aren't too eager to see Hogarth succeed, other ranchers with their own plans for the future, and a mysterious rustler on a barefoot horse. Nobody told Hogarth his dreams would come easy . . . but he knows they are worth fighting for.

___4444-7 $4.50 US/$5.50 CAN

Dorchester Publishing Co., Inc.
P.O. Box 6640
Wayne, PA 19087-8640

Please add $1.75 for shipping and handling for the first book and $.50 for each book thereafter. NY, NYC, and PA residents, please add appropriate sales tax. No cash, stamps, or C.O.D.s. All orders shipped within 6 weeks via postal service book rate. Canadian orders require $2.00 extra postage and must be paid in U.S. dollars through a U.S. banking facility.

Name_____
Address_____
City_____ State_____ Zip_____
I have enclosed $_____ in payment for the checked book(s).
Payment <u>must</u> accompany all orders. ❏ Please send a free catalog.
CHECK OUT OUR WEBSITE! www.dorchesterpub.com

COPPER BLUFFS

LES SAVAGE, JR.

Kenny Blacklaws returns to the East Texas town of Copper Bluffs nine years after the brutal murder of his stepfather, only to find himself smack dab in the middle of a war with cutthroat rustlers. But that isn't his only problem. His return also awakens the feelings of Corsica, the beautiful woman his stepbrother has claimed as his own. It's not long at all before just about everyone in Copper Bluffs is itching to see Kenny dead—just like his stepfather.

____4478-1 $4.50 US/$5.50 CAN

SPUR AWARD-WINNING AUTHOR

GORDON D. SHIRREFFS

Southwest Drifter. Wes Yardigan's luck is beginning to run dry. It kept him alive all the years he's drifted the territory, a stubborn saddle tramp chasing the wind. Now he wants to settle down, and has even managed to scratch up a stake—just in time for the Indians to sweep down out of the hills and leave him with nothing but his own thick skin. One more day in this blistering country and he won't even have that. But Yardigan's luck hasn't quite run out. Two men ride in with a curious proposition—a deal that will give him a chance to stake himself again. And after he agrees, he realizes he should have taken his chances in the desert.

_4207-X $3.99 US/$4.99 CAN

To read the work of Max Brand is to experience the Old West in all of its glory, energy, and humanity. And here, all restored to their original length, and collected in paperback for the first time, are three of Max Brand's greatest short novels. In "Winking Lights," a chance encounter and burning curiosity lead a rider to an ancient hacienda and a trapped young woman. A tenderfoot in a Mexican border town learns hard lessons about trusting gunfighters in "The Best Bandit." And in the title novel, a frontier gambler is given a rare second chance in life . . . if he's willing to take it.

___4508-7 $4.99 US/$5.99 CAN

Dorchester Publishing Co., Inc.
P.O. Box 6640
Wayne, PA 19087-8640

Please add $1.75 for shipping and handling for the first book and $.50 for each book thereafter. NY, NYC, and PA residents, please add appropriate sales tax. No cash, stamps, or C.O.D.s. All orders shipped within 6 weeks via postal service book rate. Canadian orders require $2.00 extra postage and must be paid in U.S. dollars through a U.S. banking facility.

Name_____
Address_____
City_____State_____Zip_____
I have enclosed $_____ in payment for the checked book(s).
Payment <u>must</u> accompany all orders. ❑ Please send a free catalog.
       CHECK OUT OUR WEBSITE! www.dorchesterpub.com